MOURNING IN THEIR TRIBE

Enjoy !

Tom Sherwood

A NOVEL BY

THOMAS W. SHERWOOD

For my wife, Marilyn Foss.

...The most interesting thing about the terrorist movement…is that while women have been approaching equality with men in other fields of crime, this is the only one in which they have come to be dominant.

San Antonio Express. Thursday, February 10, 1977. Excerpted from "Women: The New Criminals"; Copyright 1977 by Richard Deming; Published by Nelson

PROLOGUE

September 1985

The regret of Heavenly Valley Police Officer Robert James Butler's life came when his name was pulled from a police officer's cap during a private ceremony held in County Sheriff Dan Briggs' office thirty days prior to the date of Paulson's execution. One hundred and twenty-two peace officers from jurisdictions throughout the state responded to the sheriff's request for volunteers to staff a firing squad. A committee of two police chiefs and the sheriff of an adjoining county pared the list down to the best twenty candidates, according to their records and recommendations from supervisors.

"We looked for men of substance," Sheriff Briggs reported at a news conference. "We wanted, and I am assured that we got, qualified marksmen who are physically and psychologically fit to meet the challenge of carrying out the job. The qualifying committee presented me with the names of twenty volunteers, any of whom, they felt confident could carry out society's work. This morning in front of several witnesses I drew six names, five for the firing squad plus one alternate, from a hat in my office. We are set to proceed with the execution of cop killer Horace Paulson."

The state of Utah had reinstated capital punishment following the U.S. Supreme Court decision on January 1, 1977. Horace Benjamin Paulson was tried and convicted of first-degree murder on August 7, 1977, of Corporal Halverne Franklyn Halverson of the Heavenly Valley Police Department. After all the last-ditch efforts to save Paulson's life failed, the sentence of death by firing squad, which he had chosen over hanging, was scheduled at the Utah State Penitentiary at the Point of the Mountain, Draper, Utah.

Before dawn, two unmarked 1982 Chevrolet Impala sedans drove away from the Hotel Utah in Salt Lake City destined for Draper. There, Horace Benjamin Paulson, named after his maternal grandfather, and the prison chaplain knelt side-by-side, waiting for the men to arrive. The men were coming to shoot out Paulson's heart.

———————

By the summer of 1992, retired Officer Jim Butler wanted to tell his story. He sought out a reporter named Susan O'Brien.

O'Brien placed a tape recorder on the table between them. The interview would be conducted professionally, without regard to the fact that they had known each other for several years.

"Tell me about your experience as a member of a firing squad that executed Horace B. Paulson back in 1985?"

He grimaced, turning the deep contours on his face into Shar-Pei pup-like rolls. Butler had been a cop for almost thirty years. Hawaiian born and constructed like a cinder block, Butler spoke with a raspy voice of one who smoked too much and enjoyed too many whiskeys, straight up.

"What motivated you to volunteer for what surely must ... for most people ... seem like such a ... ahem ... grisly task?"

Butler wrung his hands. "I guess it was because I knew Hal. He was younger than I was, but I knew him from the time he joined the force. When he was killed ... the way he was killed ... I wanted to have the man responsible in my sights."

O'Brien continued cautiously, "It has been reported in the ... some ... newspapers that the state pays the volunteers for the service. You know ... some ... have reported that it seems very much like a murder for hire."

Butler's back stiffened. He had, after all, asked for this interview.

"I felt," Butler twisted his fingers, "that the extra money and two days at the hotel offered as perks were difficult to pass up."

O'Brien's article was published in the Sunday edition of the newspaper entitled "Firing Squad: Someone Must Do It. Would You?" It read:

A murder, a crime for which there is no excuse, is committed by a person who, by his own admission, committed other similar crimes and would do so again if let free, and you have an opportunity to volunteer to cull society of this mad man: would you do it? Can you sight down the barrel of a deer rifle and shoot another human being strapped to a chair not more than five or six paces away from you?

For Officer James Butler the answer was yes. He joined four other young men on the firing squad and shot and killed convicted cop killer, Horace Benjamin Paulson.

Perhaps Butler's story serves as a cautionary tale to those who may be called upon to serve on yet another firing squad.

At dawn on September 30, 1985, Officer Robert James Butler's world was compressed into a Chevrolet with the car's windows covered by black contact paper to conceal the identities of those inside.

"Ordinary things were happening outside the car. I had a tough time with that," Butler said staring blankly. "I could hear the clinking of bottles as milkmen made deliveries. It really irritated me, even the squawk of the car radio. It didn't seem right that people didn't know what we were going through to protect them from people like Paulson."

In the car, he felt like he was suffocating.

"God, I couldn't breathe. I had to pee. That is all I could think about. I wanted the driver to speed up. Slow down. Stop. I hoped for a wreck. I wanted out."

He wanted to run away but knew that he couldn't. He felt caught in a trap of his own making.

The night he looked forward to spending at the Hotel Utah, a perk for the volunteers, crawled by with tossing and turning. He would never set foot in the hotel again or drive by it in the years to come.

"We're here, gentlemen."

The group marched into a large room within cell block 'D,' where an office chair, surrounded by sand bags, loomed with heavy leather straps suspended from its polished arms, legs and seat. The men paused and beheld the scene until they were prompted to keep moving to their assigned places behind a canvas curtain separating them and the chair. Five three-inch wide gun slits had been cut into the canvas curtain. Five pre-loaded Winchester .30 caliber rifles lay in front of the shooters on a table. One contained a blank, the 'conscience' round.

Butler and the four other peace officers listened as witnesses tramped into the room next to the chamber. The marksmen stood and the cellblock became silent.

He heard the guards strap Paulson to the chair. He realized he would actually be shooting a human being strapped to a chair. The thought robbed him of breath.

A prison guard asked in a small voice that trembled, "Not to tight, Hoss?"

4

"My name's Horace. Remember, Bill?" Paulson admonished in a surprisingly calm but high pitched, nasally voice.

A small, round white cloth targeted Paulson's beating heart.

"I thought I was going to pass out. Even when we first saw the chair standing alone, straps hanging loosely, for some reason it did not register with me. But when the guard asked him if the straps were too tight… The killer I volunteered to shoot became a living, breathing, thinking, human being."

As for last words, Butler recalled that Paulson said words to the effect, "There will be no tribe to mourn for me."

Overcome by anxiety, needing to urinate, Butler's legs trembled as the county sheriff read the lengthy death warrant. Arms grew heavy. He wanted this anxiety filled moment in time to pass quickly. It did not.

The county sheriff read the lengthy death warrant, "so, so slow." Officer Butler's discomfort stretched on and on. He wondered what the man strapped to the chair was thinking. "What are a man's last thoughts?" He vaguely listened as the sheriff coughed and read the legal jargon contained within the warrant in a strained voice without enough volume to drown out the long, slow, deep-breathing sounds of the man strapped to the office chair, polished for the occasion, on the other side of the canvas curtain. Finally came the commands to get ready, to aim.

"The small target looked like a smudge," he recalled with the clarity of one who had replayed the event many times in his mind. He had opened the chest kept in the attic, and that is where he was now as he continued. "My heart was beating so hard, so fast. The rifle in my hands weighed a ton. I could smell the gun-oiled stock as I brought it up to eye level. The sights were jumping around with my heartbeat."

Apparently, all of the marksmen—chosen for their ability to shoot, as well as their physical and psychological toughness—were having difficulties steadying their aim. *Two of the four "live rounds" missed the small white cloth target, with one striking Paulson in the upper thigh and the other in his lower stomach. The other two "live rounds" missed the mark marginally, penetrating the edges of the "smudge."*

The next few minutes would haunt Butler the rest of his life. "We heard Paulson thrashing about. He wasn't dead. Good God, we thought we would have to shoot him again."

A second volley would not be necessary.

Eight minutes later, amid hurried, whispered discussions among prison officials, the doctor pronounced Paulson dead.

"I still see that target moving with the man's deep breathing," Butler said. "I hear his voice [responding] to the doctor's pin prick while attaching the target to the man's shirt. Sometimes it is a screaming voice. I still see the hood over the man's face being sucked in and out with his last breaths."

Butler admitted to having an irrational and unnatural fear, but very real to him, following the execution. "I couldn't get Paulson's words out of my head. He told the guard who strapped him to the chair that we just didn't want to walk in here wearing the hood. He said we. Who'd he mean by we?"

Perhaps it was Butler who had fired the 'conscience round.' Butler cleared that up. "No, the man on my right fired the blank. You could tell. Not as loud as the rest. His rifle, he said, did not have much of kick. He knew he had fired the blank. Afterward, he was in much better spirits than the rest of us."

The man's shoulders sagged. "I couldn't trust myself with a gun anymore, and I took a job in the evidence room."

Volunteers yet to be, too, will learn how to cope with the gruesome task that they, most likely, will forever feel that they should have never volunteered for, and would advise anyone else not to do. No matter; only the volunteer executioners will know the dread of coming of night—that grey pre-dawn interface when the cruel events of their choosing will come calling for the rest of their lives. Will they, like Officer Butler, be forever revisited by the sight of that "little white target heaving up and down, closer then farther away, closer again," then "torn and shredded like the human heart beneath it?"

Butler sighed and concluded, "It was as if I freed Paulson from prison, only to take his place."

———————————

Susan placed the Daily News to expose her article on the table next to her coffee cup. She glanced over at the Hellman Award, gathering dust on the bookshelf, which she had received for her reporting on the events that had consumed her husband's life in 1976. Chasing a shadow, a vengeful cop killer, led him into a den of terrorists.

Her son walked into Susan's home-office and picked up the paper. After reading his mother's article, he reflected, "That's a bit jarring."

Susan thinking back, replied, "1976, Riley, was a year thought to be a demarcation of rebirth after Vietnam, the protests, race riots, cities burned, Watergate, and Nixon. The country started to overcome all that. The protests and counter culture movements had begun to sputter and grind to an end. In the years prior to the bicentennial, we weren't sure that our democracy would survive. We came through, though not unscathed." Susan chuckled sardonically. "You know what, Riley? There were so many bombings in the early seventies that people got used to them. For example, the patrons of a movie theater in New York actually became angry with police for shutting down a film after a bomb was set off in the back of the theater."

"No kidding?"

"No kidding," Susan responded

"However, not all of the terrorist cells faded away."

"No. And one of the deadliest made their way to our little burg, and your dad and Mo walked right into the mouth of that beast."

"Mo Reynolds…" Riley mused.

Susan responded with a distant look in her eyes. "Poor Morris Reynolds. I guess I'll always hold a soft spot in my heart for him."

Preoccupied with thoughts of the past, Susan repeated, "The bicentennial…what a summer…"

PART 1

Horace

Gone was the cowboy. He stopped dropping *g*'s from verbs. "Whaddya mean you're 'talking?' You only talk the way your teachers say is proper at school. Around here, you talk like a man. You got that?" On this matter, his mother agreed. "Horace, we are country folk. We walk like country folk, and we talk like country folk. Around our people, you talk right. Listen to your dad." Horace became Hoss at home, at the stables and around his friends. Horace and Hoss resided side by side. He found that Hoss made friends easily. Though his size would always separate him from his peers, Hoss discovered that he could temper the intimidation factor with his country accent, and it worked. On the other hand, Horace could impress with his eloquence, and he found solace in this ability to flit back and forth between Horace and Hoss.

Chapter One

"He's a lazy son of a bitch. All that bastard does is sleep and eat," Ben screamed at Mary, whom he referred to as "bitch," especially when he had been drinking after a day's work on the oil rigs of Rifle, Colorado.

Ben drank beer and then turned to whiskey to enhance the experience and push him more quickly into a place where he was king, and powerful, and had hope; a place where the dream of a ranch and horses was real. A vision that saw him, Ben Paulson, ride up on the big bay horse to the front door of a large white two-story house with a wrap-around porch that seemed without end or beginning, complete with gleaming white rocking chairs on polished dark wood decking. A dream that saw him greeted by a young Mary Paulson like Mary once was: young, independent, fierce in her love of Ben, with hair still full and yellow as straw, eyes that narrowed just enough as she looked up at him under a soft hand that shaded her blue eyes perched above flushed cheeks that gave way to a perfect smile reflecting the afternoon sun.

Mary had been down this road all too often. Ben would start drinking at the Main Street Saloon after a day of being a Roustabout on the big oilrigs that shimmered mirage-like in the high desert sun. Quenching his thirst, as Ben called it, not dream chasing, which is what it was, he would come home bitter and full of anger. She would walk softly and make sure that his supper was prepared just right. She would have the stove burner turned on, the frying pan set off the burner, then on the burner, when a car would pull up, then off the burner if it was not Ben. Any little thing would set him off. But nothing set him off like their son Horace Benjamin.

Mary lived for the early mornings when Ben, who never missed a day of work, would drive away in the battered GMC pick-up truck at five fifteen. She knew he would stagger in about six thirty after spending two hours pouring down as much alcohol as he could in Rifle to "quench that goddamn thirst."

Even with his shortcomings, Mary kept telling herself that Ben was a good provider and therefore a good man. In her less forgiving moments, she knew he could be a mean son-of-a-bitch. He did not realize how close he came to pushing Mary into that place where she remembered her mother's abuse. She was taught to take "no guff from no man." She could shoot and owned a .32 caliber revolver that she kept under the bed. Some nights Mary wished she could find the courage to pull the revolver from under the bed.

Horace used to protect her, but now he didn't. All he does is sleep and eat. She missed that Horace.

Horace Paulson, known as Hoss to his teammates, at six foot five and 240 pounds had been the pride of Grand Junction High School football. He was an all-conference, all state, linebacker for the team that took the state championship, and had college recruiters drooling. His physical bearing and emotional strength also brought his mother relief from the beatings that his father liked to administer regularly to both mother and son throughout the boy's life.

When Horace came into his size the summer after high school junior year, the beatings came to a halt. One Saturday Ben and Horace were in a rented stall where Mary's horse, a bay named Junior, was kept. Ben was drunk. They argued briefly over the mixture of oats and grains to feed the horse. Ben's sucker punch landed behind his son's right ear. Horace took the punch. He turned, eyes fierce, and he snatched up Ben by his throat and threw him against the wall.

"Listen to me, old man," Horace hissed. "If you ever lay a hand on Mom again, I will kill you."

All of the beatings, all of the nights used up cringing as his father waylaid his mother while Horace lay in bed powerless; the seventeen years of misery caused by the man squirming in his grasp burst forth with a crushing right fist that smashed the man's nose and left eye socket. Ben went completely stiff, then limp as Horace released him. Ben wilted onto the straw covered floor. A sobbing Horace ran to the office and phoned for help. He thought he had killed his dad.

Ben was admitted to St. Francis Hospital with a concussion and a detached retina. Horace and Mary sat in the waiting area.

Placing a hand on her son's shoulder, Mary asked, "I don't want to know what happened at the stables this mornin' son, but what have I always told you?"

"Fight fair," Horace nodded and replied.

Mary grew pensive then said, "He wasn't always this way. When he was ridin' them big old bulls, he was somethin' to see. We were at our best back then," she smiled. "There are times I still see the old Ben in him. I always used to admire the way he rode them big beasts. He still looks the same, except when he drinks.

"If you say so, Mom."

Mary knew there were no words that she could say that would lessen the loathing Horace felt for Ben. She also knew that Ben supplied ample fuel for that fire.

Ben refused to discuss the incident with police or anyone. Not that Ben came out of the hospital a changed man, his anger remained but smoldered under the surface like a coal seem fire. He would get even someday.

Horace signed a letter of intent to play football at the University of Utah. By his junior year Horace made most All-America lists. Mary and Ben, especially Ben, were caught up in Horace's celebrity. Before the short fight in the stable, Ben often referred to Horace as a "Momma's boy," and now he became "My All-American son."

Ben and Mary made the two hundred fifty-mile road trip to attend all of the university's home games in Salt Lake City. They made the shorter trek to Provo for the last game of Horace's junior year as Utah faced off against its archrival Brigham Young University.

On that hazy autumn Saturday afternoon, the happy respite of the last three years ended quickly in the first quarter of the big game. Horace fell victim to a crack-back block that tore the anterior cruciate ligament of his left knee. The cart that carried Horace off the field that afternoon also held the hopes and dreams of the two parents standing in the west stands dressed in matching University of Utah fire-engine red western shirts, blue jeans and sweat stained cowboy hats. Mary covered her face with her hands. Ben, with thumbs in belt loops of his Lee blue jeans, sneered as his son was carted off the field.

An operation on Horace's left knee successfully reattached the ACL, but complications followed. During the healing process, Horace contracted cellulitis. Two more surgeries and a year of little activity healed Horace's knee, but left him confused, depressed, and with little energy.

Months passed. It took everything within him to get out of bed. Mary took him back to the hospital for further evaluation, however the answers were always the same. "Don't worry Mary, lethargy is common after surgery." The white-coated doctor slapped Horace on the back and continued with his learned opinion, "This big ole Hoss has been through a lot with that damned old knee. He'll be fine. Give him time. All will be okay. He'll get over it." In nineteen seventy-four, post-operative depression was thought to be transitory, if thought of at all, following orthopedic procedures.

Horace didn't get over it. He didn't return to the "same ole Hoss." He stayed in bed most of the time. He gained thirty pounds. He lost most of his hair. He could not bring himself to even speak much. He mumbled. An old blue terry cloth robe and slippers too small for him became his daily uniform, as he shuffled about the small apartment from his room to the couch in front of the television and then back to bed.

Horace's incapacitation emboldened Ben. Horace heard his father's insults. He heard his mother's screams muffled under Ben's hands. He could do nothing but lay in the bed too short for him and cover his head with his pillow. He cried. He cried often. He hated himself. He wanted most of all to die, but even in that, he could not bring himself to do it. He cried.

———————

On an unusually warm February day, the Paulson's lives changed again, this time forever. Ben left for work as usual. Mary had other plans. It all started with the rush of air that streamed into the apartment as Ben left for work. The fragrance drew Mary from the kitchen and she stepped outside and stood on the landing for several minutes and just breathed deeply, one long inhalation after another. She could not get enough of it. It felt like spring, and it enveloped her with want, desire, and hope.

After cleaning up after Ben's breakfast and stopping by her son's room to peek in on him, Mary went to her closet and dressed quickly.

She drove to the stables where she worked three days a week just to maintain a stall for Junior.

"Wow. Mary what's the occasion? It ain't your day to work, but I can see you ain't here to work," commented the always-friendly owner of the stables.

"Well Robby, it's a pretty day, and I am here on my own accord today. No shovelin' shit today. Nope. Today, I am goin' to ride old Junior here till I wear out my thighs."

Mary did ride. She rode Junior all day along the many trails and over the mesas of the open spaces accessible from Robby's stables. She rode until the fickle February sun found high thin clouds to hide behind, and it turned cold.

Mary brought Junior back to the stables. While brushing and cooling the mount, her mood grew dark like the day outside at the thought of having to return to the bleak apartment. She stopped brushing the horse and held tightly to Junior's neck. All the optimism she felt earlier seeped out of her. She tried to stem the flow by holding tighter to Junior, but gloom flowed back in with the emptying hope and the fissure in her soul widened.

"Robby! You out there?"

Robby came running. "What is it? What the hell is wrong?"

Surprised by Robby's concern, Mary laughed. "Nothin's wrong, you old fool," Mary said while catching her breath between convulsed laughs. "Hell sake man. You wanna get drunk?"

"You sure, Mary?" Robby knew Ben and hated him. He had seen Mary limp into the barn on too many mornings holding her side and looking pale and worn out——far more worn out than a woman her age should look.

"Hell yes, I'm sure. You comin' or not?"

13

Mary and Robby spun this way and that in a flirty way, thought Robby at any rate, on round chrome bar stools cushioned with faux red leather, drinking whiskey, laughing, joking, and occasionally slow dancing to melancholy refrains of country music from the three-songs for a quarter juke box in the small bar called Lucy's. At nine forty-five Robbie begged off and said he had to feed his dogs, and left the bar. He would always remember the lingering sorrow he felt while driving home that night. For the rest of his life, whenever he heard Hank Williams' *Your Cheatin' Heart,* he would recollect the unsettling potency with which Mary clung to him while swaying a two-step that terrible night in Lucy's Bar.

Mary sat and drank for another hour and a half. In her sodden reasoning, she knew that she would pay a high price for this day. She further rationalized, and emboldened by liquor, that she deserved to have fun every once in a while and may as well get as much out of it as possible. A man she did not know came in and she had danced with him before Robby left the bar. Now she and the man, a Forest Service employee, found themselves in his truck with his hand tugging at her belt. Laughing, she helped him unbuckle it.

———————

Ben happily seethed while drinking whiskey from the bottle waiting for Mary's return. When Mary stepped inside the apartment, she, with once golden hair, now lank, greying and mussed, at once saw the fire in Ben's eyes. She knew what was coming, but this time she was different.

"Where've you been, bitch?"

"I went to take a shit and the hogs ate me, you asshole."

Mary lunged at the man she loathed. In the ensuing melee, she grabbed for a table lamp, and smashed it on Ben's face. He staggered, and she ran for the bedroom.

Chapter Two

Ben regained his senses and a rancorous calm replaced his rage. "I'm comin' in there to kill you, Mary," Ben said serenely.

Mary grew cold. Icy fear spread over her. She searched beneath the bed.

"You know what, Mary? I'm sorry it had to come to this," Ben said soothingly. Swiping blood from his face, he examined his stained fingers with distracted fascination. "But you've forced me into this, haven't you?"

Ben slowly removed the belt from his jeans and smiled as he held it in both hands and swung the large silver buckle side to side with the deliberate rhythm of a clock's pendulum, tick-tock, click-clack. He unhurriedly swaggered towards the bedroom door, the buckle clanking off the wall and the doorframe with metronomic pulse as he neared the woman clawing her way beneath the bed. He smirked and whispered, "Oh Mary, you can't hide, baby. I'm comin', comin', comin' for you."

Horrified as never before, Mary searched furiously beneath the bed. Her hand struck the small revolver and sent it spinning.

"What the hell you doin' under there, babe? Come on out and take your medicine. Come out. Come out," he cooed. Aroused as never before. Voice husky by the anticipation of what was to come, he croaked, "You know you've left me no choice."

Mary pushed herself out from under the bed on the other side. Her knee thumped into the revolver, and she reached for it, and turned it over and over in her hands as she fumbled for the trigger. Wedged between the bed and the wall, Mary plopped her arms on the bed, holding the pistol in both hands, and aimed the gun at the shadowy figure standing in the doorway, belt swinging with deliberate menace side to side, backlit by the stark glare coming from the living room.

At the sight of the pistol, Ben quickly transmogrified: stimulation lost by the fog of unbridled hate. Robbed of the moment, his rage boiled over, "You done it again, haven't you, bitch. This could have been so easy. But look at you. Cowering behind your little fucking gun."

He lurched forward fuming, "I am going to shove that thing down your throat."

A moment later the report of the revolver filled the apartment. The bullet hit Ben in the stomach. He stumbled out to the living room and fell onto the dirty, once beige, linen-covered recliner.

Mary screamed for Horace. Leaping out of bed believing that his father had finally shot his mother, Horace crept down the hallway and saw his father, eyes wide and face pale. Mary stood menacingly over the man. The pistol hung loosely at her side.

"Horace, call the goddamn cops," Mary yelled frantically. "Now, Horace, before this pig-fuck bleeds out."

Horace dialed the operator and was passed through to the Grand Junction Police Department dispatcher.

"There's been a shootin'."

"What is your address?"

"Bayview Apartments. Number 210."

"Okay. Are you shot or hurt?"

"No."

"Who is shot?"

"My dad."

"Okay, sir. Do you know who shot him and is that person still present?"

"Ah… Yes."

"Okay units are on the way. Please stay on the phone with me until they get there."

Horace hung up the phone.

The first police unit arrived. Sergeant Stu Greenwall and Officer Sandra Ebbitson exited the cruiser and headed toward apartment 210.

The two officers went to the staircase and climbed about halfway up to gain a visual of the apartment. They stopped and knelt on the cement stairs, guns drawn, peering through the wrought iron railing.

Mary, now on hands and knees vomiting, told Horace to get a towel and help Ben. Trundling from the bathroom with a thin pink bath towel, Horace saw his mother open the door and step out onto the narrow walkway that serviced the second-floor apartments.

Still holding the revolver, Mary heard commotion below as she stepped out of the apartment.

The residents of the building were being led by an officer. Another cruiser driven by the shift lieutenant, Gibson, pulled into the parking lot.

Mary waved at the car driven by the lieutenant.

"It's about time," she screamed.

"Police! Drop the gun." Came a command from somewhere near the stairwell to her left, but Mary could not see anyone.

"Police! Drop the gun. Now!" Came a second command now louder, again from the darkened staircase.

Mary lifted her right hand to shield her eyes from the glare of the bare bulb overhead. She still held the gun, and she turned towards the commanding voice.

The round from Sergeant Greenwall's service revolver struck Mary in the left lower abdomen.

Holding the gun in her hand shielding her eyes, Mary looked down at the puncture wound in her belly. The second round fired by Sergeant Greenwall struck Mary through her left hand as she attempted to cover the stomach wound. Almost simultaneously with the sergeant's second shot came a loud crack from Officer Ebbitson's service revolver. It struck Mary in the upper chest and exited through her right scapula and punched a hole in the large front window to apartment 210. Ebbitson's second round struck the railing to her front, ricocheted, and smashed into Sergeant Greenwall just below his left armpit.

Lieutenant Gibson had climbed to the second floor using the back stairwell. He heard Officer Ebbitson yelling "Officer down! Officer down!" as more units of the Grand Junction PD stormed into the parking area and officers fanned out.

The lieutenant fell to his stomach while drawing his service revolver and carefully aimed at Mary, who, apparently attempting to re-enter her apartment, had slowly, feebly turned towards him. Both rounds fired from the lieutenant hit the intended mark. She collapsed against the brick wall and died.

———————————

For weeks the police department deflected questions from the public and women's organizations about how an abused woman had been shot five times by three different officers. Diagrams of the scene were distributed to the newspapers; a transcript of the audiotape from the call into the dispatcher was mysteriously leaked; and a subsequent statement from Sergeant Greenwall found its way into reporters' hands.

The reporting and outright leaking of information were enough to placate the majority of the public. The community's scorn slithered off Ben, the police officers, and settled on Horace Paulson, who slept while his mother had to fight for her life night after night.

Chapter Three

The consequence that came from that horrible night was that Horace Paulson emerged from the cocoon of his depression at least to a degree that he appeared to become a fully functioning person again. Arising from hypersomnia, Horace stepped from his bed that February night only to run headlong into the vortex of revenge. At twenty-four years of age, he began his personal rampage. In that rampage against anyone, real and or imagined, that he believed would bring *fair* retribution for his mother's death.

Horace would emulate his mother's teachings and life as often as possible. He did not return to college. He took jobs around stables and horses. He purchased a horse trailer for Junior, and left the prying scrutiny and sadness of Grand Junction behind and ended up in Tucson, Arizona.

Ben fled Grand Junction without a word leaving most of Mary's possessions behind. Horace rummaged through them and settled on his mother's books that she had collected since she was ten years old. All were westerns, and many dealt with the life and times of Kit Carson, with whom Mary shared her birthplace and his chosen home, Taos, New Mexico. She often quoted sayings attributed to Carson and applied them to any situation she thought fit. Many of those quotes related to fairness, but others noted vengeance, no matter how long it may take.

Mary often quoted lines of a story told by Carson and confirmed by many. According to Mary's favorite yarn, it took Carson and his band of mountain men over three years to avenge the theft of a season's worth of pelts by Blackfoot Indians that the mountain men viewed as an act of war. According to Carson, "It was three years before we could get back and thank them. But our time came, and we left mourning in their tribe."

Aggrieved, no matter how slight, whether by a clerk in a market or by splash back from a passing eighteen-wheeler on a slushy highway, Mary would mutter in anger, "I'd like to leave *mourning in their tribe*."

19

After arriving in Tucson, Horace realized how much work he had to do to avenge his mother's death. He knew that his vengeful quest must begin with his father.

He discovered his journey while reading one of Mary's books. At first, he didn't know what to make of the strange note written on a dog-eared page:

> 7 Jun 50. Shreveport. Cops here are assholes. Grabbed us both. Got beat by a club.

The phrase had no apparent relationship with the novel on that particular page, however by the date noting the event Horace knew it occurred during Ben's rodeo years.

Throughout his early life, Horace listened to his father's drunken recollections of his run-ins with the law. It never occurred to him that his mom was involved in those scrapes. It disturbed him nonetheless.

He browsed through the books looking for dog-ear bookmarks and found a total of six that contained similar entries. All were dated between 1949 and 1954 and spoke of brutal treatment at the hands of police:

> 24 Jul 53. Heavenly Valley (ha!). Threw us in the jail elevator and kept us there by smashing us behind a steel gate. Hooked my fingers in the gate tryin to stand up. Cop broke my fingers with a sap.

Horace realized that his mother noted these wrongs and bookmarked them for a reason. He felt that his mother's notes spoke directly to him from the past.

He read his mother's experiences with the police until they became embedded in his memory. Whispering her words quietly while alone, he made a list of his mother's run-ins with the law noting where and when they occurred. He visited libraries and found microfiche copies of newspapers for each of the days in question to better understand the times in which they occurred.

A plan - a reason - a life - evolved. Working his mother's scribbled words found in the paperback books over in his mind formed a rationalization that crystalized into a blueprint for his future and validation for his existence. Horace warmed to the expectation, felt a burgeoning motivation to breathe, to get out of bed each morning. Cold thought replaced anger. He understood the purpose behind his mother's notes. A plan evolved.

———————

One afternoon in late May, Horace read a story in the newspaper titled, "Strange Saga of Mary Paulson." The reporter interviewed several people regarding the events of that February night. "However, no one seems to know the whereabouts of former football star Horace Paulson. Fully recovered from a gunshot wound suffered at the hand of his wife, Ben Paulson now works at the oil rigs in Corpus Christi, Texas, and has not heard from his son since his wife's death."

"It begins," Horace whispered.

———————

It didn't take long to locate a roustabout named Ben Paulson in Corpus Christi. After visiting several waterfront bars and buying a few rounds of drinks, Horace learned all he needed to know about his father's whereabouts.

Horace located the trailer park and was pleased to find his father's trailer next to a small grove of trees that separated the park from the beach that was protected by a breakwater.

He rented a motorboat from a marina on the far side of the bay and drove along the beach. He made land near his father's trailer park. Horace found a comfortable spot on the sand where he could see Ben's trailer and waited and watched.

Horace heard Ben before he saw him. Ben sang a bit too loudly as he parked his truck next to the trailer.

Hastily making his way to the trailer, he tried the doorknob; it wasn't locked. He quickly opened the door and stepped inside.

A startled Ben stood in the kitchen. "Son?" Ben breathed.

Horace flashed a toothy grin. "Dad. How've you been?"

"I'm doin' okay, boy," Ben replied eyeing the gun on his son's hip.

"Come on. You and me are goin' boatin'."

"B-B-Boatin' son? It's dark. Why don't we open a beer and talk this over?"

Horace pushed the man out the door. The two men marched through the trees and down to the boat. Horace threw Ben in and pushed the boat from the shore and climbed in.

Horace powered the boat along the shore for about a mile before turning seaward. After a few minutes, he idled the motor.

"Okay, Dad," Horace seethed, "start swimming."

"Swimmin'? I can't swim too good son. You know that, don't you?" Ben peered hysterically into the dark water.

"Now, bitch." Horace drew the pistol and pointed at Ben's face and yelled, "Jump in!"

Reluctantly Ben clambered into the water, but he clung to the side of the boat. "Please, Horace don't do this," he cried.

Horace hammered the man's hands with the butt of the gun.

Ben released his grip and began flailing in the water. He screamed for help, but no one would be coming to his aid. The screams could not be heard above the surf.

Days later a short newspaper article noted, "The father of All-America football player, Horace Paulson, and the man involved in a police shooting in Colorado that claimed the life of his wife, drowned not far from his home at the Coastal Calm Mobile Home Park in Corpus Christi, Texas. Police have closed the investigation, ruling the man's death an accident." The report noted that the man "was legally intoxicated at the time of death."

Back in Tucson, Horace sat in his truck as he re-read the article. He noted that the article never mentioned his father's name.

PART 2

La Ligue des Terroristes Environnementeaux

To the press and law enforcement, they were just another "minor group of crackpots who are nothing more than two-bit criminals." Jonathon and his three associates believed they were urban warriors, who knew their cause was far more important than their lives or the lives they would take to insure the rebellion that began in the streets would be sustained.

Chapter Four

Tall and athletic-looking, most first impressions of Jonathon were dead wrong. He abhorred athletics. Although he labeled himself an environmentalist, he disdained the outdoors, because he sunburned easily. He found, to his great satisfaction, in high school that his size and his ability to grow facial hair were intimidating. Moreover, he could be charming, intelligent and supremely self-confident.

Jonathon scoffed at Martin Luther King Jr. "Nonviolence only begets defeat according to those who are not opposed to using violence to achieve their program," Jonathon concluded in his senior seminar in political science at Princeton, the year following King's assassination. He had not written about civil rights, however. His paper on environmental protectionism was built on the argument that the environment could be saved only by destroying the destroyers of the land before they could do any more harm. His approach worried his mentor, Dr. Amundson, who knew that such an inflammatory hypothesis detracted from the overall research and writing Jonathon presented; more to the point, the paper would not pass muster of the review board. The professor managed to convince Jonathon to temper his approach from one calling for civil violence to that of using aggressive legal action to prevent corporations from damaging environmental practices. Jonathon agreed with Dr. A, but privately hated himself for selling out.

He revealed his feelings to Amundson several months before graduation over beers at a local bar that catered to students. They argued. Amundson worried that Jonathon was becoming more and more agitated, and it became more difficult to push him away from his ever more radical ideas.

Jonathon insisted that using legal methods would take too long and would ultimately accomplish little change. Political interests and compromise would water down any legislation, and the only way to deal with those who make money killing our planet was to kill them. Amundson was shocked and disheartened by Jonathon's passion for lawlessness and violence.

"The Cuyahoga River doesn't support life! If you fall into the goddamn river you won't drown, you decay. It fucking catches on fire and these so-called student environmentalists are more concerned with their draft statuses than figuring out how to save the water that someday these assholes will need," he ranted. He grew more and more restive. On the sly, he accused Professor Amundson of misusing his lofty teaching platform to imprison real change in mumbo jumbo, while rebuking any real change that can be grasped only through revolution; an uprising that sets aside a government of law and rule based on compromise and venality of legislators bought and sold by corporations.

"First of all, Jonathon, violence begets violence," the professor began. "Let me be very clear, you can't win that way. You simply cannot bring about social and cultural change using armed insurrection. Yes, I said it. Armed insurrection is what you are talking about. It didn't work a hundred years ago, it certainly won't work now."

"Armed insurrection is really not what I am getting at," Jonathon lied. "I really mean that we must take a stand against the perpetrators of crimes. The predatory corporate mucky mucks who refuse to heed scientific analysis that strongly indicates that the practices used to fuel our appetites are, in fact, killing us. Professor, please hear me out. How different is a board of directors of any tobacco company, who know their products cause death, and yet they continue to spend large amounts of money advertising the benefits of their fine tobacco products, from say, Adolph Hitler and his henchmen telling Jews that they are simply being asked to take showers?"

"Oh, Jonathon," the professor began but rose above condescension. "I know your peculiar dilemma. Your father works for an ad agency whose major client is tobacco, and I know your mother died of complications from lung cancer. I can't even imagine how I would deal with that."

Jonathon lifted is hand to cut the professor off. "No, you have no idea." Jonathon's temper scaled its limit quickly and burst through the protective barrier worn thin by years of repression. He simply stopped fighting it. It overpowered him. He lost control.

Jonathon turned on his bar stool and with those cold, calm, ice blue irises, locked onto the professor's eyes, and stilled the professor. Amundson felt as if he were standing on the rim of a caldera feeling the seismic shift that precedes the eruption that would surely envelope him. Jonathon's sharp whisper washed over Amundson, "I could kill you right here, right now, if I thought it would serve my cause."

25

Amundson believed him. No matter how he tried to rationalize his fear away by thoughtful introspection, he could not repress his instincts. He decided to steer clear of Jonathon.

Jonathon grew weary of the student bars and the never-ending discussions of the Vietnam War and anti-government attitudes, all expressed in Ivy League trained language citing statistics and learned political science terminology. All talk, no actions.

Jonathon began frequenting bars along the waterfront in Newark. He met other men who only knew one method to dispute resolution: violence. Men like Bingo, who he saw rip the lower jaw off an unsuspecting, fat man, sitting next to Bingo at the bar and laughing heartily at Bingo's never-ending retorts at being one-armed. "Someone once asked me to give him a hand. I told him that's all I have to offer." At each punch line, Bingo would hold up his transradial prosthesis that replaced his lower right arm. He professed to have lost the arm in Vietnam, but his story could change with whoever his audience may be at the time. Seldom did his wordplay end with violence. Bingo was unpredictable, and that is what drew Jonathon to him.

Few people knew him by his given name. His father named him Marion, after his father, but he could not bring himself to call the boy, Marion. His mother provided his middle name as tribute to her family name, Leaf. Marion Leaf Jankowski became "Bingo," the first word that he allegedly ever garbled. He lost his arm in junior high while playing around cement mixing equipment at a building site after the workers had left for the day. The boy's parents passed along their obsession with not allowing him to become entrenched in self-consciousness because of the loss of the arm. The boy's father was a machinist by trade and a mountain climber by avocation. He perfected various prosthetic devices for his son that allowed the boy to perform almost any task from ice climbing to weight lifting. The fourteen-year-old became fixated with physical conditioning and, though not tall at five foot nine, he was powerfully constructed. He wore his blonde hair straight, parted in the middle and long enough to cover his rather large ears.

His beard grew in patches, so he settled for a goatee that enhanced a jutting jaw that supplemented his confrontational appearance and demeanor. Most women thought him handsome. Some were attracted to his ruggedness, while others were attracted to the bad boy in him.

After graduating from high school, Bingo had no interest continuing with school. He preferred to pursue his education by doing, not by studying. He hitchhiked across the country from his home in Newark with full consent by his progressive parents, searching for adventure. He fell in with hippy communities and communes in Northern California, but his need for aggressive physical activity didn't fit with the flower child lifestyle. He made his way to Alaska where he discovered community with the rugged individualism of frontier living, where the vast, dangerous wilderness loomed at the city limits.

He liked to drink. Drinking in bars in and around Fairbanks, inevitably led to physical clashes in a place where a man is measured by his ability to "handle himself," code-speak for a man's ability to fight other men. The more ferocious the man fought, the better the man. By that standard, Bingo became the better man, better than most. He developed the ability to flash violence, quickly, without warning at any perceived provocation. In his world, equilibrium in life came from keeping those around him off-balance.

Bingo's world unraveled three months before he met Jonathon. His parents were killed in a car crash on the New Jersey turnpike. Although he had been away from his parents for years, the loss of them bore a hole into his being. They had always been foremost in his thoughts. He reveled in their pride. Now he felt directionless and alone. He returned to Newark, but the rules under which he had thrived in Alaska were the opposite in New Jersey. Instead of flourishing as he had in Alaska, he found himself in police precinct lockups.

The fat man found himself caught up in Bingo's raillery, and he joined in the merriment. Amused, Jonathon looked on from the far end of the bar, and he detected nuanced changes in Bingo as the fat man roared, "Let's give him a hand." Bingo's eyes narrowed, back straightened and smile tightened. He leaned towards the man and whispered something to him. Both men roared with laughter.

Jonathon followed Bingo and the fat man as they strode from the bar together. Bingo's prosthetic right arm affixed with a two-pronged hook rested brotherly over the fat man's shoulders as they pushed their way out the door. Jonathon followed them as they turned and entered an alley by the bar. Peering around the corner, Jonathon watched as Bingo smashed his left fist into the fat man's stomach, causing the man to regurgitate ten dollars of cheap beer. The prosthetic device flung in uppercut fashion, caught the fat man under his jaw as the man lunged forward. The force of the upward blow from the powerful Bingo and the downward fall of the heavy man tore most of the man's jaw from his face, dangling from Bingo's prosthesis.

The sight was too much even for Bingo. He slumped to his knees and apologized to the man who convulsed with horror and pain clutching the wound.

The sight had a different effect on Jonathon. He approached the two men and gently pushed Bingo aside. Bingo looked up at him fiercely, but he was so transfixed by the calm of Jonathon's voice that he could only look on dumb struck.

"Well, we can't leave the poor man like that now, can we?" Jonathon said soothingly and smiled. He bent over the man, who squirmed and gurgled for help. Jonathon calmly forced the man's hands away from the gaping wound and pinned them to the ground by standing on them. Reaching down, Jonathon found the man's throat and strangled him to death with such calm that terrified Bingo. After issuing quick commands, Jonathon ran for his car.

They struggled but managed to lift the dead man into the trunk of Jonathon's car. A short distance from the bar, they turned into an industrial site. To Bingo's horror, Jonathon told him exactly what he intended to do with the body. As if in a nightmare, Bingo obeyed orders, and the two men carved the cadaver into four sections, using sharp carpet knives and shoved each section into large trash bags. Bingo didn't question Jonathon's apparent preparedness.

Driving around the dark edges of the city like butchers looking to store their product, they found a site. They stuffed the sectioned fat man into rusting, fifty-five gallon drums behind a gas station. There the drums would remain unnoticed among several other similar containers for years.

The improvised actions of the two strangers that night cemented a relationship that would last the rest of their lives. It wasn't friendship. The pair developed rather quickly a co-dependency, a symbiosis. A leader in need of a loyal lieutenant discovered one in need of someone with whom to be loyal. What emerged from that night of carnage in Newark was a lasting relationship with terrible consequences, someone to give orders and someone to carry them out, no matter what. From then on, Bingo would do anything Jonathon asked. Anything.

But, Jonathon had to be sure. He devised to use the Mafia-tested measure of absolute loyalty: you can trust only those who are as dirty as you.

———————

On a chilly June night, following the graduation ceremony at Princeton, Jonathon feted with other Poly Sci grads at the local student bar called The Folly. Professor Amundson shared in the celebration and left the bar just before midnight amid slaps on the back, handshakes and hugs from his now former students, acknowledging their admiration with well-practiced humility and warmth. The professor pulled up the lapel of his sports jacket replete with the requisite elbow patches and pulled his trademark fedora low to fend off the sharp gusts.

Bingo lurked in a parking lot across the street from The Folly in Jonathon's car. He rolled his knit cap up to uncover his ears to remove any impedance of his senses as he followed the professor on foot towards the doctor's home. He closed in on the professor and smiled at the tune the professor whistled softly between his teeth. Bingo moved with the silence and agility of Fenimore Cooper's Natty Bumppo, or at least, that is what he thought. Although he was not someone you would find in a library, Bingo worshipped the *Leatherstocking Series,* and he had read them several times.

Bingo was upon the unsuspecting professor as Amundson broke from whistling to softly singing as he unlocked the door of his professorial looking, two-story Tudor home. Bingo snapped the prosthetic hooks shut on the professor's upturned collar and pushed him into the house. He forced the professor to the floor and told him to kneel with hands behind his head. He then pulled a .38 caliber semiautomatic pistol from his jacket pocket and pressed it to the back of the professor's head.

"You'll never be the fucking mouthpiece for The Establishment again Prof, spewing their corporate bullshit," Bingo hissed and fired two rounds into the doctor's brain as the professor protested the accusation.

Bingo ransacked the house and used a pillowcase to carry off a small CB radio, a clock radio and the professor's watch and wallet.

The official finding by the Princeton Police Department was a burglary gone wrong. The pillowcase containing the small electronics, wallet and watch and the .38 caliber automatic pistol would not be recovered from Carnegie Lake. The League of Environmental Terrorists, or as Jonathon termed it in French for its international—if grandiose—appeal: La *Ligue des Terroristes Environnementeaux*, LTE, although a team of two, was born. Soon, it became three.

Chapter Five

It was in an overcrowded, smoke filled, apartment in Greenwich Village. He and Bingo met with a group of young people through Jonathon's connection with the Students for a Democratic Society. But, this group was different. Most had affiliations with the SDS, however their message struck home with Jonathon, and, therefore, Bingo. They advocated violence as a means to social change and justice. And, they were devout communists, who called themselves The Weatherman Organization.

Bingo had struck up a conversation with an African-American woman, who seemed disinterested with the ardent speak going on around her. Bingo thought he had found a kindred spirit in Beatrice's indifference to what he secretly thought was a bullshit meeting. They laughed and rolled their eyes at some of the speeches. Jonathon made his way back to Bingo who introduced him to Beatrice.

Jonathon had been moved by the conversations, and he was excited to take up with this group, until Beatrice intervened.

Over the coming weeks, Beatrice and Bingo developed a relationship, and she became a fixture in the apartment that Jonathon and Bingo shared. They shared experiences from the counterculture movement, and over time, it became obvious that she shared Jonathon's views on the need for change, but only through violence.

"Why not join forces with the Weatherman?" Jonathon asked.

Beatrice argued that they were sloppy. "Take that meeting we attended, for example," she began. "How long do you think it will take the FBI to infiltrate them? Maybe the FBI already has. True, there are benefits to belonging to a large organization like having established safe houses around the country. They talk a good game, but they think going public about who they are and blowing up a few government buildings will result in a full-scale revolution. We can do better as a small, well-organized group of true revolutionaries, who are equal participants in the decision-making. Think back to that meeting in the Village. You could feel the lack of agreement and organization."

31

Beatrice added, "I am far more intrigued by the LTE than I am with the Weatherman. Don't look at Bingo that way, Jonathon. He did let me in on some of what you have been up to. I want in, but not if you plan on associating with large, disorganized counter-culture groups. In short, I want to cause the establishment pain and grief for all the pain and grief they shower us with under the guise of the establishment. Their so-called adherence to American values is killing us, especially those of us on the lower end of the economic spectrum. They pollute our water, for profits. They pollute the air we all breathe, to profit a very few. They poison the life-giving rivers and our bodies, to make rich fucks richer. They poison our minds with their bullshit television, the opiate for the masses someone called it, correctly. They are sending thousands of our poor to their deaths in Vietnam, and call it patriotism, as long as it does not reach the sons and daughters of the wealthy class, because being rich is patriotic enough. For they are the ones held on high——our gods and goddesses perched on the Mount Olympus of the American dream. And we should all feel nothing but gratitude for these God's gifts to humanity for the sacrifice of their risk taking. After all, aren't we the beneficiaries of their inspired speculation that ultimately lifts us all as if by invisible hand? Oh, what benevolent, prescient ones they are. The least we can do is sacrifice ourselves in beating back the red scare in the jungles of Vietnam to preserve what they have worked so hard to achieve: mind numbing jobs for us, beach homes for them. Fuck me. Let's do, not talk. Give me an assignment that you feel will prove my loyalty."

And so, it became a team of three. The assignment she requested landed Beatrice in a penitentiary for four years and her loyalty never wavered. She did her time without any outward sign of remorse, and she found Chrissy.

Chapter Six

Christina Baker was a freshman in high school when her infatuation with George Rogers Clark began. At first, the Bakers rationalized that their daughter's obsession was normal curiosity of adolescent romanticism and love fantasy: a healthy approach in her attempt at understanding physical and emotional changes that all young people experience.

Two years later, after the sixteen-year-old girl went missing and turned up at a Rogers-Clark family reunion in Kentucky, several hundred miles from home, the Bakers realized that their daughter's fixation with the long-dead frontiersman resided outside the realm of typical behavior. They sought treatment, but when doctors said, "Obsessive compulsive disorder," the parents refused any further therapy that suggested, even remotely, that their brilliant daughter might be sick. Mrs. Baker's trepidation with psychiatry was well founded. She saw the affects of lobotomy on her beautiful mother in 1953.

Christina Baker went on living in her parents' blind spot throughout high school and college. She excelled, therefore how could she be ill? As she made honor roll each year, she regressed deeper into her own world.

Mr. and Mrs. Baker often remarked how cute it was that six-year-old Chrissy knew the number of steps between the front door and the mailbox, and the number of paces from home to school. No one thought twice that as the girl grew older she would insure the number of steps it took to get there remained the same. Upon learning how to drive a car, Chrissy always looked over her right shoulder exactly three times and checked the left mirror twice and the right one once before reversing.

Danny, her older brother, saw a girl unable to escape a fantasy. He worried how she would handle real-life crises that he knew all people experience. But, he remained hopeful, and he did not want to appear overly critical for fear of driving her from him. He was her last connection with reality, and, as long as they could talk about it, everything would be all right.

In a time when IQ testing was mandatory for all grammar school children in Montana, Christina Ann Baker scored the highest in the Missoula School District, which came as no surprise to her parents or Danny. Mrs. Baker taught her children to read long before they attended public school. Danny taught his precocious younger sister algebra, then advanced algebra, plane geometry, solid geometry and so on as he was taught the same subjects in junior and senior high schools. Chrissy, therefore, was always far ahead of her classmates, and that was where she longed to remain. Her biggest challenge in school was overcoming boredom, and then she discovered the Carnegie Free Library, her sanctuary. Here she found George Rogers Clark, Venice and King Lear. Her curiosity was only exceeded by her imagination that transported her through time and space and to emotional attachments that reality had no chance of keeping pace with. Most of her schoolmates thought she was weird, and teachers thought she was brilliant though lacking in social skills. However, her high school counselor nailed her by concluding in a letter of recommendation for Chrissy's use in the college application process: *Christina Baker demonstrated, throughout her time here at Missoula High School, the remarkable ability to simply overwhelm a subject with hard work to a degree I have not witnessed in my seventeen years in the field of education.* Other than Danny, Chrissy had no real friends.

On Thursday, May 27, 1971, Christina Baker prepared for her college graduation party that she initially planned not to attend. But, she gave in to the Bakers' idea of celebration and felt she owed them that much. Her parents proudly informed even the most disinterested acquaintances that their daughter earned her bachelor's degree in science from the University of Montana in just three years "in chemistry, no less."

The celebration came to a halt when Major Douglas and Captain Shapiro stopped by the Baker residence.

Army protocol called for the delivery of death notices by two officers for two reasons: it may take two officers to console the families and the safety of the purveyors. You never knew how the family would take the news of a deceased loved one.

The officers stood ramrod straight in the Baker's living room and delivered the news with textbook precision. The Bakers took the news of Danny's death with unusual stoicism. Mr. and Mrs. Baker had feared the worst since their son's deployment to Vietnam seven months earlier. In a house decorated for her college graduation, which would take place the next day, Christina Baker sobbed inconsolably at the reading of the citation by the major:

THE UNITED STATES OF AMERICA

TO ALL WHO SHALL SEE THESE PRESENTS, GREETING:

THIS IS TO CERTIFY THAT THE PRESIDENT OF THE UNITED STATES

HAS AWARDED THE

PURPLE HEART

ESTABLISHED BY GENERAL GEORGE WASHINGTON

AT NEWBURGH, NEW YORK, AUGUST 7, 1782,

TO

DANIEL HENRY BAKER

SPECIALIST 4 E4

FOR WOUNDS RECEIVED IN ACTION

19 MAY 1971

REPUBLIC OF VIETNAM

GIVEN UNDER MY HAND IN THE CITY OF WASHINGTON

THIS 22ND DAY OF MAY 1971

Malcolm E. McDonald   Lt. Colonel

Stanley R. Resor   Secretary of the Army

The major then read the official letter from the president that regretted to inform the family that their son died of wounds received in action. Chrissy jerked the papers from the major's hands and ripped a corner from the Purple Heart citation. "Look at this," she sobbed. "It is a fucking form with my brother's name and dates typed in, sloppily I might fucking add. Look at how some of the letters and numbers jump up like they didn't want to be a part of this bullshit."

Kenneth Baker tried to put his arms around his daughter, but she pulled free and pushed through the two officers and out the front door. The officers stood silently and nodded ever so slightly as the parents apologized for their daughter's behavior. Loud banging and the sound of glass breaking interrupted the parents' expression of regret. The officers hurried outside with the horrified parents to find Chrissy hammering at the olive drab Chevrolet with a sixteen-pound sledgehammer.

The officers maintained their disciplined emotionless demeanor as Mr. Baker pulled the hammer from his distraught daughter. Mrs. Baker took the girl in her arms and rocked side to side. The two officers exchanged glances and Captain Shapiro retrieved a small book of procedures from the glove compartment in the car. They stepped away from the grieving family and returned to them after a short discussion.

"Sir," the major addressed Mr. Baker, "procedures require that we notify local authorities to report the destruction to the vehicle. We need a police report to verify how the damage occurred. I am very sorry, but we do not have a choice in the matter."

The events of the last fifteen minutes caught up with Mr. Baker, tears streaming down his face. "Chrissy, you hammered their car. They are just doing their duty."

"Sir, may I use your phone? I have to notify the police."

"Yes, of course," cried Mr. Baker. "We are in an unincorporated area. Call the sheriff's office. Come in, please."

"Oh, for Christ's sake," Chrissy screeched. "I can't fucking believe this." She broke free of her mother's embrace and ran to the back of the small home counting aloud through her tears as she ran.

MOURNING IN THEIR TRIBE

"She'll be okay, sir," Mrs. Baker spoke evenly, unemotionally. They were people who were taught at an early age not to show emotion in front of strangers. Mrs. Baker remained loyal to that tenet, though her voice shook.

The major stood in the living room speaking softly with the sheriff's office. Captain Shapiro stood nearby with hands clasped behind his back, but purposely positioned himself between the major and the Bakers to follow security protocol.

Those procedures broke down as Chrissy burst through the back door of the home, carrying her father's twelve gauge shotgun.

"No!" Mr. Baker screamed.

The major half-turned towards Chrissy and dropped the receiver of the phone, bouncing crazily on its chord.

Captain Shapiro broke from his stance and rushed towards Chrissy as the room exploded in a deafening blast. The birdshot intended for the major ripped into Captain Shapiro's left thigh as he lunged toward the gun.

Chrissy attempted to pump another round into the chamber of the shotgun, but Major Douglas and her dad wrestled the gun from her before she could get off another shot.

Captain Shapiro would recover fully from his wound. Christina Ann Baker would not. During her trial for attempted murder, the judge considered the mitigating circumstances of grief and shock suffered by the young woman when he handed down a sentence of one to five years in the penitentiary.

Chrissy served out her sentence in York, Nebraska, because at the time Montana did not have a long-term prison facility for women. There, Chrissy became a model prisoner. She found that life in prison was not much different than her life in high school and college. She kept to herself and worked tirelessly in the administration building, gaining the trust of the prison officials who would reward her with parole in fifteen months.

It became easy for her to access the inmates' records, which she studied with theologian zeal. No one questioned a document that transferred Chrissy to a cell she would share with an African-American woman whose story Chrissy knew by heart.

Beatrice McCovey, at twenty-seven years old, was serving out the final year of a four-year sentence for bombing a federal building in Omaha. Though her bomb caused little structural damage to the building and no casualties, McCovey received the maximum sentence mainly for her lack of legal guidance. She proudly confessed to the bombing, saying she did it to thwart the lies used to recruit young men to fight and die to improve profits for the military industrial complex. She took the stand and read an exhaustive anti-government manifesto that Chrissy found intriguing.

Chrissy entered Beatrice's cell and stacked her few belongings neatly in one corner as Beatrice looked on. She picked up a black-and-white photograph of Beatrice, tall and pretty, standing next to a man with a prosthetic right arm wearing a tee shirt.

Beatrice snatched the photograph from Chrissy and hissed, "Leave my shit alone. What the fuck happened to Maria?"

"I don't know, but I do know that you used a primitive pipe bomb on that building. What'd you fill it with, match heads?" Chrissy scoffed, shaking her head.

Beatrice glared at the brash, skeletal woman sitting on the bunk opposite her. As Beatrice mulled over her choices of indecorous retorts, Chrissy broke the silence. Her voice turned icy, and her gray eyes held Beatrice's eyes, "On the other hand, I could have assembled a device so elegant, it would have taken down the entire fucking block." She smiled brightly and extended her hand. "I'm Chrissy, and a damn good chemist."

Chapter Seven

On the night of July 4, 1974, Beatrice and Chrissy watched from a van parked at a sharp bend in the road that separated the armory from a sports field. She saw the moon's shadow playing off the long, single-story stucco building as Jonathon and Bingo carrying large canvas bags made their way along North Parmelee Avenue in Compton, California.

The men cut the chain securing the gate with bolt cutters, quickly shuffled to the side entrance and turned toward Beatrice in the truck. A short blink of the headlights signaled the all clear. Using hammers and crowbars, the men easily battered down the door.

Once inside, the men wore headlamps to efficiently work their way to the weapons vault. Employing a vacuum drill, the taller of the two men went to work on the lock.

Beatrice saw one of the men emerge from the broken door and wave at her. She blinked the lights, leaving Chrissy on the sidewalk standing guard, and drove the van towards the gate. The man ran from the doorway to push the gate open and directed Beatrice to back the van up to the side door.

She sat behind the wheel keeping an eye on Chrissy as she heard her male compatriots quickly load the van with heavy boxes.

In a bar frequented by National Guardsmen in South Los Angeles in May 1974, Beatrice overheard a group of young men talking boisterously. Speaking over one another ever more loudly with each round of beer, each man offered his opinion on the surge in burglaries of armories around the country. One of the men, sporting a shorter afro than the others, said, "Oh man, I'll tell you what. It would be like taking candy from a baby at our armory." The other three leaned in closely. "Yes, if you're a guardsman, all you got to do is request a copy of the floor plans, and just like that, the

Guard will mail them to you. Do you know how many people we are talking about? Hundreds. That's an awful lot of trust."

"You got to be shittin' me, man."

"Charles would know … he, being in the guard and all."

"Charles, are you telling us that the Compton Armory is not protected by an alarm system? What about armed guards?"

Charles lowered his voice, and Beatrice passed by them heading towards the restroom. "Guys, we are going to install the alarm this summer, but our unit does not even have the funds to pay for armed guards. There's something like fourteen hundred armories in California. The cost to guard them all would be huge." He looked around and finished sarcastically, "We have strong locks."

Beatrice returned to her bar stool and stared at the man called Charles. After one of the others nudged Charles to look her way, she stood up and approached him.

She smiled bashfully and said, "Excuse me, I did not mean to eavesdrop, but did I hear you're in the National Guard?"

"Yes, ma'am," he replied. Charles straightened up in his chair.

"Were you in Vietnam?" she demurred.

"Yes, I was, but I'm continuing my career in the Guard. Why do you ask?"

Beatrice looked downcast and raised her eyes to meet his. "My brother was killed over there two years ago. May I buy you a drink?"

Charles looked at the others, and they gave him the "If you don't, you're a fool" look.

He stood up and followed her to the bar. After several rounds of drinks and dancing in between Beatrice's soft grilling of his experiences in Vietnam, they left the bar together. "Where are you parked?"

"That's me in the red Mustang."

"Very, very nice," Beatrice responded.

"I paid cash for this baby with my re-up money. It's my pride and joy. Can I give you a lift?" Charles responded confidently.

"It's gorgeous and sure. As I told you, I work near here, and usually take the bus … " Beatrice slurred.

He opened the door for her, and she plopped down into the seat while he skipped around to the driver side. Beatrice pushed two fingers into her throat, and just as Charles opened his door, she threw up, spraying the steering wheel, the dash and the windshield with puke.

"Jesus Christ," Charles raged. "What have you done to my car? Shit."

Charles slammed the door and ran back into the bar to find something to clean up the mess.

Beatrice flipped the driver-side visor down and yanked the plastic pouch free, containing the registration for the car. She quickly noted the man's full name and, more importantly, his address.

She was outside the car when Charles jogged back to the car with a hand full of paper napkins and a bar towel.

"I'm so sorry. I shouldn't drink that much."

He scowled at her and began wiping down the interior of the car. She stuck her head in her side of the car and said, "Look, I'll just take the bus home. Again, I'm so sorry."

"Yeah, whatever. Jesus, careful, you're dripping."

Two days later, Beatrice and her crew watched as Charles drove away from his house. Five minutes later she stood at the front door and pressed the doorbell to insure no one was at home. On her signal, two of her compatriots walked to the back of the house.

Beatrice heard glass breaking and a moment later, one of the men opened the front door. She entered, taking position near the front window as the men went to work.

The men found a small desk in the bedroom containing Charles' military file, neatly labeled. They jotted down his full name, rank, service number and social security number. Carefully they returned the file to its place in the drawer. One of the men grabbed a 13" television from the desk, and they nonchalantly departed through the front door.

Maintaining her vigil inside Charles' home, Beatrice kept an eye on the area for several minutes before following the men down the street to the waiting car driven by Chrissy.

In the coming days, Beatrice set up a mailbox in the name of Mr. and Mrs. Charles Walters, Compton, CA. She sent a letter to the California National Guard, Sacramento, using Charles' service information, requesting a floor plan of the Compton Armory. The main office obliged by sending a form back with a note attached from Staff Sergeant Dayton saying, "I assume this is for the upcoming installation of the burglar alarm to be completed by the end of July. Please fill out the attached form and return." Beatrice completed the form and noted the reason as "installation of alarm system." In about one week, the urban warriors had a complete set of floor plans for the Compton Armory.

———————

Once they had all that they had come for, the men jumped into the back of the van, and Beatrice drove through the gate. Chrissy shut the gate behind the van, restrung the broken chain where it had been and climbed into the passenger seat.

After a short drive, Beatrice stopped near a pickup truck equipped with a camper shell into which they quickly transferred the stolen property. Once fully loaded, Chrissy, driving the pickup truck, followed Beatrice and the others in the van for less than half a mile. Beatrice parked the van at the spot from which it had been stolen behind The Federal Cleaners, and Bingo quickly reversed the "hot wiring" of the van. The foursome drove away in the pickup truck. The entire operation took less than ninety minutes to complete.

In the days to come, the foursome contemptuously noted that the newspapers all failed to mention the most important missing property and the central objective of their mission, solely focusing on the stolen weapons.

The military chose not to release the fact that an enormous amount of plastic explosives was also stolen. The group shared a toast at the expense of local authorities and the FBI, who insisted the burglary was an inside job due to the obvious knowledge of the armory and the timing of it.

Interviewed by several news outlets, the chief of police stated unequivocally, "This [burglary] was an inside job. The thieves knew exactly what tools they needed. They had to use a truck to haul the vacuum drill they used on the fence, the doors and the vault. We will first check with all the truck rental agencies in Southern California for leads."

Weeks later, Sergeant First Class Walters could not explain to the FBI the form sent to headquarters in his name requesting a copy of the armory floor plan nor the mailbox rented in his name by a fictional wife. Samples of his handwriting were secured by the government agents and sent off to the IRS to be analyzed by world-renowned graphologists. His typewriter was confiscated, and its type analyzed. They re-examined the burglary of Walters' home. Nothing was found to tie the sergeant to the armory crime.

Chapter Eight

On a desert rise known as Promontory Summit, Utah, a steam engine named Jupiter of the Central Pacific Railroad met with Engine Number 119 of the Union Pacific Railroad. Promontory Summit lay at the transection of routes that provided the easiest way around the north side of the Great Salt Lake for the two railroads. Celebrants made their way to this obscure spot on May 10, 1869, to witness one of the nation's historical events: the joining of the nation by rail that was commemorated by the driving of a golden spike. The once castle in the sky of a transcontinental railroad was realized.

The Freedom Train, conceived to bring history by rail to the American people, would not bypass an important geographical place in U.S. railroad history. Promontory would become the cornerstone of Utah's grand bicentennial celebration.

So many months ago…

The group sat in a small Philadelphia apartment looking over the itinerary of the proposed scheduled stops for the Freedom Train that Beatrice had secured. Bingo, of course, pointed to the next stop in Harrisburg, Pennsylvania.

"That's my choice. Right there, and we're done with this shit in a week."

"Right. How like you, Bing," Jonathon said. "Get it done. Move on, right?"

"Right on. Right on."

"As usual," Jonathon soothed. Then he sneered, "Wrong. We aren't ready yet."

Chrissy jumped in, "Let's wait. Let's get out of the east. I like that crowds will be larger here, but…" She looked at Beatrice.

44

Beatrice took the cue, "But," she focused on Jonathon knowing she had secured Chrissy's vote of approval before hand. "What are we trying to achieve? The biggest bang for our buck." She smiled at the obvious use of words. "Look down the line to Promontory Point, Utah." She paged through the itinerary to that location.

"Fucking Utah?" Bingo interrupted and added sarcastically, "Wow, that'll get their attention."

Jonathon shut him off with a look. "Yes. Of course." Stroking his beard, he continued. "I like your thinking, Trish. Promontory Point is brilliant," he agreed. "Promontory Point, a redundancy of words to be sure, since promontory and point mean one and the same," he said with more than a little pedantic air. "Still, one cannot overlook the huge historical significance of the place."

"Exactly," Beatrice breathed easy. She had not expected Jonathon to so quickly accept her target. Since she had been prepared to complete her argument, she swiftly added, "Here at this remote site, the corporate pigs completed their railroad using essentially Chinese slaves and poor Euro immigrants. Christ, they probably paid more for the final celebration with their precious spikes and whiskey than they paid to lay the last fifty miles of track." She looked at the faces of her companions and knew she was preaching to the choir.

She completed her thoughts with notably less gusto, "It is a softer target, far from a major city, and far enough down the line. That will give us time to thoroughly plan our assault. Test our equipment and so on."

"Promontory, it is," Jonathon roared.

Chapter Nine

"The history of steam starts with James Watt's mother's kettle and progressed to this magnificent machine. To celebrate our nation's two hundredth birthday, this locomotive will bring our history to our citizens across the country. In the next year and a half, we will have visited eighty cities located in all forty-eight contiguous states and have traveled more than 25,000 miles by rail. The Freedom Train is made up of 26 cars with 12 specially constructed cars to preserve and show more than 500 artifacts and memorabilia that represent American history. It will be delivered by locomotive, a masterpiece of steel and steam rescued from the scrap yard, given a second chance like so many of our citizens," said Pierce.

A man not noted for verbosity, Pierce had made a fortune in the stock market. When asked to what he attributed his success, he would simply say, "luck," if he answered at all. But if trains made it into the conversation, he became an out-and-out Cicero.

"Now, ladies and gentlemen, allow me to lead you through the multi-media exposition. You will be the first of thousands to view a slice of our great history using modern methods. Follow me to car one, designated as our Revolutionary Beginnings."

An attendant supplied the audience with state-of-the-art transistorized receivers whereby they would hear a running narrative of what they would view in the first ten cars. Each car is equipped with moving floors using conveyor belts that ensured those who would come to see the grand show did not interrupt the constant flow of traffic. In eighteen minutes the audience is transported briskly from car to car, each designed to show a particular time period of American life. Examples of American achievements in art and architecture, entertainment, exploration, literature, science, sports and transportation are on display. After zipping through the ten cars that include memorabilia such as Shirley Temple's toys, World Series pennants, Jim Thorpe's Olympic scroll and George Washington's draft of the Constitution, the audience spilled out of car ten. Pierce unveiled the final two display cars. These were designed with large picture windows where a large replica of the Liberty Bell, a 1904 Oldsmobile and other historical transportation items could be viewed at the audience's leisure.

Grumbling arose in part of the crowd, especially from members of the press. One reporter complained that the conveyor belts moved people along at a pace greater than the transistorized audio narrative. Another calculated that two dollars a head was an exorbitant price to pay for an eighteen-minute presentation that she called a "whirlwind tour" and amounted to paying twenty cents per minute per couple to see and not hear well. She also noted that the projection mechanism by which mannequins appeared to speak was "spooky and too Disneyesque" and did not afford the proper "gravity" of presenting a true picture of Americana to the people. Another reporter wrote that the train designated by Pierce as a "museum on wheels" was more circus than historical enlightenment. He also recorded that the squalor of inner cities, immigrant shacks, ramshackle medical facilities and schools on Indian reservations did not make the "historical tour." All that being said, most of the inaugural audience was mesmerized by the spectacle.

Pierce noticed a young woman kneeling near the front of the engine. She ran her hand along the track below a drive wheel of the huge engine and brought her fingers to her nose. Peering under the engine near the wheel, the woman closely inspected the lengths of metal tubing. She lightly traced one of the lines with her left hand stopping at a junction box.

"What have you found?" asked Pierce amused.

Straightening up, the woman turned to face him. "Mr. Pierce," she said, "hydraulic fluid is leaking from the pressure valve in the medial junction. Well, in my opinion."

Pierce tried to hide his skepticism, "You'll find oil around this massive machine. The drive rods will … "

"Yes, I know. But this is a pressure valve problem. It will not leak when hot … "

"But, it will leak when the valve has cooled. When heated, the metal will expand, thus closing the imperfection," Pierce noted.

"Exactly," the woman answered confidently.

"How is it you know so much about this locomotive? It has been out of general service for years."

"I grew up in Reading, Pennsylvania. My dad was a railroader and devoted time rebuilding the old 2-8-0 and the T1 class, 4-8-4 engines, like this one for the Reading Company," she said, using the wheel configurations to describe the types of locomotives. "Due to war time restrictions on building new locomotives, the railroad rebuilt the old ones. I spent my childhood crawling over these beauties. I find something comforting about being close to them and the way they smell."

"Beauty and the beast," Pierce blurted, embarrassed.

The woman laughed, "She is a beauty, all right."

"That isn't what I meant. I was struck by the look in your eyes, and, well … "

The woman touched his arm to ease Pierce's discomfiture.

"What brings you out here today?" Pierce asked. "Other than your adoration of steam locomotion."

"I wanted to see it up close. I heard of your project to use this magnificent behemoth to bring history to the masses. Now, I would like to be a part of it. Are you still hiring?"

"Well, no." The woman was pretty, and pretty women evoked an anxiety in him that he was never quite able to control.

"No problem, I should have come forward before now. I found the announcement for today's presentation intriguing, and I really didn't think about being employed with the project before just this minute," she lied.

Turning she spoke in a low tone as if speaking to the train, "I didn't realize until I came out here how much I miss … the sight, the smells that swept me back to grand memories. Gone now, forever … "

Trying to regain her composure, Pierce interrupted her. "We do have a few security positions open," he lied. "We will fill many of these positions city by city, but we have had difficulty in hiring individuals for the long haul. You will learn our safety requirements for preserving the priceless cargo and security features like our state-of-the-art closed-circuit television system and instruct the volunteers. If you're interested, see Jason Bigelow in car two."

She held out her hand, "Beatrice Donaldson. It would be my pleasure to work for you, and an absolute joy to ride the rails behind this grand machine."

Pierce smiled. "Come, why don't I introduce you to Jason."

Beatrice stopped. "There is one thing I need to make clear."

"Of course. What is it?"

"The kettle," Beatrice stated.

"Kettle?"

"James Watt and the kettle," Beatrice instructed. "He didn't invent the steam engine after watching steam lifting a lid from his mom's boiling kettle. Thomas Newcomen invented the steam engine."

Pierce added, "You're right. But, Watt did greatly improve the design, and his steam engine company, started with Matthew Boulton in 1775, changed the world."

Beatrice thought, *just what I expected, the train is presenting history to match the current narrative.* Like most of what she knew and thought of the train, *it would pay small homage to Martin Luther King, Jr. by including his bible among the artifacts it carried, and would carry little of the strife for freedom that African-Americans are still fighting for some two hundred years after the signing of the Declaration of Independence and more than one hundred years after the end of the Civil War ... Not to mention excluding the part about the genocide of Native Americans.* She did not say how she would try not to revel in victory when the whole goddamn thing is reduced to rubble.

"Touché, Mr. Pierce. Shall we go find Mr. Bigelow?"

Chapter Ten

Thursday, April 22, 1976. Kentucky

The Freedom Train

Dear MMI,

Can't sleep.

Black-and-white. Conway doesn't know the difference! Incredulous as it may seem. Skin pigment!

He's shitting me, right?

In this day and age, how can anyone believe that being black, or being white, is just a matter of skin pigment?

Beatrice's diary entry was motivated by a conversation she had earlier that day with a workmate when he said, "I don't think there is any difference between black and white people. It is just pigment, if you ask me."

The surprise showed on his face as she responded, "There's a difference. You can say that we all experience the same emotions—love, hate, empathy—have the same color of blood, and so on, and no one will disagree."

He nodded.

"Though true," Beatrice said, "that is overly simplistic. Being black in America is more complicated than that. It starts with history, memory and bigotry. The printed signs, as a safety measure, telling you that you are not good enough to use certain bathrooms and water fountains, to sit wherever you can afford in a stadium or to enter certain cafes. It is about living in a country where it is okay to fight and die for it, but not to vote. It is about being brought up with the notion that you are second class, no matter how much money you make or how educated you are, and having to deal with that. Saying that we are all the same may sound good, but that is a cop out."

"Okay, Beatrice. I apologize for over simplifying the issue."

"I know you meant well. Believing people are the same beneath the surface is a small step in the right direction. There are actually people in this country that feel black people are less than human. Race relations are complicated.

He's not a bad sort really. He may have understood my point, but how can I be sure? At first impression, I thought we had little in common: different upbringings, different family situations. After getting to know him, I could like him, if I had the luxury.

My workmate was reared in a place where routine was expected, and he considered that dull. I had routine in my life, but continuity escaped my upbringing. We relocated every couple of years. I would have traded places with him in a heartbeat, and that has nothing to do with being black or white. No matter. That's not my truth.

We will be in Cincinnati tomorrow and then Cleveland.

More importantly:

The nightly security details are less serious now. Three officers made the rounds in the beginning and now one at predictable times.

Routine has replaced the awareness everyone had in the beginning. Bitterness over wages, long hours and loss of staff has crept into conversations. If something were to go wrong, we don't have the staff to deal with it. Decay will be the downfall.

Notes on watch times:

Each security officer patrols the same path, even though Mr. Bigelow told us to alter our routes and start times. Observation: the foot patrol never alters his schedule.

Need: 1. Take pix of crowds at various times of day.

2. Analyze itineraries and look for consistencies.

3. Predict with confidence what happens and when.

4. Make sample itineraries to predict what to expect at Promontory.

Satisfied with the day's entry, Beatrice closed the book and locked it. She turned off the lamp and waited for the rhythmic clickety-clack of the rails to bring sleep that eluded her often. She looked out the window as the Freedom Train sped towards its next destination.

She replayed the conversation with her workmate in her mind and reprimanded herself for exposing too much. That is not the way of "The Chameleon," that she had worked so diligently to perfect. Her good looks were difficult to disguise, though she tried by dressing in understated fashion.

She feared she might have overstepped her masquerade today, even though she reeled in how she really felt. It could have been worse.

"Don't give them anything more to remember you by than 'well she's pretty, but I don't recall her saying anything to make me believe she was anti-anything. Seemed nice.'" She whispered to herself.

As she drifted toward sleep, her thoughts coasted to her diary that she named *Me, Myself and I* years ago. Although she knew the hazards of keeping a written record, she felt that it was necessary for her well being.

Beatrice wrote in her diary since her eleventh birthday: a gift hastily purchased by her father, Major McCovey. This book became a refuge for her.

Her family moved too often to form friendships. For a childhood bereft of personal relationships, she found comfort in the blank pages of her diary. Beatrice's dairy became her confidant. She filled page after page with imagery. The book became a living thing that she looked forward to rushing home to and sharing her most intimate thoughts with. Lured by the stark paper, she felt the power of bringing life where nothing existed. When not writing, she spent hours reading the words within her journals. In short, she did not think in terms of writing in her journal. It was her voice.

Me, Myself and I always showed up for Beatrice. *MMI* held her disappointments, embarrassments and hopes. *MMI* was there when classmates made fun of her overbite. It held close counsel as she worked tirelessly to overcome a lisp aspersed by teachers and students alike. The little book held synonyms that replaced words beginning with and containing *s*'s that Beatrice memorized nightly and used in class to overcome her lisp, a disguise to be an effective weapon against the insults. Early on, Beatrice understood the advantages of blending in.

To the outside observer, her father provided shelter and a good home, but as a single parent and career Army officer, the Major afforded little time for nurturing his children. Emotionally, the houses in which Beatrice and her brother resided were quarters, as the Major called them, never homes. Beatrice and her brother were on their own to find their emotional way in life. The Major demanded perfect school attendance, and poor grades were unacceptable. Beatrice immersed herself in her schoolwork and confided in her diary.

Unable to sleep, she re-opened the diary and wrote the following entry:

Dear MMI,

Looking out my window, I see everything close up whiz by quickly, while the distant objects hardly move. Like the telephone poles along the track, the here and now whizzes by quickly forgotten while there, in the distance, always visible, looms my past, my father, disappointments, humiliations. Maybe tomorrow they will be out of sight.

She dozed.

Chapter Eleven

Thursday, May 19, 1976, Texas

The Freedom train

Dear MMI,

Black-and-white, again.

My workmate is very curious about black people. Is he a racist? Does he keep asking questions about how black people think, because he cannot fathom us being as intuitive or forming thoughts in the same way, or is he genuinely interested?

I know I was certain that that was the case, in the beginning. Now, I'm not sure.

I think he is struggling to understand today's world and race relations. He is besieged with concern and thinking about how we communicate with each other. The fact that he wants to understand is basically good. After months of working with him, I really do think his heart is in the right place.

PART 3

Heavy

A sprawling city extending north and south along the foothills that separated the western front of the Wasatch Mountains and the Great Salt Lake, Heavenly Valley was one of the fastest growing communities in Utah. In 1870, the city had sprung up around a railroad water stop where the main line track passed over the Wasatch River before the track bent west towards Nevada. Following World War II, the city's population exploded and outdistanced the growth of the government to service it. Heavenly Valley gained the reputation much more applicably fitting the portmanteau, Heavy, for which it was widely known.

Chapter Twelve

The bad language—profanities, obscenities and slurs—was as much a part of the job as the ten-code. *Shop talk. Tools of the trade.* He would never speak that way at home in front of Lizzy and the kids. Of course, he wore his Temple garments under his uniform and that eased his mind some. Hal Halverson believed that his sacred underwear, embroidered with meaningful symbols of God's endowment, not only provided protection from temptation and evil, but also from physical harm especially after he had witnessed such protection first hand. Halverson's friend and fellow officer, Reed Johnson, while investigating an auto accident during a severe thunderstorm that included a downed power line, was electrocuted and survived. Johnson experienced burns over his body except for the areas, neck to knee, covered by his Mormon underwear. Hal Halverson fretted over life's contradictions and how his chosen occupation tested his religion nightly on the streets of Heavenly Valley, Utah.

Corporal Halverson, oh, how he loved the sound of that. He was one of the first selected for the newly minted position by the police department. As a team lead, he seldom took direct calls for service. He was free to provide backup whenever and wherever the need arose. Free to roam the entire city and not confined to a certain patrol area was liberating. Free to do real police work—less paperwork—more beat work.

Truth is, Hal Halverson loved the work. He likened the Motorola two-way radio in his police car to a doctor's stethoscope. The city could look so benign, but the crackle of the radio told a different story. The radio was his connection to the inner workings of the community. Few citizens knew the hidden dangers of the town that only the radio revealed. Most days he could not wait to go to work and climb into the cruiser and turn on the radio. Tonight, was no different. Corporal Halverson returned to work following three days off.

The radio revealed no maladies tonight. State law prohibited bars from staying open past midnight on weeknights, and 1 A.M. on weekends. It had been over an hour since the bars had closed and most of the employees and proprietors had gone home. Halverson loved the silence.

MOURNING IN THEIR TRIBE

The summer night turning to morning was warm. It was time to check the bars. He headed for the center of town and Fifth Street, known by those who frequented it as "The Street." Fifth Street connected the train depot with Main Street. Bars, fleabag hotels and greasy cafes, lined both sides of The Street for a half mile.

The corporal doused the headlights and flipped the toggle switch that turned off the brake lights on the cruiser as he made a slow right turn into the "Electric Alley" that serviced the businesses on that side of The Street. He stopped often, turned the engine off, and listened for the telltale sounds that would tip him off to a burglary in progress: breaking glass, a scream or a gunshot. Nothing. The only sounds emanating along The Street were the rustling leaves and rubbish in the summer breeze.

Pushing on through the back alley, the cruiser idled through the intersection and entered the alley on the other side. Watching the darkened cruiser slip through the alleys and crossing the street, a lone man sat in a black Ford pickup truck with a short wide bed, which was parked beneath the trees lining the cross street. The dull light from the streetlight, interrupted by the swaying branches of the large oak tree, glittered off the truck's highly polished chrome wheels.

The man in the truck hung an elbow from the driver's window and listened. Suddenly, he thought he heard the muffled sound of a car door closing. He sat up and leaned towards the windshield. Moments later, the corporal emerged from around the opposite corner in front of the man in the truck. He watched as the officer silently walked along the street peering into windows and trying doors to ensure they were locked. The officer moved deliberately from building to building. He often stopped under the awnings of the storefronts, remaining in the shadows listening.

Feeling his pulse quicken and breathing grow heavy, the man reached over and opened the glove box. He snatched the black gun belt and holster that held the Colt .45 western-style revolver. He pulled the pistol from the holster and thumbed the loading hinge open. The man spun the cylinder and noted that it was loaded with five shells.

The man stepped from the truck and fastened the gun belt around his waist, then closed the door to the truck quietly without taking his eyes from the approaching officer. The man moved along behind parked cars whenever the corporal turned his back to try another door. He waited as the officer moved up the street rattling more doors, stopping in the darkened areas, listening and moving on.

Jogging up the alley in the same direction as the officer but behind the buildings on his side of the street, the man stopped abruptly at the sight of two men speaking loudly as they crossed through the intersection. The two men turned away from the watcher standing in the shadows, and they sauntered towards the town's police station.

One of the men threw his car keys in the air and pretended to shoot them with his finger. The other man laughed loudly into the night air. They disappeared around the far street corner.

The man stepped from the shadows and crept slowly to the corner of a building. He removed his large black Stetson hat and peeked around the corner. The corporal had made his way to the man's side of the street, and the man quickly stepped back, surprisingly agile for someone his size. He pulled the revolver partially from the holster and let it fall lightly back into place. He listened as the corporal rattled the handle of the door to yet another bar.

Stepping back from the corner, the man carefully put his hat back on his head, lowering the hat above his eyes. The big man faced the corner of the building where he knew the officer would appear.

Halverson decided to walk around the building and make his way back to the cruiser through the alley. He tried the doorknob to another bar and stepped out into the glare of the street light on the corner. Looking up past the light into the starless night, the officer breathed deeply and let his breath slowly escape as he thought how very few people in the town had the opportunity to roam it like he did. "Man, oh man, what a night," he whispered.

He turned and was surprised by the man wearing a large cowboy hat, standing shoulders square, right hand hovering above the holstered Colt, feet shoulder width apart.

"Geez, man, you gave me a start," the corporal breathed, but the hair on the back of his neck arose. *Danger.* He shaded his eyes from the glare of the arc light with his left hand to get a better view of the man.

"Draw, sheriff," the big man drawled calmly.

Fear spread through the corporal's body and settled in his chest. He tried to smile, and instead his lips stretched to bare his teeth, "What the fuck did you say?"

The man shook his right hand as if to loosen the tension. Calmly, the big man repeated his command. "I said, draw, share-eefe."

The corporal attempted to diffuse the situation. "I'm no sheriff." He tried to smile again, and his teeth remained bared. "I work for the city," he reasoned while carefully and slowly unsnapping the leather strap that secured his police revolver in its holster. He spoke louder to disguise the sound of the snap of the safety strap and to conceal the sudden fear welling in his gut. "See, the county police are called deputies and work for the sheriff, so I'm not ... "

Bang!

Chapter Thirteen

The Roof Bar took its name from a mostly decorative gable shaped canopy over the front door that gave the impression of a roof replete with bright green shingles. The bar was located on the first floor of a three-story parking structure that provided parking for midtown businesses and a watering hole for the off-duty officers whose police station was less than a block away.

A big man burst through the front door and stood, hands on hips, surveying the patrons of the bar. Detective Reynolds, sitting at the bar, eyed his partner, O'Brien, who occupied a table in the far corner entertaining two young women. O'Brien met his glance but continued talking to the women.

Sonya, the bar owner, quickly walked around the bar and approached the big man blocking the door.

"Rick, I want no problems from you tonight, or you can leave right now." She placed both hands on the man's chest and pushed.

The big man didn't budge. He continued eyeing the bar patrons, and then looked down at the bar owner and smiled. He boomed, "Nice crowd in here tonight. I am just making sure I have some nice people to share a few drinks with."

"Uh-huh. I know the look, Rick. You've already had plenty to drink, and now you look like you wanna top off the evening with a little extracurricular activity. Leave now, or promise no trouble."

"Okay, okay. Geez, Sonya," he lowered his voice. "I had that one little spat in here a couple of months ago. Are you ever going to let me live it down?"

"All right, you can come in. But, one complaint, and you're out." The bar owner was adamant, and Rick knew it.

Rick ambled around the bar and settled onto a stool at the far end. Reynolds knew Rick liked to fight when he drank. Despite Rick's love of drinking and fighting, he managed to have a successful business.

Six years before, he started one of Utah's first free classified ads newspaper called *Big Dollar*. People advertised anything they wanted to sell or buy and paid little for the space to do so. Businesses could purchase larger ad space, but the backbone was its access for selling and buying second-hand goods. New editions hit the stands every Wednesday. People in and around Heavenly Valley looked forward to the new editions to such a degree that many altered their grocery shopping schedules to coincide with the days the new editions hit the stands.

Rick Benson was respected and mostly liked by his employees. When sober, he could be thoughtful, but when drinking, the large man transformed into an imposing bully. He was referred to as "Big Rick" in the bars, and he was too willing to embrace the epithet, using the third person vernacular the more he drank. "Hey, honey, Big Rick needs another." Big Rick found pleasure in pushing people around, but he rarely fought. Most of his victims chose to back down, which would bring a loud, derisive laugh. "No one wants to mess with Big Rick."

Two months back, the man, who Big Rick chose to pick on, did not back down. They had been shooting pool together in the back room of The Roof. When the bar owner responded to the commotion, she found the man under the pool table bleeding and cowering to avoid Big Rick's boots. Sonya didn't have to call the police, because The Roof is known as a cop bar. Several off-duty police officers, drinking at the bar, rushed to her aid. It took four of them to subdue Big Rick. He was booked into jail and freed the next morning, because the victim refused to press charges.

Sheila Henry stood up from a table that included her boss, Russell Gates, and her mentor Phyllis Lucas. Gates had been the District Attorney since Sheila attended grammar school. Gates' directness bordered on brusque. He could be outspoken on any topic favored by his constituents; moreover, his suave good looks and noted family man image—a wife of twenty-three years and five strapping boys—made him extremely popular with the voters. He hired Phyllis Lucas as assistant district attorney after she passed the bar and

61

after winning his first election eighteen years ago. They had been carrying on a "secret" affair ever since. The affair had remained a secret apparently to only the voters of the county and his family.

"Sheila, do me a favor," Gates commanded.

"Sure thing, Boss." Everyone in the office, and, most who worked for the city and county, called him "The Boss."

The Boss took pride in keeping his finger on the pulse of the community; little escaped his attention. Sheila secretly thought he stuck his nose where it didn't belong, but she was young and ambitious. She knew that she lacked political savvy and for that she leaned on Phyllis and The Boss. She attached herself to them, and she did not care what the others in her office thought of her. A big future lay ahead, and she planned to take full advantage of every opportunity.

"Go see why Detective Reynolds talked to the press about being against the death penalty. The voters agree. We don't want some impudent cop giving the public the wrong impression. He was not expressing the views of my office," said The Boss.

Sheila slid onto the stool next to Reynolds, who wore a blue and white striped sear sucker sports jacket and light blue pants that matched the stripe in the jacket, and asked with a straight face, "How'd the ice cream sales go today?"

Reynolds didn't look up from his drink that he slowly stirred with a swizzle stick. "I made $16.50. Would have done better but the music machine broke down."

"Probably a good thing. How do you ever get that jingly-jangly music out of your head at night?" Sheila continued.

"Vodka tonic."

"Ahh, so that's what it is? I thought you were drinking perfume."

They both sat looking straight ahead but at each other in the mirror behind the bar. Reynolds knew that Henry was on a mission, but he played along.

Reynolds turned and exaggerated an elevator look at the woman with the straight blonde hair, trim figure, wearing a two-piece dark suit popular with the professional set. She sat on the high bar stool showing a lot of thigh and crossed knees next to him. "My, you must have worked late tonight. Big night at the mortuary?"

"Where's your shadow?" Sheila asked, paying no attention to the detective's assessment of her clothes. She thought his remark a poor counter to her ever more applicable opening salvo.

Reynolds nodded to a table in the corner where O'Brien, known to most as OB, amused the two women with his magic cigarette trick. Reynolds and Henry looked on as O'Brien slid an unlit cigarette back and forth on the tabletop after making a show of wiping the tabletop clean with a napkin. He then bent a little closer to the table and looked at the cigarette not far from his nose. He skimmed his index finger along the table a few inches in front of the cigarette, and the cigarette magically followed. One woman applauded and screeched, "How did you do that?" The other said, "It is static electricity between the table and the cigarette. That's why you rubbed the cigarette on the table so many times."

"Okay, you try it then," O'Brien said confidently.

She did, and, after repeating O'Brien's actions, nothing happened.

"Wow, how impressive," Sheila remarked flatly, shaking her head. "Jesus, does that shit really work?"

"Sometimes."

"I'm surprised that you're not over there taking advantage of the obvious situation. The two rocket scientists with your partner in crime would seem right up your alley."

"I would've been, but that would have meant missing out on the repartee with the assistant district attorney. And by the way, they're not rocket scientists, they're architects. Rocket scientists would have noticed him blowing on the cigarette."

"Ooooh, is that how it's done?" she replied in astonishment aping the women at O'Brien's table. "Gee, I thought it was O'Brien's personal magnetism." Sheila almost smiled, but perhaps didn't, as the two continued their conversation into the mirror.

Sheila did not know what to make of the detectives. O'Brien and Reynolds were longtime partners, who "somehow managed not to get fired," according to The Boss. They were often referred to as the "odd couple" by the district attorney's office. O'Brien, gregarious and affable, dark haired with a mustache many of Henry's peers admired for its perfection. And as The Boss said often, "He has a face made for a mustache." For reasons that Sheila only vaguely understood, the women in her office always laughed coyly at O'Brien's sexist humor and attitude that she found demeaning and appalling. She knew they were attracted to the brawny man who had been something of a high school sports legend in the valley. *But,* Sheila thought, *he is slippery. You can never get a straight answer out of him. He disguises his intentions whether personal or professional in incessant mocking jabs and jibes that he passes off as humor. Admittedly, he is handsome, but I agree with The Boss. He's a bruiser. He's also married. Yet, look at him obviously trying to get into the panties of the women at his table. Jesus, how disgusting.*

As she bantered with Reynolds she thought, *Reynolds on the other hand appears almost fastidious, thus the "odd couple" tag seems appropriate, but not entirely. True enough they are opposite looking: O'Brien, dark complexioned and muscular, perfect mustache and all; and Reynolds taller, light complexion, wavy… more brown than blonde… hair, could do without the wispy mustache. Perhaps it's true that opposites attract.*

Sheila then held her thumb up to Reynolds' mouth as a pretend microphone. She said in her deepened radio voice, "Tell me, Detective, how do you feel about the Supreme Court's possible lifting of the ban on capital punishment?"

She alluded to the interview that Reynolds participated in at a local radio station the day before. He surprised the host and most listeners, especially the police officers who had tuned in, by saying he was against capital punishment. The host cut him off, and the DJ muted his microphone as he attempted to explain.

Sheila, now serious, asked, "You were about to clarify your answer, but that jerk on the radio jumped in. I know most in my office were astonished by your answer. I was. I haven't met a cop who is against capital punishment. Why?"

Reynolds faced her. "Who do you get to do it? That's my question, and my concern. You say murder is terrible, unlawful, against most religious precepts. What citizen do you ask to commit murder? Strap a defenseless person into a chair, then pull the handle?"

"Legally, it isn't murder."

"Right, legally," Reynolds sneered.

"Well, I would think that someone would be willing to do it. I mean, it happened in the past. Someone pulled all those switches before Furman v. Georgia struck down the death penalty in the states. Most in our office believe that the cases currently under review by the Supreme Court will result in reinstatement of capital punishment with certain qualifications. The decision should come down before long. The Court is working through the issues of the past that showed determinately that capital punishment was applied to certain minority groups far more frequently than to the majority. I'm sure that finding executioners will not be difficult."

"Probably not, finding them is one thing and then performing the grisly shit is another. I know the arguments for capital punishment. We all know that white people get away with murder while black and brown people are executed. I get that. It is true. What do you do with serial killers? Convicts who kill fellow inmates? All the arguments center around deterrence," Reynolds replied.

"There has been little evidence brought forth that the death penalty deters murder," Henry inserted. "Capital punishment advocates argue that it is needed as a societal retribution for extremely heinous murders and other terrible crimes."

"As far as societal retribution, there's a valid argument for that. You know, what do you do with them? I get all of that. Still, who do you persuade to kill another human being, who is not trying to kill you? Who do you get to kill another human who is totally rendered harmless and shackled? Seems pretty cold-blooded to me."

"I don't know," Sheila Henry said softly. "I know I couldn't do it."

65

"No, me either. Tell me, how would you like an executioner living next door to you?"

"I hadn't thought about that, frankly." Amusement showed in Sheila's eyes in the mirror.

"Yes, I can see you leaving your condo for work just as your neighbor is heading out for work too; a shirtless fat guy in a black hood and tights carrying a huge axe fumbling with the keys to his door. 'Morning Gary. How goes it?' 'Heads will roll, Sheila, heads *will* roll. Have a nice day.'"

Sheila smiled showing teeth, now perfectly straight after having endured two years in braces, that she couldn't help but admire in the mirror while noting how the subdued lighting of the bar also masked the pock marks in the hollow of her cheeks, remnants of teenaged acne. "So," she said, "I guess I would feel a little more comfortable living next door to a doctor than a head chopper."

"Oh, so you'd have a doctor do it?"

"We are hearing that lethal injection is now thought of as the most humane way to go. When the death penalty is reinstated, I suspect that will be the way most states go."

"I can't imagine too many doctors willing to concoct a killing injection. How does that square with the Hippocratic Oath?"

"I will prescribe regimens for the good of my patients according to my ability and my judgment and never do harm to anyone," Sheila replied absently as she quoted from a translation of the original Greek oath.

"However we do it—hangman, head chopper or doctor—my question remains the same. Who do you get to perform the act, and what are we doing to those who have to carry it out?" Reynolds asked.

"I don't know, Reynolds. You may be over thinking it. Who knows? Even if The Court reinstates the penalty, it will still be up to the states. Who knows, maybe Utah will choose not to reinstate it."

"Yeah, right. We both know that reinstatement is very popular here and throughout the country, especially after Charlie Manson. But, how popular would the death penalty be if the person chosen to flip the switch or inject the needle had to be a citizen chosen the same random way that we choose jurors? It's like going to war. Many are all for it as long as they don't have to go themselves. You should talk to old Sergeant Bob Jensen. He volunteered for a firing squad back in the fifties. It changed him. Talk to him. He will tell you what it is like to shoot a man strapped to a chair."

"Okay, I will have to talk with Jensen," Sheila replied.

She turned suddenly when she heard loud voices coming from the front of the bar. O'Brien was poking Big Rick in the chest and repeating, "Maybe some people have to take your shit, but I'm not one of them."

Big Rick held both hands shoulder level in a "hands up" position. "Looky here, O'Brien, I'm not going to fight you."

"You came in here looking to fucking fight. You've got one." With that O'Brien pushed Big Rick hard, and he fell back against the closed door. Big Rick looked befuddled, but he knew his reputation was on the line. His response came halfheartedly, and that was no match for O'Brien. O'Brien loved to box with quick hands that contradicted his size. Still, Big Rick stood a half head taller than the detective.

O'Brien struck Big Rick twice before Rick knew what hit him. Rick went down in a big heap.

Sheila turned to Reynolds who sat looking straight ahead into the mirror behind the bar unfazed by the ruckus. He knew that O'Brien had been laying for Big Rick since Rick had caused the disturbance in the poolroom months before. It wasn't that O'Brien wanted to right an injustice. He wanted to ensure that the sanctity of The Roof as cop territory was maintained. No one was allowed to come in here and cause trouble. The territory had to be protected.

"Are you just going to sit there while your partner pummels that man?" Sheila gasped.

"I have no idea what you are talking about, Sheila." With that, Reynolds stood up and walked over to Big Rick, who by now was on hands and knees shaking his head and bleeding from the nose.

Reynolds bent over Big Rick and asked into his ear so that all could hear, "What happened here?"

Big Rick shook his head and stood up shakily. "Nothing happened here, Reynolds. I ran into the door. My mistake."

"Okay. I'll have Sonya call you a taxi." Reynolds walked back to the bar. O'Brien stood at the far end talking amiably with The Boss and Phyllis.

The Boss asked Reynolds, "Any problems?"

"No, just an unfortunate accident."

After a taxi picked up Big Rick, the bar closed, but Reynolds and O'Brien stayed behind.

Sonya mixed drinks for the three of them from mini bottles, which was the weird law of the day. "I thought that worked out well," she beamed. "OB, you were terrific. You really thought that out too. Not bringing your gun. Well done."

"What do you mean? How did OB not wearing his gun play into any of this?" Reynolds asked.

She continued, while O'Brien sat in self-satisfied glow. "While you were talking to Big Rick, The Boss came up to OB and said something like, well, you know O'Brien, any time an armed man fights with an unarmed man there could be dire consequences, even if the guy had it coming." She laughed, "O'Brien opened his jacket and twirled around and said, 'Who's armed? Search me.'"

Reynolds laughed along. O'Brien absorbed the praise with his usual simulated humility. Reynolds revealed, "Oh, man. So, let's not get too carried away with praising his plan. OB forgets his gun half the time. In fact, I thought you were going to stop Rick from coming in. That would have ruined all O'Brien's fun."

O'Brien looked up from his drink and with a grin and yawn, stretched his arms side to side, and said, "You know, you just have to do that every now and then. Going fist city is good for the soul. I'll sleep well tonight. Besides, nobody fucks with The Roof."

"Here, here," the bar owner raised her glass to the toast, and they all clicked glasses.

After a game of pool and more mini bottle drinks, Sonya pushed her erstwhile protectors from the bar.

Walking back to the police station to their cars, O'Brien and Reynolds laughed as they recounted the Big Rick story again. Their loud talk echoed off the darkened buildings. O'Brien pulled his car keys from his pocket and threw them in the air as he shot them with his index finger, signaling a job well done.

They were parked a few stalls from each other in the officers' parking area, now almost empty, behind the police station. O'Brien said, "You hear that?"

"Yep." Reynolds and O'Brien listened and looked around. "Fireworks?"

"Maybe, see you tomorrow."

"Good night, OB. Hope you didn't hurt your hands."

Reynolds watched O'Brien drive off. Then he drove out of the parking lot, made a right turn, and slowly made his way to the parking structure above The Roof. Walking down the darkened ramp to the back door of the bar he felt a chill.

He turned quickly and cried out, "Who's there?" Nothing. He waited. Nothing. *City sounds. Scraping? What's that? Familiar clamor from the far-off train yard?* "Jesus, Mo. Get hold of yourself," he scolded.

Chapter Fourteen

Standing at the back door to The Roof, Reynolds raised a hand to tap out his passcode knock for Sonya. The SOS, *rap, rap, rap; rap — rap — rap; rap, rap, rap,* was Sonya's idea. He chuckled to himself and wondered why they did not use the familiar 'shave and a haircut' knock. "I suppose, that would have been too ordinary, and if there is anything that dear Sone loathes, it is all things ordinary," he said aloud, therefore drowning out the sound of footfalls approaching from the shadows.

The first sharp blow to his right kidney robbed him of his strength. The pain shot deep within him and he felt as if he were about to experience explosive diarrhea, or was it acute constipation, or was he about to shit an organ? All of these thoughts raced through his brain. The kidney punch dropped him to his knees. But it was the kick into his ribs beneath his armpit that caused him to cry out and crumple against the metal door unable to breathe. He lost consciousness though momentarily felt eternally.

Hurrying to clean up the last of the bar glasses, Sonya leaned against the wash basin behind the bar and thought about going downstairs to change the sheets on the bed in the small apartment she maintained in the basement next to a supply room and office.

Reynolds slumped to the cement floor. He attempted to push himself up, but a large boot pressed his right hand into the floor while Reynolds stared at the foot crushing his hand. He almost blacked out again after the malefactor's other boot kicked him in the stomach. The footsteps faded away from him, but Reynolds looked up to see a shadowy figure disappearing out of the garage and around the corner of the building.

Rolling over and struggling to sit up, he leaned against the wall next to the door and tried to process what had just happened. *Who was it? Big Rick? Was Rick wearing cowboy boots? A boot, a shadow, not much to go on. But, the boot. What was it about the boot?*

After several minutes, he forced himself to his feet and rapped on the door. Moments later Sonya opened the door and Reynolds gingerly entered.

"What the hell, Mo?" Sonya blurted. "What happened? You're a mess."

"I don't know, Sone. I got rolled and I have no idea who did it."

She supported him under his right arm and they made their way downstairs to the small apartment.

"You don't know who did it? What exactly happened?"

"No," he puffed. "I don't know who did it. Kidney punches mainly. Kicks. Will leave no visible marks. Don't know."

"Well, it was that fucking Big Rick. Who else could it be? Who else would do this to you?"

"I don't know, Sone. I really don't know. Didn't see him."

"I'm gonna call OB. He'll know what to do."

Sonya's words hurt almost as much as another kidney shot, and she knew it. He stopped in front of the small bathroom in the basement and looked down at her. Dismay showed through the pain. *How do you know OBs phone number? Why do you know his number?*

"Oh, Mo," Sonya bemoaned. "You know I didn't mean it that way. You're hurt. I was just thinking that OB would find Big Rick in no time, before he can work up an alibi."

"Sure, Sone," Reynolds smiled. "An alibi. Right… No, we will not call OB or anybody else for that matter. By the way, why do you know OB's phone number?"

Sonya held her ground and anger lifted her voice. "I don't know his goddam number. But I'll bet you do. How could you think such fucked up thoughts?"

"Sorry Sone. I apologize." Reynolds wheezed.

"Accepted." Sonya replied, but thought, *don't go there again, mister.*

"Look. Really. Finding Big Rick will not be a problem. We know he got into a taxi. I'll check with Yellow Cab tomorrow about where they dropped him off, and so on. Not to worry, I got this. Right now, I need a shower."

Chapter Fifteen

The big man straddled and gazed down at the officer lying on his back gasping for air, eyes twitching. His right leg had buckled under him revealing that he had pissed himself.

"It ain't like it is in the movies is it, sheriff?" The big man spoke softly and easily as if talking to the person sitting next to him at a bar. He held the revolver lightly and easily in his hand and waved it casually as he spoke. "They always show somebody gettin' shot and jerkin' around like they been hit with a ball bat. It don't work that-a-way does it, sheriff?"

The corporal, still disbelieving what had happened, looked up at the man standing over him. He tried to focus, tried to speak, but he could not manage to form words. He thought he was dreaming for he couldn't move no matter how hard he tried.

The big man lifted the Colt .45 and pushed his hat back with the barrel of the gun, so the hat perched on the back of his head where he liked to wear it.

"Nope, it don't work that-a-way, does it, sheriff? In my experience anyway, it don't work that-a-way. More like a hot knife through butter. Whadya think?" The man's voice was nasally and rather high pitched for a big man. "Looks like the first one went through your liver by the looks o' things. Maybe caught your spine, by the way you can't move."

The corporal's eyes rolled, but he found his voice that sounded unfamiliar to him. He squeaked, "But–I–not–a–sheriff." His mouth continued to move, but no sound escaped.

The big man's face grew dark and forehead furrowed as his eyebrows rose with the widening of his eyes. His hat moved farther back on his head with the action of his expression. He lowered the Colt .45 directly over the officer's forehead and he watched the officer's eyes cross as they focused on the path of the muzzle of the gun.

The man slowly thumbed the hammer of the Colt back into a fully cocked position. His eyes glared, and his nose flared as he peered over the length of his arm and down the barrel of the gun into the eyes of the dying officer. He squeezed the trigger on the revolver.

MOURNING IN THEIR TRIBE

The bullet crushed through the corporal's forehead. The big man bent down and opened a bullet pouch on the officer's Sam Browne belt, taking a bullet from the pouch.

The man looked around, listening. He then turned and backed slowly to the alley as he slid the revolver back into the holster. Turning quickly, he jogged easily back through the alley, and passed a stand of garbage cans overflowing with several days waste, and behind which sat a man who closed his eyes as the big cowboy ran by.

The big man stopped at the end of the alley and listened momentarily as he unbuckled the gun belt and curled it around the holstered revolver. He walked unhurriedly to his awaiting pick-up truck with cat-like nimbleness, eased into the driver's seat, and slowly rolled down the window. He sat behind the steering wheel covered in faux snakeskin and secured by a tightly wound leather lace and listened to the night sounds.

The truck started with a low rumble and the man turned the truck onto the street and proceeded slowly through the intersection. He looked to his right and saw the corporal's black and white police cruiser parked under a large tree in the alley. The car looked nonthreatening and lifeless, under the shifting light from the nearby street lamp diffused and softened by the leaves and branches of the tree swaying slowly in the early morning warm summer breeze.

The man gunned the engine to bring the truck to the speed limit, signaled a right turn and slowly made his way to Main and then east up a short hill. Soon he was cruising on a road next to the Wasatch River that found its way into the mountains from which it was named.

Seven miles up the canyon, the truck turned left off the road and over a small bridge that serviced several small dirty-white clapboard cabins with screened-in porches that faced the small river. Built by city folk as summer getaways fifty years ago, the cabins, though run down, had been shabbily converted to four season, one and two bedroom houses by a developer now dead, but whose sons, now middle aged, rented out to back-to-nature hippies, an elderly couple from Salt Lake City and one big cowboy.

The big man parked next to the door of his cabin and removed the revolver from the glove box of the Ford truck and went inside. He cautiously flipped the switch that illuminated the kitchen and looked around. He walked through the small bungalow stopping before each window and carefully pulled the blind down before proceeding to the next one until he came to a short hallway. Unlocking the padlock that secured the spare bedroom on the right, the man entered the room and removed his hat and held it respectfully in front of him. He lit an oil lamp with a stick match from a box that sat next to the lamp. The lamp had been his mother's. A water-stained yellowing blind almost covered the room's lone window leaving a two-inch gap at the bottom. Next to the window stood a small roll top desk and oak swivel desk chair equipped with rollers. The floor was of bare plywood that strained and creaked beneath the man's weight as he strode through the room.

He unlocked the roll top desk. Pushing back the tambour revealed a desktop backed by a single shelf surrounded by several small cubbyhole box shelves. A photograph of a middle-aged woman in western wear astride a big bay horse stood in an ornate brass frame on the shelf. Five of the cubbies contained a single bullet standing neatly upright, like small statuettes. The man dug the bullet from his breast pocket and carefully placed it in one of the empty cubbyholes.

He located a bound scholastic notebook under several newspapers and found the carefully folded graph paper sheet containing a neat columnar list under the headings: Location, Book, Page, and Name of Tribal Member. There were six entries below the Location column. The columnar entries to the right of five of the six locations were complete. Next to the last location, Heavenly Valley, UT, he traced his finger along the page to the final column, which was blank. Thinking back to the small silver nametag attached to the corporal's chest, he wrote "Halverson."

Holding his black Stetson hat on his lap, he sobbed. Wiping his eyes and blowing his nose now and then into a handkerchief that he kept in his left rear pocket beneath the can of Skol tobacco. He then heard the kitchen door squeak open.

"Hoss, you awake?" came a woman's voice from the kitchen. "You can't be asleep that quick. I heard you drive up."

He locked the desk and shouted over his shoulder, "Chrissy, I'll be right out. Why don't you put on the coffee?"

"Will do," Chrissy hollered from the other room.

Chrissy lived next door with two men and occasionally another woman who seemed to come and go at odd times. One of the men was Jonathon and the other man was Bingo. In fact, Horace paid little attention to his neighbors, although he felt especially protective of Chrissy for reasons he did not understand.

Horace walked out of the room and padlocked the door.

"I was beginning to think that you forgot that you and me were supposed to go fishing this morning," Chrissy said over her shoulder as she was lighting the gas-stove burner under the stained and dented coffee percolator.

"Nope, I didn't forget," Horace blushed.

Chrissy wore sandals, very short cut-off blue jeans, and a yellow triangular shaped top that tied in the back that Jonathon termed "an ode to trigonometry" that exposed her stomach and all of her back. She was sun bronzed and she wore her long dark, stringy hair pulled back tightly into pigtails. Her addiction to speed, mostly cross tops, insured that she remained underweight and sleepless most nights.

"I know it's a bit early, but we need to be out on the river by 4:30 A.M."

It was a little before 3 A.M. Horace smiled, knowing Chrissy simply wanted company.

"You know after the sun comes up, the trout stop biting," Chrissy scolded. "I promised the guys a trout dinner tonight."

"I had to work over tonight," Horace replied as he approached the sink.

"What have you done?" Chrissy gasped.

Horace, confused and quickly overtaken by fear, said breathlessly, "What?"

"Your hand. Is that blood? Are you hurt?" Chrissy thought Hoss reminded her of Danny.

Horace looked dumbly at his right hand, which was splattered with dried blood.

He thought quickly and pushed his hat back and grinned that *big ole country boy* grin. "Oh heavens, Chrissy, I ran over a damned ole porcupine, and the thing got stuck under my truck. I had to dig it out of the under carriage, very careful like, cause of them big ole spines. Must'a bled on me."

Chrissy frowned and shook her head in mock anger. "You gotta be careful driving that canyon at night. There are all kinds of critters out there. You have to be more careful."

Horace wasn't sure if she was concerned for his safety or the safety of the critters.

He washed his hands and went to his bedroom to change his shirt. He dressed quickly in a shirt identical to the one he had changed out of.

"I know that's your look, but wouldn't you be more comfortable in a tee shirt? Oh, never mind, you are who you are, and that's fine with me," Chrissy responded as Horace came back to the kitchen buttoning his sleeves.

They took their coffee in tin cups and wandered down to the river. Chrissy carried a small bait box made of cork that contained a couple dozen night crawlers. They carried rods with spinning reels to the large pools under the bridge where they liked to start fishing. This morning was no different.

"You know, Hoss, it's against the law to fish at night." Chrissy laughed at their small rebellion.

"Yeah, I s'pose it is, but really what's the difference when you catch the critters so long as you stay within the limit?"

"Exactly, Hoss. But, Jonathon doesn't like to needlessly attract attention to us," Chrissy's voice trailed off. She knew she had spoken unwisely and quickly added, "But, he worries too much. He's way too law abiding, especially when it comes to the environment."

Horace looked around. He hadn't thought about that. It would be stupid to attract the attention of the law on any level. He squirmed on the riverbank and almost stood up to go back to the cabin. Instead, he leaned back against the bank and dozed to the sounds of Chrissy's never ending chitchat.

The cutthroat trout jumped randomly at bugs, flitting about the stream in the gray morning light.

Horace and Chrissy sat a few yards apart casting worm-baited hooks wherever they saw a fish jump. Soon, Chrissy caught her second trout. Horace smiled at her excitement but sat silently.

"You're awfully quiet," Chrissy quipped as she took another speed pill from an old tobacco tin she kept in her pants pocket.

Horace knew that soon Chrissy's voice would be filling the air with nonstop random talk about anything that entered her thoughts. He didn't mind though. He liked listening to her speed-induced narrative, but this morning she troubled him greatly.

"You want a cross top? It'll improve your gloominess."

"No thanks."

"I don't know how you stay awake all night, fish in the morning and cry in that secret room of yours without it. What's with that, anyway? Are you sad, Hoss? How can you be sad on such a beautiful morning as this? You should have one of my happy pills," Chrissy stopped speaking, mesmerized by the sun as it peeked through the forest mist.

Horace didn't move. He didn't pay attention to the jerking tip of his fishing pole. He stared with furrowed brow into the dark water.

Chrissy pretended not to notice. "I know I shouldn't peek in windows, but I did this morning. Sorry. You looked so sad. I wanted to come in and give you a big hug. Jonathon says your secret room is none of our concern." Chrissy knew full well that is not what Jonathon had said. No, he felt just the opposite and ordered Chrissy to find out what was so valuable behind that padlocked door. Chrissy, even in her speed-induced thinking knew also to be careful and not raise suspicion that could in any way alert him to their plans.

Horace looked at Chrissy for a long moment. "What else do Jonathon and Bingo say?" Horace asked, his voice hollow.

"Bingo? Who said anything about Bingo? You're getting a bite there, Hoss. Your pole is going nuts."

With a sharp snap of his wrist, Horace set the hook and reeled in the trout that Chrissy netted.

"Wow, nice one. A couple more and we'll have a nice dinner tonight. Can you come over, or do you gotta work?"

"I'll be over," Horace said sullenly.

Chapter Sixteen

Jonathon sprayed charcoal lighter fluid over the briquettes he carefully stacked in a well-organized pyramid on the bottom of the broiler. He struck the match on the side of the metal barbeque pit and dropped it on the stacked briquettes.

Whoomph!

"Think you used enough lighter fluid, there Jonathon?" cackled Bingo. "It's a wonder you got any hair left."

Jonathon stood wide-eyed, stroking his heavy beard and his shoulder length, reddish brown hair to insure it was all still there.

Horace bent over the Styrofoam cooler and found an orange soda and turned towards the others sitting around a picnic table behind Jonathon's cabin.

Bingo, sitting nearest the cooler, sipped whiskey from a plastic cup, said in his twang, "Careful there, big'n, that soda comes with quite a kick." He chuckled; there was something about Horace that unsettled Bingo. Perhaps the man's size had something to do with it, but not exactly. He kept an eye on Horace nonetheless, and probed everything the big man did with cloying comments meant to annoy and anger. It frustrated Bingo that his comments failed their intended missions.

Horace found the trio of neighbors perplexing as well. Bingo, he simply did not like. He found him insulting and bullying, but he had dealt with those types all his life. He did not worry about Bingo. Jonathon, however, was another story. Jonathon seemed to be seething below the courteous, but never polite, exterior. Horace felt Jonathon pushed his emotions below the calm sea, exposing only a periscope at times before it was gone, slipping below before you could get a fix on it. Chrissy, on the other hand, appeared open and defenseless. That was her unique adaptation. That was her survival technique. She relied upon others' clouded judgment. Like many others, Horace misread Chrissy. Horace thought Jonathon provided direction; the rudder, Chrissy, needed to navigate life's circumstances, and that frightened him for her sake. He felt a connection with Chrissy, though he cautioned himself that he did not know any of them. He must be careful.

Horace walked around the table and sat next to Chrissy.

Bingo's nonstop banter and pinched grumbling continued, "Careful, there Jonathon, Big'n here seems to be real comfortable with your woman."

Jonathon paid no attention and preoccupied himself with the six trout that simmered over the hot coals. He perspired profusely as he attempted to turn the fish without losing them to the coals.

"Oh, Bingo," Chrissy chirped, trying to keep it light, but the amphetamines she had been taking all day long had taken their predictive toll on her patience. She added flatly, "Just shut the fuck up, I've had enough of you for one day."

"Sure, whatever you say, your royal highness." Bingo laughed and then blurted, "Boy, oh boy, some fucking body executed a cop downtown early this morning. Whaddya know about that? In tired little Heavenly Valley. Who said nothing exciting ever happens here?"

Jonathon looked up from the fish, and he and Chrissy exchanged looks. "Most unfortunate," Jonathon said shaking his head. He carefully pushed a trout onto a spatula with a fork and plopped it on a plate. He was not so fortunate with the other five. Each one broke in feathered pieces as he tried to pick them up. He quickly piled the remains of the fish on a plate and said with exasperation and nods toward Chrissy and Horace, "That will have to do. My apologies all, perhaps we should have left the cooking to the fishermen."

Chrissy picked at the plate of fish as it passed her way, added a tablespoon of macaroni salad that she had prepared earlier in the day, and tore off a piece of a dinner roll and added it to her plate.

"Chrissy," noted Jonathon, "you should try to eat a little more. Have you eaten anything at all today?"

Chrissy raised her beer towards Jonathon. "Good calories here, baby."

"I think your old man would like to see a few more pounds on yer skinny ass, there Chrissy," Bingo chipped in as he loaded his plate up with healthy portions of everything. He handed the plate of fish to Horace, who, being at the end of the table, was last to be served. Very little trout remained, and Bingo did not leave him much salad. Horace put a couple of rolls on his plate as Bingo giggled.

Chrissy glared at Bingo.

"What?" Bingo smiled.

"It's okay, Chrissy. I could use a few less calories, and a few less pounds on my bones." Horace did not look away from his plate.

"I'll bet you've always been a big'n, there Hoss. Your mother's big too, I'll bet, bigger than your daddy." Bingo said, glaring at Horace. "Is she, Hoss? Bigger than your daddy, in that big ole western way in a house dress and apron? Is she there, Big'n?" Holding his prosthetic arm up, Bingo concluded, "I gotta hand it to you."

The color rose in Horace's face as he took a bite of dinner roll, which had hardened in the hot dry breeze. He stared straight ahead, and stood up.

Amused, Jonathon merely looked on.

Peripherally, as he poured himself another four fingers of whiskey, Bingo saw the man rise.

Chrissy glared at Jonathon. Jonathon just sat, head cocked taking it all in. He did not take his eyes off Horace.

The big man stretched and pushed his hat back on his head, and said, not outwardly disturbed by Bingo's goading, "Thank you all for the nice dinner, but I gotta git to work at the stockyard. I have the late shift again tonight." He turned and walked towards his cabin.

Chrissy ran after him. "Hoss. Hoss! Wait up."

Horace stopped and turned serenely towards Chrissy. Confused by the man's lack of reaction, she continued her course of action with a shake of her head. "I'm sorry, Hoss. Bingo can be a pig, especially when he drinks, but he didn't mean anything by it."

"Yes, he did, Chrissy." Horace smiled broadly, "Don't worry, it's water off a big ole duck's back. I gotta git."

"Whoa, okay. You're something else, Hoss. Same time tomorrow morning?"

"Sure thing."

Chrissy watched him drive off. She seethed as she stomped back to her bungalow.

"What is fucking wrong with you, Bingo?" Chrissy screeched. "Jesus fucking Christ. The last thing we need right now is for you to have a testosterone eruption and need to prove your manhood, yet again. And you," she turned towards Jonathon, "just sitting there and letting this Neanderthal ruin everything. We have worked too hard. Jesus, what is wrong with you two?"

Bingo chuckled, "Chrissy … "

Jonathon cut Bingo off, "You're right, Chrissy. I think we do have to act natural." Bingo nodded, thinking Jonathon agreed with his behavior.

Jonathon continued, ignoring Bingo. "You are absolutely right, Chris. We have to be cognizant of the fact that we do not need unwarranted attention. We do not need slipups. You got that, Bingo? You stupid fuck. It was obvious you were trying to get under the cowboy's skin. Had you succeeded, and he kicked your ass, what would you have done? I think we both know the answer to that, don't we?" Jonathon threw his cup of ice at Bingo.

The reprimand stung Bingo. Gone was the bravado. Bingo looked into his empty cup and turned slightly away from Jonathon.

"I asked you a question, Bingo." Jonathon lived for these moments. He controlled the situation, and he wasn't about to let up. "Well? Speak up, goddamn you."

"Yeah, I am really sorry, Jonathon. I gotcha, man. Sorry, Chrissy. Gotcha, Jay."

"That fucking train is coming in a little more than a week," Chrissy whispered as she bent over the table separating the two men and looked right and left into each of their faces. "Almost everything is in place. Keep it together, will you? Beatrice will be back in a few days. The groundwork is complete. Each of us must be absolutely disciplined if we are going to pull this off. Do you understand?"

Both men nodded.

PART 4

Discovery

Despite the crime scene investigator's promising report, the detectives knew they had little to go on. Even if the fingerprints were salvageable, they still needed a suspect from whom to compare prints. Even in a case of the magnitude of a police officer's murder, they knew that the FBI, with a national file of more than ninety million fingerprint cards, needed more qualifying information to limit the range of possible suspects in order to match the prints, which at that time had to be done manually.

Chapter Seventeen

Reynolds entered his home and pressed the receive button on the Ansaphone dual cassette tape answering machine as he walked by it. He seldom received messages, but he loved the machine.

Two small dings indicated a message. It was O'Brien. "Where the fuck are you?" He always began his recorded messages the same way, as if he figured Reynolds was present but ignoring him. Reynolds listened half-heartedly and headed up the narrow stairway to his bedroom.

O'Brien's message droned on below, though clearly audible throughout the small home. "How come, Reynolds, that I'm married, and you know everybody I'm fuckin', and you're single, and I don't ever know who you're fuckin'? Makes no sense."

"Because you're fuckin' everyone, OB." Reynolds yelled back down the stairs at the answering machine. At least, he thought, Sonya had not talked to O'Brien about last night's assault.

O'Brien's tone changed and froze Reynolds as he unbuttoned his shirt. "Look, man, get down to Fifth and Wells just as soon as you get this. Halverson's been murdered. They found his body in the alley behind the The Street. Shot between the eyes."

"Holy shit!" Reynolds hurriedly stripped off his clothes and dressed in a dark suit, tan shirt and bold red tie, bolting out the front door.

Reynolds parked in the detectives' parking lot at the police station, but he could see cruisers filled the intersection two blocks away. The scene unfolded before him as he walked quickly toward the police cars.

O'Brien stood on the corner near a lamp pole with his hands clasped behind his back. Reynolds noted OB following the fundamentals of crime scene investigation that begins with keeping your hands behind your back or in your pockets. *Pick up nothing, touch nothing.* If your hands are out of the way, you're less likely to pick up or touch anything.

Reynolds noticed several detectives peering into the taped-off area, and many uniformed patrolmen protecting the scene from various spots around the perimeter. They were not going to allow anyone to enter.

Reynolds approached O'Brien. "He was killed over here under the streetlamp, but they found him over there in the alley."

"Let me guess, it happened a little after 2 A.M.?" Reynolds asked.

"That's my guess, so let's keep that under our hat for now," O'Brien hissed.

"Understood." Until more was known, neither detective saw the need to disclose that they may have heard the fatal shots earlier that morning and did not report them. That would present more questions than answers. Right now, there were enough questions.

"When did they find him? And, what do we know?"

"By the look of that stain, he was already on the ground when he was shot through the forehead," O'Brien began.

"Yeah, I can see it was a through-and-through wound. The bullet passed through Halverson's head and chipped the pavement there near the center of the blood stain," Reynolds reflected. "So how did he become prostrate in the first place? Shot, fell, then shot again?"

"So, the bullet that passed through his head is somewhere around here," O'Brien swung left and right, "in fragments most likely. But, the body contained a gut wound with the bullet still inside him. They took him away while you were ignoring your phone. A small break he was found," O'Brien cleared his throat and gave Reynolds a sidelong look, "at 4:26 A.M. by garbage truck operators who almost ran over him with that big-assed truck blocking the alley over there."

"Another break," Reynolds matched his partner's glance. "What else? Why did it take so long to find him? Where's his fucking car?"

"One block west of here. Seems Halverson signed out on a routine building check at 1:16 A.M. The dispatcher, who took the call from Halverson, Amanda, left work just after taking the call, going home sick. The other dispatcher was away from the console when Amanda took the call, and Amanda made no note of it. She just happened to forget to tell the other dispatcher about it before she left for the night."

"It was a slow night, right?" Reynolds ventured, "How many calls came in between 1:30-4:30 A.M.?"

O'Brien, as he liked to do, saved the most obvious and best for last. "Looks like a simple robbery. His gun, Sam Browne, wallet, and flashlight are missing. Could it be that he was shot with his own gun."

"Jesus, we need those individual personal walkie-talkies that most departments have," said Chief Hansen, who now stood behind Reynolds and O'Brien. "Christ almighty, I have been trying to get the goddamn city manager to approve a new communications system that would bring us into the modern age now for more than two years. And now, look what happened. A seasoned officer is gunned down two blocks from the fucking police station, and it takes a couple of garbage men to find him. He is away from his radio for three hours. Three hours. That shouldn't happen, men." The chief was visibly upset.

"No shit, Chief," agreed O'Brien.

"Good morning, Chief," Reynolds said in a hushed tone. It was a fellow officer's murder, and one with whom they were all more than a little familiar. He was family. *This is a fallen brother, let's not forget that,* Reynolds thought, and his tone of voice and bowed head emphasized why they were all here.

Chief Hansen briefly offered a grim face. "Good morning, Morris," the Chief replied. Then, he added in a conspiratorial whisper, "I want you two to find out who did this. If anyone can do it—quickly—I know you two can." Hansen leaned in closer to both detectives. "You know what I need. Take whatever measures necessary to bring the son-of-a-bitch in. You got that?"

"You bet, Chief. We'll take it from here," O'Brien said with mustered confidence.

"Loud and clear, Chief," agreed Reynolds with less bravado and head bowed.

As the Chief walked away, Reynolds turned to O'Brien. "Well, that answers who is going to be assigned to this mess."

"He knows we will get it done. And he gave us the green light to do it our way."

"Easy, big guy. One step at a time," Reynolds rasped a whisper. Sensations of unease spread down his spine at his partner's misplaced delight at being assigned a big case by the Chief himself.

The detectives stepped over the taped barrier at the behest of Sergeant Shanahan, who headed the Heavy PD crime scene lab.

The detectives dared not cross the barrier until given the go-ahead. Shanahan walked them to where the body was found.

"We've completely photographed the scene and removed all the physical evidence that we found. It appears the officer was shot by someone standing about where we are now. The officer would have been more than three feet from the shooter, and he fell near the arc light. The officer grabbed his stomach with his right hand, dropped to the ground with his head towards the intersection, feet this way towards the attacker."

"What makes you think so, Shanahan?" O'Brien asked.

"There is a slight impression of the victim's palm on the right side of the taped figure. The victim grabbed his stomach, and then tried to break his fall with his right hand." For the first time, Shanahan's normally strained voice seemed more strained. He gathered himself and continued, "The officer left a massive amount of blood. The shooter then approached the victim with a large caliber weapon and shot him in the forehead at a close range. Judging by the powder burns on the officer's face, I can determine he was shot from between eight and sixteen inches away."

"The shooter then dragged the body from the street corner and into the shadows of the alley. The victim's boot must have come off as the body was being dragged back here." Shanahan's emotion and personal knowledge surfaced. "Hal's meticulous about the appearance of his uniform. He polished his boots before every shift. The back of the boot contains an impression of someone's palm. Left palm, I think. And three fingerprint impressions on the top of the foot section of the boot. These had to have been left by someone pulling on that boot with terrific force. Pulling the body with both hands by the right foot until the boot came off in the shooter's hands."

"Shanahan, do you think he was shot with his own gun?" Reynolds asked.

"It is a possibility. We'll know more when the bullet is recovered from the body."

"We will know more when the autopsy is performed, and hopefully the bullet that is recovered from the victim's body is in decent shape," O'Brien muttered.

Several detectives combed the immediate area, but they failed to find any discernable part of the bullet that had passed through Corporal Halverson's head. Bone fragments had been photographed, bagged and removed by the crime scene investigators.

Although uniformed officers and other detectives had walked the length of The Street, knocking on doors and interviewing everyone they came into contact with, Reynolds and O'Brien repeated the chore.

They began by searching the alley on one side, and then trading sides, repeating the process. They combed the alley for any sign that both felt certain existed: a scuffmark or a cigarette butt.

Reynolds waved his partner over, "Hey, look here. It's a cowboy boot print. Grab that empty box over there and we'll cover the thing so Shanahan can get a picture of it. I can't believe he missed it."

They covered the footprint that Shanahan later photographed, but he was skeptical of its usefulness, saying that half the people that frequented this part of town wore cowboy boots. But, "There's a distinctive notch worn into the front of the heel. It comes from wear caused by a certain type stirrup worn while riding horses. It just may be something we can use. Good work Robert and Morris."

"Thanks, George," O'Brien said. "It's a start, but a long shot, no doubt."

Chapter Eighteen

The Chief entered the police department building through the south door to avoid the crush of reporters at the main east entrance. Cecie, the chief's long time secretary and personal protector and gatekeeper, looked up from her typewriter. She was crying.

"Are they all in there, Cecie?" The Chief asked softly.

Disheveled Cynthia Andrews, with rarely a greying brown hair out of place, removed her glasses and let them hang from the silver chain onto her bosom. She tried in vain to push a strand of misbehaving hair from her cheek back into place.

Leaning heavily on both hands on the front of the desk as much to steady his shaking knees as to look his secretary in the eye, The Chief whispered, "Cecie, this is the worst day of my career, of our career." And when the teary-eyed Cynthia patted the back of his hand, The Chief broke down. His knees buckled and he dropped to one knee, head bowed, arms extended over her desk, and he held firm to the secretary's hand.

Captain Paul "Nellie" Nelson, leading his two lieutenants, stopped from entering the secretary's office that provided entrance to the chief's office on the right and a conference room on the left. He stepped back out into the hall and ordered his lieutenants to stop. "Hold up, men. Let's give The Chief and Cecie a moment.

Cynthia looked up long enough to notice Nelson back tracking into the hall.

"Gerry, pull it together. The guys are all here now." Cecie gave Hansen's hand a small tug.

The Chief stood and buttoned his suit coat and smiled at his secretary. "Okay. I'm good to go now, Cee." The Chief then called out for the captain and his lieutenants to enter. As they did, The Chief greeted each man with a firm handshake that included warmly grasping each by the elbow with his left hand. They entered the conference room where the other three captains and three lieutenants were already seated.

MOURNING IN THEIR TRIBE

Captain Sherman Oswald, commander of the Patrol Division, stood and greeted The Chief. He felt compelled to open the meeting since Corporal Halverson was assigned to his division. He turned to address to the group, but the Chief took over. "Please have a seat, Sherm," The Chief began. He gave a short speech that sounded like a eulogy for the fallen corporal. He spoke of the man's wife and four children and how the Police Benevolent Association needed to step up and make every fund-raising effort to see that family "has everything they need."

Each man at the long table covered with protective glass that Cecie had polished and would again after the meeting and, as was her wont, she offered an under-breath complaint about the finger prints and coffee cup rings left behind by the attendees stood and paid their respects to the murdered officer.

Nellie Nelson, Captain of Detectives seethed. He was last to speak and sat at The Chief's right. He was known as the "City Manager's Man." Wide speculation had it that Nelson coveted the Chief's job. He had already held an "informal briefing" with the City Manager Louis Withers earlier that morning. The other captains, Nelson's peers, detested him. He was tall, young— *"thirty-three, for Christ's sake,"*—too young to be a captain they all thought. Good looking with blonde hair and mustache, piercing blue eyes, fit, tanned—*"even in winter, for Christ's sake."* Nelson was known as super smooth, especially with the ladies. It took all of Nelson's well-concocted cool to suppress his anger with The Chief for assigning Reynolds and O'Brien to the Halverson case without consulting with him first. But the detectives were known as "The Chief's Boys," and that thought simmered.

After making a brief condolences statement about Halverson and his widow, Nelson launched into the investigation. "I am going to personally insure that we bring the perpetrator of Corporal Halverson's murder to justice. I am putting all of MY detectives on this case until it is solved. I…"

"To be clear, Nellie," The Chief interrupted. "Reynolds and O'Brien will spearhead the investigation. I don't want anyone, Nellie…" The Chief looked up at Nelson who continued to stand, "…anyone to slow Robert and Morris down."

The Chief left Nelson standing and continued speaking to the men seated at the table. "In addition to the two detectives, I spoke with the District Attorney this morning and I agreed that we should have someone from his office work with Robert and Morris to ensure that no one from MY department," The Chief glanced at Nelson who was reseating himself, "makes any, ANY legal blunders that will cost us conviction of the son-of-a-bitch who gunned down MY officer."

Nelson's tanned face darkened, deeply reddened with anger. The other captains exchanged quick, '*good for The Chief*' looks.

"When do you plan on briefing The Manager, Chief?" Nelson all but sneered.

"Soon, Nellie," The Chief purred. "I have a meeting with him and The Boss right after this one. We, along with the mayor, will make a statement to the press in about an hour. Captain Nelson, advise O'Brien and Reynolds I want them to lead a daily briefing on the investigation right here and with all of you present, every day at one PM sharp. Got that? I want all of you to hear directly from them so that we all know, first hand, what is going on. No filters, got that?"

Nelson nodded and then asked, "Do you know who The Boss is going to assign from his office?"

"Nope."

Captain Nelson and his right-hand man, Lieutenant Brand, were the last to leave, when The Chief asked Nelson and Brand to "hold on."

Perturbed, Nelson turned and faced The Chief as did Lieutenant Brand, but he looked far less agitated. Meetings with his supervisor and The Chief made him anxious. He walked a tight rope in such settings. He strongly felt, as did most in the know, that Captain Nelson would most likely be the next chief, but The Chief "drove the bus," at least for now.

"There is one thing, Captain. I know this may not be the right time, but this is the right place. What have you done about that graffiti in the men's room down there next to your office?" The Chief's forehead furrowed and his eyes widened.

"What?" Nelson searched his assistant's face for the answer. Brand shrugged ever so slightly.

The Chief, enjoying the moment, continued, "The thing reads 'Flush twice. It's a long way to the chief's office.'"

The captain was truly perplexed. "What are you… um… huh?"

The Chief leaned in towards the two men and whispered, "I'm fucking with you Captain. Lighten up." The Chief turned and walked out past Cecie's desk.

"I will be meeting with the District Attorney and the City Manager, Cee; then we will hold the press conference."

Cynthia, covering the mouthpiece of the phone with one hand, stopped The Chief. "I have Amanda Blakely on the phone, Chief. Do you want to take it?"

The Chief stopped and directed his secretary to forward the call into his office.

"Mandy? Chief Hansen here," the Chief said hurriedly.

"Good Morning Chief," Dispatcher Amanda Blakely replied tentatively.

"Yes. Mandy, have you heard the terrible news about last night?" the Chief asked, hesitantly. He heard a noticeable intake of breath on the other end.

"No, what happened?"

The Chief then relayed the events of Corporal Halverson's death, the time of Halverson's last call-in, and the time he was found. Then he paused and allowed all of that to sink in. Silence. "Amanda, we know that you were alone on the console when Hal last called in. We know that you went home ill just after taking the call. First, how are you feeling?"

Silence.

The Chief waited. "Amanda, are you still there?"

"I am. I am feeling a little better. I should be able to make it in tonight," Amanda replied. "If that is what you mean."

93

"It isn't. But I am glad to hear that you are feeling better." The Chief then warned, "There will be many questions of you. Like why didn't you tell the other dispatcher that Hal had signed off the air and his location. Why didn't you do that Amanda?"

Silence.

"Amanda?"

"I don't know, Chief. I really don't know why I didn't do that. I just didn't. I just was not thinking right. I wish I had done my job right, Chief. I really do." Then she added, a bit too quickly, "Other than saving a couple of hours in finding Hal, my telling Maria would not have saved his life."

"I know, Amanda. Mistakes happen every day. Most never amount to anything. This time it did. There will be questions. If you don't feel up to coming in tonight, I understand. Okay? I know how sorry you must feel, Mandy. Believe me."

"Thank you, Chief, but I am planning on making it to work," the relieved dispatcher replied.

The Chief walked out and stopped in front of Cecie, who sat expectantly.

"She already knew, Cee. I'm sure of it." The Chief outlined an infinity sign on the top of the secretary's desk with his finger.

"Captain Nelson, Chief?"

"Hmm. Who else." It was not a question. "Remind me to talk with Maria Gutierrez later today. I know she worked until eight this morning. I need to speak to her once she gets a good day's sleep."

Cynthia Andrews gave The Chief a knowing look, and said, "I spoke to Maria this morning before she got off."

Briefly stunned, but knowing better, The Chief lifted his eyebrows.

"Amanda received a phone call from Captain Nelson at about one AM." Cecie replied, but not without some remorse at giving up a confidence, but an officer's death outweighed keeping office secrets. "The dispatchers are close friends, Gerry… They talk."

"Where'd he call from? The Roof? No, no... check that. Captain Nelson would have called from The Valley Club."

The Valley Club was *The Country Club* in the area, and that would meet Captain Nelson's view of himself and his standing within the community. Although his annual salary from the department would barely cover the membership dues of the exclusive club and golf course, his trust fund more than provided for a very comfortable life above that of his salary from the city.

Cecie saluted The Chief with her pen.

Chapter Nineteen

O'Brien and Reynolds sat in their cruiser, lunching on gyro sandwiches.

"Look, here comes our favorite snitch." O'Brien motioned towards Willis Givens who was staggering towards them. Drunk as usual, but he did not approach the car, which was not his practice. O'Brien and Reynolds knew that little happened on The Street that escaped Givens' attention. He lived in one of the fleabag hotels. For five bucks the detectives could count on Givens, known by all as Sarge, giving them the latest scuttlebutt. Most of the time it amounted to nothing the officers could use, but Givens always needed the five bucks. Not this time.

Givens was almost past the car and ignored Reynolds' commands to come over. The detectives jumped from the car, and O'Brien grabbed Givens roughly by the arm, causing the drunk to stumble. O'Brien held firm and kept the man upright.

"Hey, Sarge, where's the fire?" Reynolds asked as the man struggled in vain against O'Brien's grasp. "Where you been, man? We haven't seen you around for a few days now. We need to talk, and you know what we want to talk about."

"Get the fuck away from me. Goddamn it, OB, leggo my arm. I got something to do. Get the fuck away from me," Givens screamed.

Passersby looked on, but no one cared enough to stop. Most knew the detectives, and all knew Givens.

He was known as a scrapper. In his younger days, he was considered a rough son-of-a-bitch. But years of boozing and drugs had sapped his strength and had stolen the pride of his youth. Givens' days were taken up with finding enough scratch for a bottle or two of Mogen David Twenty-Twenty wine, commonly known on The Street as Mad Dog Twenty-Twenty or just Mad Dog or just Twenty-Twenty. That he was not interested in making a quick five dollars from the detectives just for shooting the breeze about the biggest crime to have been committed on The Street in anyone's memory was most unusual.

MOURNING IN THEIR TRIBE

Now O'Brien slammed Givens against the red brick wall of the building behind him. "Look, you little bastard. You know something, don't you? Let's see what you have in your pockets."

The man struggled mightily and began screaming, "Help me. These fuckers are robbing me."

Reynolds patted Givens down as his partner kept the man pinned against the wall. He found a flat, round rock and a faded purple and yellow ribbon, all that remained from an Armed Services medal, in the man's pockets. His wallet contained his Social Security card and a faded, torn photo of a young woman and nothing else. Reynolds pulled a wad of cash from the man's dirty grey, once white, sock.

Reynolds counted the money and hissed, "Where the fuck did you get $143?"

"I earned it. It's none of your fucking business, Reynolds." Givens then seemed less drunk. He stopped struggling and looked into O'Brien's eyes and said, "Take me in if you think I'm public drunk, unless you're going to steal my money. But, you ain't like that, are ya? Not you two."

"OK, talk to us. Where'd you earn that much money? And, why haven't you drank yourself to death with all that scratch, man?" O'Brien released him. Reynolds handed the cash back to the man.

"I told you, OB," Givens said as he put the wad back into his sock after looking around to see if anyone noticed that he was carrying that much cash. "I have been working out in Corinne for the railroad. You know they are paying good money for people to tear up and lay down the new track out to Promontory."

"I do know that they are laying a new spur out there, but that is all mechanized these days. Why would they hire you?" Reynolds asked derisively.

"Check with the railroad. They'll tell you. They need laborers to help out those big fuckin' machines. We just put shit down and pick shit up. A guy comes around in a truck and picks up laborers down by the shelter. I have been out there a week or so. I know one of your brothers in blue got his self killed out here the other night," the man whispered, "but I been out at the

97

Point. I haven't heard a thing. Not one fuckin' thing." The man was getting worked up again. "Now, let me go or take me in, goddamn it."

The detectives stepped aside, and the man hustled off looking back over his shoulder. "Where you living these days?" O'Brien called after Givens.

"Where you think, OB? I'm down at the James." Givens turned and waited impatiently for the next question that did not come. O'Brien waved the man on.

"You believe him?" Reynolds asked as the two officers returned to the car.

"No, no way. I can see him going out there for a day or two, but he's unable to sustain a job for longer than that. But I figured checking out his story is easy enough. If we ran him in for Public Intox, they would have kept him for four hours and he'd be out with a fifteen-dollar bail. Four hours wouldn't buy us much time," O'Brien mused.

"You think that little fuck is crazy enough to shoot a cop?" Reynolds looked at O'Brien. "If he got the chance, I think he is nuts enough, or drunk enough to do almost anything for a couple of bucks."

"Yep, and according to Hal's wife, he had around $230 in his wallet that night, and payday was just last Friday."

"We need to check out the James."

"D-3, D-18," the dispatcher said over the under dash two-way radio.

"D-3, D-18, go ahead."

"D-3, D-18, see the Chief in his office immediately."

"Ten-Four," O'Brien replaced the hand-held microphone and drove into the station parking lot.

Chapter Twenty

Still grumbling over his exchange with the detectives, Willis Givens burst through the door of the Utah State Liquor Store. He approached the clerk who stood behind the counter protected by a chain link fencing that extended to the ceiling.

"Twenty-Twenty?" the clerk asked and turned to fetch a bottle from the shelves behind him.

"Fuck you and your Twenty-Twenty. Two fifths of Wild Turkey," Givens growled.

"Watch your tongue, or you will have to find another store." The clerk turned and scowled at Givens.

"You damn well know there ain't another liquor store for miles," Givens' tone softened. "Come on man, I meant no offense. Can I have my booze?"

The clerk's eyes narrowed, and he looked Givens up and down. "I'll need to see the color of your money first."

While giving the clerk a disdainful look for impugning his integrity, Givens pushed $25 through the opening in the chain link barrier.

The clerk slowly and carefully smoothed out the bills and scooted them out of the customer's reach. The clerk removed two bottles of whiskey from the shelf and asked Givens if he would like a bag, which set the man off again.

"Fuck yes, I want a goddamn bag just like any other motherfucker that comes through these doors."

The clerk placed the bottles in a brown paper bag and handed them to Givens along with his change. "Careful now, Willis, your so-called friends out there will put a knife in you for that kind of merchandise."

"Fuck you."

Givens scurried out the door and down the street.

He approached the small brown brick house with the large porch that had once been painted bright green. The paint had peeled, leaving bare the grey cracked wood beneath. Two of the three stairs leading up to the porch were broken, and Willis had to climb them gingerly along the only railing on the right side. The grey-white door stood open behind the torn screen door.

"Big Jane? Big Jane, you home?" Willis yelled through the screen door and bent to look through the area where the screen had detached and curled away from its mooring.

A tall middle-aged woman, heavy in the middle, wearing a stained blue sleeveless house dress and dirty pink slippers, duck-walked up to the door with her head tilted to the right to allow the smoke from the cigarette dangling from the left side of her mouth to escape her eyes. The woman wore her long grey-blonde hair in a single braid that hung over her ample right breast. She habitually stroked the braid with her right hand, which she did now.

"Whadya want, Sarge? I thought I told you not to come pokin' around here anymore." The woman's girth blocked the door, but her eyes did not move from the brown paper bag in Willis' grasp.

Willis, eyes down and respectful said, "That you did Big Jane. I come with a peace offering. I got us, er, ah… you a special treat today."

Big Jane replied as if speaking to the brown paper bag, "What you got in the sack?"

Willis' confidence returned and he found his regular voice. He said excitedly, "I got us not one, but two bottles of our favorite. Wild Turkey, Big Jane. I got two fifths of Wild fucking Turkey."

Big Jane still staring at the bag said, "You can come in. But not until you give me that bag." She removed the hook from the eye-lock on the inside of the screen door and pushed the door open far enough to grab the sack from Willis. She blocked the door, however, and looked inside the bag. She handed the bag to a dark-haired woman who had materialized behind her.

Big Jane opened the screen door and stepped out pushing Willis back a step. She looked down at the man. The cigarette between her lips bounced as she spoke. "Any shit outa you and out you go. You got that?" the woman barked.

"Sure thing, Big Jane. Sure thing. I'll behave myself."

100

Jane peered into the man's eyes and blew smoke in his face. She turned and stood in front of the screen door. Willis quickly stepped around her and opened the door for Big Jane, who defiantly walked through it in front of the small man.

Ninety minutes later, the bottles were empty. Jane sprawled on a large overstuffed living room chair with threadbare, once red print, upholstery. Cigarette butts overflowed the large ashtray on the end table next to her. She lit a cigarette from a diminishing one that she removed from the indentation in her lips. The dark woman called Jewel lay on well-worn faux leather sofa reading a movie magazine. A tumbler half full of whiskey set on the hardwood floor within easy reach.

Willis sat on the floor in the far corner. He was crying. He held an empty glass between his outstretched legs. "Fuck, Big Jane. I cooked those Japs. You know that. I cooked 'em. Jesus Christ, the screams. The fuckin' screams, Big Jane." Willis put his hands over his ears and sobbed, "Those poor goddamn Japs."

"You watch your fuckin' language, Sarge. I'll have none of that 'Jap' shit here. Not in front of Jewel. Ain't right. You have to respect her."

"I'm Chinese." Jewel didn't look up from her magazine.

"Same difference," Big Jane shot back. "Sarge, you promised you'd behave yourself."

"I'm sorry, Jewel. I'm so, so sorry," Willis cried, and wiped his nose on his bare arm.

"I'm Chinese."

"Sarge, you got more money, ain't ya? I need another bottle." Jane tried to push out of the chair but managed only to re-position herself. "You got more money?"

"Yeah, I do," Sarge said dully and pulled the wad of bills from his sock.

Jane's eyes widened slightly as she watched the man peel a twenty from the roll.

"Jewel, baby, get your Jap ass off the couch and go get me and my good buddy Sarge another bottle."

The woman let the magazine slide off onto the floor. She stood and grabbed the twenty-dollar bill from Willis' outstretched hand and went to the door.

"I'm Chinese."

The screen door slapped the door jamb as the woman, wearing a blue tee shirt, yellow shorts and red flip flops padded out onto the porch and past the window without looking back.

Willis pulled his knees up under his chin and wrapped his arms tightly around his legs, resting his chin on his knees. "Okinawa, Big Jane," he whispered. "It was fucking Okinawa. And a flamethrower, Big Jane. It was Okinawa and a flamethrower. I cooked 'em. I cooked all of 'em."

"Okinawa, Big Jane. Okinawa in nineteen and forty-five. They said it would be a big battle, but we walked right in. Right off the boats and nothin'. For a couple of days, we just walked right across that goddamn place and then, and then, all hell broke loose."

Givens was right. The Japanese chose not to defend against the onslaught of Americans landing on the shoreline. They dug in and waited. They fortified and waited. Against an enemy in pillboxes, holes, tunnels, caves and castles, the flamethrower was thought to be most effective.

The man-portable flamethrower consists of two elements: a backpack and the gun. The backpack element comprises two cylinders. One cylinder contains compressed, inert nitrogen, and the other holds flammable liquid gas with some form of fuel thickener added to it. The Army manual spoke to the profound psychological impact that the weapon imparted on the unsuspecting enemy, but was silent on the effect the weapon parlayed to its operator other than to point out its excessive weight.

Twenty-year old buck sergeant Willis Givens boarded one of the first landing craft to sail towards the gnarly coast of Okinawa on April first. He would spend all eighty-two days of the campaign burdened by the extreme weight of an M2 flamethrower. The morbidity wrought by the weapon that his aching back supported would plague him for the next thirty years.

The Okinawa campaign crawled along yards at a time. Day by day, hour-by-hour, casualty-by-casualty, the men of the invasion force methodically destroyed an enemy who refused to give up, and who knew they were defeated, yet proudly gave their lives to slow the inevitable assault of their beloved home islands. More and more often would come the cry, "Sarge! Hey Sarge, fry 'em up," as the infantrymen who somehow had survived when so many others had not, would approach another hole or tunnel. "Bring up Sarge," the platoon leader would command. "We got another hole. Cook 'em Sarge. Cook 'em."

Sergeant Givens would creep up as close as possible to the enemy position. The flamethrower had only a maximum range of about eighty yards, but he liked to get closer. He knew the limited amount of fuel the small canister reservoir on his back held. He knew to conserve the fuel, to make every drop count. He discovered the most efficient and effective methods of using the cruel device. Spray a stream of fire into the tunnel opening and then listen for the screams of the affected enemy. He became adept at estimating how many he had killed by the number of screams from within a chamber such as a pillbox or a tunnel. He knew that the screams on June Second were not soldiers at all but women and children who had hidden in a mineshaft.

On that sultry afternoon came the cry from villagers that the Americans were coming. Believing Japanese propaganda leaflets that the American invaders were barbaric, rapacious, bent on the most visceral behavior, two teachers led thirty-two four-year-old to eleven-year-old students to a vacant mine shaft in the hill above their village to hide from the invaders. Ten-year-old Akio lagged behind the other students who, with practiced discipline, formed up two-by-two and marched swiftly to the safety of the mineshaft above. Akio dashed to the rear of the small schoolhouse and reached into the crawl space under the building to find the cap of a Japanese Imperial soldier he had found and stored there, and with it he located the Arisaka Type 99 bolt-action 6.5 millimeter rifle. Such items were plentiful on the war-ravaged island. Akio, named for his intelligence, had never fired the cumbersome weapon, but he was steadfast in his resolve to defend his classmates from the American scourge.

103

Akio carried the cap with one hand and the rifle with the other as he raced up the hill through the trees to the mineshaft. As the others clambered over the gravel funnel of the old excavated mine and skidded down to the small opening to the mine, Akio took up a position at the crest of the site, held guard, and awaited the invaders. Soon he saw an American soldier for the first time in his life. The soldier slowly emerged from the surrounding tree line and stopped to carefully inspect the dig site above him. He knew from the experience of the last month operating on this "God forsaken place" that such places offered excellent concealment and protection from American air raids and artillery for the Japanese Army. The point man saw movement from above and quickly dove behind the protection of the trees.

Akio carefully positioned the cap too large on his head and took aim with the rifle at the American below. The American jumped behind a tree before Akio could fire. Akio kept his position and barely breathed as his heart pounded wildly in his chest. A shot rang out from below and threw shattered rock into his face. Startled, but not hurt, Akio jerked the trigger of the rifle and its subsequent recoil from the errant blast slammed the butt of the weapon into his cheek and he fell backwards. Now, out of the line of fire from below, Akio huddled against the slope of the mine site and tears rolled down his cheeks as he pressed against the earthen shelter. A maelstrom of booming and screeching ricochets of several rounds fired from below kicked up sprays of rocks and dirt off the summit above him. He tried in vain to operate the bolt action of the weapon. Finally, he kicked it aside and the cap fell from his head as he scrambled down and disappeared deep into the mineshaft below.

The point man signaled to his squad to approach the mine opening from the right and left as he kept up steady cover fire. The first soldier from the left found the top of the excavation site and quickly craned his neck over the top. He saw the rifle and cap on the down-slope to the mineshaft opening below and pulled back to safety. He signaled the remainder of the squad to take positions around the crater-shaped entrance then he cried out.

"Sarge, come on up! Cook 'em up. Do it Sarge. Fry 'em up."

Givens scrambled quickly up the face of the conical shaped crater and slipped often in the gravel under the weight of the heavy equipment strapped to his back. He glanced over the top then kneeled on the top of the excavation site and shot a stream of fuel into the entrance of the mine. He had learned that in certain situations that pouring the deadly liquid into the opening of these holes, and then igniting the fuel by turning the weapon to full on and shooting a short stream of flame into the hole would light a conflagration deep within the tunnel, thus improving the killing effectiveness of the flame. Those who were not burned alive suffocated. He knew the more who died within the hole the greater the survival odds of the troops who would later be called upon to go into the depths to inspect the interior. None of the troops now standing on the surrounding heights above the burning mine shaft were prepared for what they heard.

High-pitched screams came from the steaming, burning mouth of the tunnel. Givens was preparing to change out the tanks on his pack with a new set of fully charged canisters carried by an assistant thrower. He sat back on his haunches and could not shift his eyes from the fire and deep black smoke emerging from the opening. All knew the screams came from the dying throats of children, and the soldiers held their positions in awestruck terror. Givens fumbled one of the tanks and it tumbled down towards the burning opening. The soldiers lining the top of the crater watched in horror as the tank of fuel slowly rolled and toppled end over end into the fiery mouth. Givens heard himself screaming, "Take cover." The men disappeared down the other side of the gravel pile. Moments later the canister exploded in a shower of Fourth of July pyrotechnics.

What he expected to see, Givens saw when he entered the cavity after the "oven cooled." The mental wounds suffered on that muggy, late spring afternoon proved, eventually, fatal to the proud sergeant. The shrieks, the sights, and noxious fumes remained ever present in the man's psyche no matter how mean of a son-of-a-bitch he tried to be with all his soul for the next thirty years. No amount of alcohol, no amount of punishment meted out or suffered by fighting any "motherfucker in the room," provided relief from the nightmare of June second, nineteen hundred and forty-five.

————————

Willis Givens found himself behind a row of garbage cans in an alley two doors down from Big Jane's house. He came to, coughing violently, dreaming that he was drowning. He was. Blood from a forehead wound puddled around his nose as he lay face down, wedged between trashcans and a wooden fence.

Givens sat up, looking around dizzily. Impulsively, he felt for the roll of money in his sock. His instincts told him before he knew for certain that the money was gone.

Slowly, the old sergeant got to his feet and wiped the blood from his eyes. It was still dark, but the sky was brightening by the minute. He pointed himself towards the street lamp at the end of the alley and started off. Falling twice before he reached the street. Regaining his bearings he headed towards the James Hotel. He pushed his hand into his pocket and pulled out the flat, black rock that he had picked up in Okinawa. He thought it was shaped like a heart. With it came what was left of the Purple Heart ribbon. As he crossed the street, he dropped his most valued possessions through a grate covering the sewer and laughed gruffly as he heard the small splash below.

The night clerk at the James did not mention the wound on Givens' face, although he did look up from his magazine. Nor did the night clerk find it out of the ordinary that Givens did not need his room key, since he had nothing anybody wants anyway.

Givens entered his room at half past five in the morning. Murky grey light filled the small room from the curtain-less window that faced the alley and parking area below. Givens turned and locked his door. He opened the tiny closet and pried up a loose floorboard and pulled out a revolver. He sat on the bed and turned on the small lamp on the nightstand and watched an army of cockroaches scamper over the linoleum floor in all directions. He watched them until they all disappeared into wherever cockroaches go. He held the service revolver in both hands, stood up and stepped slowly to a stainless-steel sheet screwed to the wall that served as the mirror above a small sink. He peered at the stranger looking back at him. The blood from the wound on his forehead coagulated on his face, but the wound continued to ooze. He asked, "Who are you? Where did you go? Where have you been?" He smiled, but the man in the mirror did not smile back at him.

MOURNING IN THEIR TRIBE

Givens saw the man in the mirror raise the revolver to his right temple. Afraid to watch what he knew the man would do next, he turned to his left and gazed at nothing. The man in the mirror slowly cocked the gun and fired.

PART 5

Solved

Rows of decaying brick buildings that made up what the cops called The Street, passersby may have wondered who or what lived behind the greasy, forlorn fenestration without curtains. Windows, some covered by stained pull shades, did little to curtail the stark glare of single bare light bulbs hanging defiantly from wall-papered ceilings decorated by random shadowy stains. One building morphed into another whose lines of demarcation were marked only by height of the structures and choice of paint on brick. Many had once been fine hotels when the railroad was in its heyday. Now, they provided housing for vermin, cockroaches and the dispossessed who counted down the days each month until the first rolled around and the welfare checks arrive.

Chapter Twenty One

Sheila Henry found the situation not as uncomfortable as she anticipated. The detectives greeted her as a welcomed addition to the Halverson investigative team in a manner that was accepting and, at least on the surface, genuine.

She met with Reynolds and O'Brien in the Chief's office along with The Boss, Chief Hansen and his staff for most of the morning. They reviewed and discussed ad infinitum all of the evidence or, more to the point, the lack of evidence in the death of Corporal Halverson, including the medical examiner's autopsy report. The detectives had hoped for more from it. The bullet had struck a rib and shattered. The pathologist noted that the bullet had separated into four major fragments. One fragment had wedged against the victim's spinal cord. The report only noted that the bullet was, "large caliber hollow point shell," and did not cause death. The shell fragments were properly packaged and sent to the FBI lab for further analysis. The report also noted that because of the amount of bleeding, the abdominal wound was the first suffered by the officer. The bullet to the head ended his life."

The meeting dragged on as each of the captains offered points of view that amounted to *"useless speculation"* as O'Brien later termed their ideas. "Total waste of time," said Reynolds. Sheila Henry silently agreed with the detectives regarding the value of the staff's remarks to the overall investigation. However, she found the dynamics of the meeting far more fascinating and noteworthy than what was said. Three of the captains seemed moderately aligned with The Chief as evidenced by body language, facial expressions, slight nods and affirming mumbles whenever The Chief made a point. Captain Nelson, alone, stood apart, antagonistic. His comments, dished out as advice, clearly pricked The Chief's sensibilities. Nelson noted (*too sharply*, in Sheila's mind: *condescending and that what he said should have gone without saying, he said it anyway*) that The Chief "hold the FBI's feet to the fire," to insure "quick work on the analysis of all of the evidence sent them by the department's crime lab and the autopsy results, after all, THIS is the biggest case in the state, for Christ's sake. The worst fucking crime in the history of the Valley." As if everyone in the room did not already know that.

The Chief winced, but held back. Color rose on his forehead and balding pate. The other department heads swapped quick glances and turned their attention to the papers in front of them. The Boss wore his usual expression of mild amusement, cool and serene: *The Maharishi*. He said little during the meeting, so Sheila followed his lead. She had questions, and looked to The Boss for any kind of go-ahead sign, but she received nothing. The Boss simply sat with that placid expression and would not return her covert pursuit for eye contact.

The Chief announced, "I left instructions with dispatch that the commanding officer be notified directly of any situation that arises in Area Three." He turned to The Boss and looked at Sheila, "That is the designation for the patrol area of Fifth Street in the vicinity of where Corporal Halverson was killed." He turned to the detectives. "Dispatch just received a call of a possible homicide at the James Hotel. O'Brien and Reynolds and Ms. Henry, go and look into this thing for any connection to your investigation. I don't want you taking on any additional work though. If there is no connection, we will reassign the investigation to another team. Patrol units are on the scene but have been instructed to wait for you. Am I clear, gentlemen?"

The detectives, relieved to be getting out of the stuffy room, jumped to their feet and blurted, "Crystal clear, Chief."

The Boss and Sheila exchanged a glance. She rose quickly, gathered her papers, and followed the detectives out the room.

"Jesus Christ, I thought that meeting would never end," O'Brien cried as the three approached the plain looking tan Plymouth Fury in the parking lot. Sheila was about to open the back door of the police unit, when she noticed Reynolds holding the front passenger door open for her.

"I thought I would just sit back here, out of the way."

"No, you should have a front row seat," Reynolds smiled, walked around her and got in the back seat.

"Let's go," shouted O'Brien, and Sheila plopped into the front seat.

O'Brien started the car, and Sheila placed a hand on his arm to stop him momentarily from continuing. "Look, there is something you two should know," she said hesitatingly.

"Well?" O'Brien asked impatiently.

"The Boss may bring up Rick Benson with the Brass."

"Big Rick?" Questioned Reynolds.

"That's right, Big Rick," Sheila said. "It seems The Boss is developing a theory in which Benson could be a suspect in Corporal Halverson's murder."

"Really?"

"Think about it," O'Brien interrupted. "He's a big guy. I embarrassed the hell out of him at The Roof in front of The Boss, among others. Rick is pissed and leaves the bar. Hal is killed around the same time."

"Right you are, O'Brien," Sheila quipped.

"And Big Rick is a big fucker, too. But, it's a bit of a stretch to say he killed Hal because his ego along with his nose were shattered by O'Brien," Reynolds completed the scenario.

"Maybe, Morris," Sheila replied quietly. "Benson is known for his temper, especially when drunk. It is not out of the realm of reasonable belief that he shot the first cop that he came into contact with following the fight that you two, quite obviously, setup the other night. And The Boss had me make a few calls this morning. It seems that Big Rick is a big horse owner, as well, according to a woman who answers the phones at The Big Dollar."

"Oh, fuck," Reynolds, responded. Connecting the dots in his mind, he was overcome with a sense of foreboding. *What is the connection? Rick. The bar fight. Hal's murder. His encounter at the back door of The Roof. The sequence of events just didn't make sense. If Rick killed Hal, why stick around to kick the shit out of me?*

The three sat contemplating the ramifications of what Sheila had just divulged. Guilt crept through Reynolds. Fighting against his instincts to mention his assault and his investigation into Big Rick's movements, he decided to hold close counsel and to let the events fall where they may.

O'Brien imagined how this would play in the newspapers: *"Cops' Arranged Humiliation Turns Deadly;" "Businessman Set Up, Turns on Cop."* Finally, O'Brien broke the silence, "The Boss didn't bring any of this up while we were present in the meeting. Why are you bringing it up now, Sheila?"

"Oh, well, I thought you should be aware of what may conspire this afternoon. Call it a heads-up, if you will."

"I suppose we should thank you for that, Sheila," Reynolds quickly added.

"Yeah, thanks," O'Brien muttered. "Let's get over to the James."

Chapter Twenty Two

In the lobby of the James Hotel, two uniformed officers were talking to the night manager. The investigators stopped near the patrol officers and close enough to hear what the officers were asking the slim manager who appeared to be in his mid-fifties with greying, thinning hair slicked straight back and, although it was ninety degrees outside and no air conditioning inside, wore a sleeveless cardigan blue sweater over a white long sleeved dress shirt opened at the neck. His head hung from his narrow shoulders and bobbed side to side as he spoke. His bulging blue left eye appeared to swim, magnified by the thick lens of his glasses that slid easily and often down his thin nose. His right eye looked straight ahead at nothing. It was glass.

Officer Dexter turned to the detectives and stared blankly at Sheila Henry.

"Mike, this is Sheila Henry from the DA's office. She is assisting us with the investigation," Reynolds said.

Sheila pushed her hand toward the officer and shook his hand with firm confidence that broke the officer's eye contact. He looked down at his notebook, "Pleased to meet you."

Annoyed, O'Brien rocked back and forth on his wide stance, hands clenched behind his back. "What we got, Mike?" He withheld the slight grin, while taking a quick glance at Sheila. He thought Sheila a *bit too perfect.* Straight blonde hair pulled into a tight ponytail, exposing skin with minor acne scarring, perfectly tanned in the manner that only those of Nordic ancestry seem to pull off so... *perfectly*, he thought, *golden.* A nonchalant, but swift elevator-glance-examination of the woman standing next to him, though cursory, was enough for O'Brien to assume that her figure, neat, trim and athletic, *though small breasted, may be fun for a one-time thing. Know what I mean?*

"This is Mr. Crowley, the night manager. He was supposed to get off duty at 8 A.M., but the guy who was supposed to relieve him didn't show," said one of the officers.

"That's right. That's right. That's right," stammered the hotel manager in machine gun staccato. "Jake is always on time. Never misses a shift. So,

I'm thinkin' that the fat bastard got drunk or somethin'. That's right. Sorry Miss, I shoudn'ta swore like that."

Sheila nodded.

An officer interrupted, "A Mr. Jacob Healey didn't show up for work, so he goes up and knocks on Mr. Healey's door about 8:30 A.M. with no response. At 9:30 A.M., Mr. Crowley calls the owner of the hotel at the law offices of Shiner and Peate."

"And… and… and… and… Tommy Peate tells me to carry on as best I can, bein' up all night and everything. Jesus, I say, 'Tommy, I mean Mr. Peate, I been up all fuckin' night.'" Sorry, sorry ma'am." He glanced at Sheila before continuing.

"At about 1:15 P.M., Mr. Crowley gets worried. He has not seen or heard from Healey, which is most unusual," the officer continued, and Crowley nodded so violently that his glasses tumbled from his nose, and he caught them at his waist.

"What took you so long?" O'Brien interjected.

"And… and… and… I don't like to stick my nose in other people's business, so I waited. Maybe something has come up. But Jake is never late. Jake is different from most of the folks in this place. And … and… and… he is just different. But I got to thinkin' I ought to check upstairs for him. Yeah, and… and… and… I goes and… and… and I got the key to 3E, and there he was with his goddamn eye shot out."

"What time did you find him?" Reynolds asked the night manager.

"By time I get the key and get Benny settled down. He got upset about why the ice machine is broke…"

"And?" The detective said impatiently.

"And… and… and… It was ten after two. I know because I looked up at the big clock there and it said it was two twenty. It's about ten minutes too fast, you see, so I figured it out. Ten minutes minus…"

"You been up there?" O'Brien asked the officer.

"Yes, but I didn't linger or disturb the scene much per the Chief's orders. The victim is a white male, sixtyish, dressed in a white undershirt, sleeveless,

114

wearing undershorts lying on the floor next to the bed. Obviously dead. I stepped in and quickly examined him. Dead as a door nail. Dispatch called the medical examiner. They should be here anytime now. The crime lab is coming too, but they haven't arrived yet. Officer Luckenbach is guarding the crime scene upstairs."

"Okay, thanks. Let's go have a look," O'Brien states.

Led by the night manager, O'Brien, Reynolds and Sheila climbed to the third floor. The pressing heat, stench of urine and cheap cleaning product and sweat increased in intensity with each flight of stairs. Pangs of nausea gripped Sheila's stomach, causing her to gag noticeably.

"Cops have a saying, Sheila," Reynolds said softly as they trudged up the narrow creaking stairs. "You'll forget what you see, but you never forget what you smell."

"You're a big help," gasped the lawyer.

"No. Probably not," wheezed Reynolds.

Sheila gained small succor that the stench was getting to Reynolds as well. *Perhaps this is not something that you do get used to*, she thought. O'Brien, on the other hand, appeared unfazed and maintained an incessant condescending chatter during their journey up, up, and up into the domain of the forsaken that did little to calm Sheila's stomach, which, of course, was the point. "Be sure to keep your purse shut, Sheila, and shake your jacket and smooth your skirt when we leave. Cockroaches, lice, and God only knows what else. I notice that you're not wearing panty hose. Could be a mistake. Don't want any hitchhikers coming home with you." He maintained that frown of a cock-sure smile. "Oh yeah, and don't sit on anything with a cushion." He was having fun at her expense, she knew.

The James Hotel was pink; perhaps it was thought to be grey by some. She allowed her mind to wander. Deep down, she feared ending up in such a place someday. Perhaps her mother occupied just such a dreadful flat in Los

115

Angeles or San Francisco—Las Vegas, most likely. "Someplace warm without nagging kids with sticky fingers pulling at me all day long while you're out schmoozing so called fucking clients," were her mother's parting words slurred by Vodka to a husband and two tow-headed children, boy and girl, aged five and seven. All of the tricks Sheila had learned since her mother's departure could not quite rid her of the badgering fear that she, Sheila Henry, Assistant District Attorney, would end up there, sitting alone, diabetic legs wrapped in soiled pressure bandages, hair grey and thinning, while peering out through gauzy window glass cracked in one corner, condemned to a room illuminated by a single bare bulb, bathroom down the hall.

Now here she was in the bowels of her nightmare. The night manager pushed open the door to room 3E that released a rush of odor so pervasive that turned all three investigators about. O'Brien lit a cigarette and waved it in front of him as a poor defense against the stagnant repugnance as the three investigators stepped into the room.

"Wait in the hall," Reynolds told the hotel employee. The room held a bed that was neatly made up. A shaving brush set precariously on the side of the small sink beneath a polished thin stainless steel sheet, ever present in each of the rooms that served as an unbreakable mirror. The man lay on his back, his bare feet under the sink. Livor mortis had set in, giving the corpse a contrasting two-tone look. Gravity had drained and pooled blood in the lower half of the body turning it deep purple, leaving the upper half opaque as bee's wax. His un-contemplative gaze from an open right eye fixed on the doorway where the officers and lawyer now stood. Blood had spread over the yellowing linoleum floor from a head wound that obliterated the man's left eye and left a larger exit wound on the back center of his head.

The window glass on the opposite side of the small room bore a neat round hole with glass cratered on the outside. The door to a narrow closet near the man's head was ajar; the investigators noted three white shirts, two

116

pair of dress pants and a thin jacket hanging neatly separated evenly on wire hangers, military style.

Reynolds stepped over the body and examined the hole in the window glass. "Shot came from inside the room."

"Uh-huh," remarked O'Brien. "Rigor mortis has passed. Been dead more than six or seven hours," remarked O'Brien. He carefully took two long strides toward the mirror and closely examined a small neat round hole right of center. He turned to Sheila and asked, "What do you make of this, counselor?"

Sheila stepped gingerly over the body and stood next to O'Brien, closely examining the hole. "It is protruding," Sheila mused.

O'Brien took a pen from his shirt pocket and nudged the mirror to the right. It swung easily on the lone screw from which it hung, exposing the wall and hundreds of cockroaches. O'Brien jumped slightly. Sheila Henry gasped and reflexively stepped back. She tripped over the dead man's leg and tumbled onto the body and tried in vain to thwart her fall by grabbing Reynolds' shoulder. Both fell into the mostly coagulated bloodstain.

O'Brien roared with laughter. Sheila, mortified and embarrassed, slipped trying to stand up in the blood puddle and landed partially in Reynolds' lap.

"Jesus Christ!" cried Reynolds. He lifted Sheila off him. "Jesus H. Chri ... " his words were drowned out in surges of laughter that he couldn't suppress.

Tears formed and poured down Sheila's face as laughter bubbled uncontrollably through tears and mucus.

The three of them stood in the room with the dead man and doubled over in uncontrollable hysterics let loose of the stress and stench and the shit-hole hotel.

Camera in hand, crime scene investigator Shanahan stood at the door of room 3E with two uniformed officers, straining to see around him at the merry-making inside the room.

"Oh, for crying out loud," Shanahan all but screamed. "What have you jackasses done to my crime scene?" He was truly pissed. He attempted to say more, but could only stammer.

Finally, O'Brien controlled himself enough to speak, "Calm down, George. You don't have a crime scene. This was an accident."

That brought Sheila and Reynolds to their senses. Reynolds knew O'Brien was on to something. He also knew his partner's flair for the dramatic. Sheila agreed, "O'Brien's mostly right. There is a crime here, something like reckless endangerment, involuntary manslaughter."

"What are you saying?" asked Shanahan incredulously.

"There's been no *real* crime here," O'Brien decreed, shaking his head at Sheila. "It's an accident, know what I mean?"

"No, I certainly do not know what you are saying or how you came to that conclusion," Shanahan responded.

Sheila Henry had recovered her voice, and she sounded indignant, "You will, Sergeant. You fucking will."

"Somebody go get the manager, will you?" O'Brien shouted at the men in the hallway. He looked at Henry admiringly.

"I'm here," came a voice from the hallway. The officers parted for the night manager.

"Who lives next door on that side?" O'Brien asked the manager while pointing in the direction of the wall next to the washbasin and mirror.

"That would be Willis Givens."

"Oh, man," moaned Reynolds.

Sheila surmised, "The shot came from the other side of the wall, causing the protruding damage to the tin mirror on this side. The bullet entered this man's face, and exited the back of his head."

"Yep, and through that window over there," Reynolds completed the thought. "The walls in this pop stand are paper thin."

Sheila looked around the sink and floor. "Shaving. Good God. The man was shaving, and…"

"Then he's dead. Shit really does happen, eh Sheila?" O'Brien said from the doorway, "Come on, let's see what we find next door."

O'Brien tried the door of 3D, "It's locked." He turned to the night manager.

"That's odd," said the manager.

"Get the key," Reynolds growled.

Shanahan examined Reynolds and Henry standing next to him. "Not too close, okay?" He was still irritated. "Come to think of it, you two better wait in the hall until I give you the all clear to come in. I doubt we are going to find much in there, and you two are dripping."

O'Brien gave Reynolds the 'you wanna bet?' look.

The manager came back with the key and handed it to O'Brien. He opened the door and stood back as the scene inside unfolded. Willis Given lay on his right side, holding a .357 magnum revolver.

O'Brien tiptoed into the room and examined the blood splattered mirror. He located a hole that he knew corresponded with the exit hole in room 3E.

Shanahan reached up and pulled the string that turned on the bare light bulb overhead. He noticed something odd in the small closet. The closet door was ajar, and Shanahan pushed it fully open with his pen. The floorboards had been pulled up and he bent to inspect them. He pushed them aside with his pen and pulled a small flash light from his breast pocket.

"Holy shit!" Shanahan exclaimed.

Chapter Twenty Three

"This is unbelievable. A derelict," the Chief beamed. Try as he might, he could not hold back the smile that spread across his face. "Thanks to you two, or three I should say, we have solved Hal's murder, before we bury him. You came through, guys."

"I'm not so sure," Reynolds began, but O'Brien cut him off.

"You know Mo, Chief. Sometimes he over analyzes. Know what I mean?" O'Brien smiled broadly, but he shot his partner a *shut the fuck up* look.

The smile evaporated from the Chief's face as he regained his composure. "I do know what you mean, Robert. We don't want to overreact, and we will know more once Shanahan completes the fingerprint comparison of the prints from Hal's boot with Givens'. He will have a preliminary report very soon. Come on, Morris, we have Hal's revolver. We have his Sam Browne belt, his flashlight. All were found in Givens' room. You guys dug his wallet from the dumpster behind the James Hotel. Morris, you said Givens had a hundred fifty bucks on him the day before he killed himself."

"Compelling evidence, Chief," said Sheila. "However, as Detective Reynolds pointed out, the medical examiner wrote that the bullet found in Officer Halverson's abdomen was a hollow point, large caliber round. We know that Halverson wasn't carrying hollow point ammunition. That is against department policy, and his pistol didn't contain that kind of ammunition."

"What about the tobacco stain? We didn't find chewing tobacco in Givens' room," Reynolds mentioned.

All three agreed to hold off discussion of the case being solved. Reynolds knew O'Brien could get carried away with his fondness of getting credit—*Credit, a myth amounting to bragging. Grandstanding is what Reynolds* thought. *Getting credit from whom? A nod from The Chief. A slap on the back? Name in the paper? Recorded in the annals of the department? Do we even have annals? In a month from now, who will care? Everyone will have moved on to something else. New men will come along. Credit will be sought. Jealousies will arise. The downside of so-called credit is spite. Envious peers will look for small mistakes in their work and will magnify them into unforgivable errors spoken of in harsh terms over drinks, and in quiet I-told-you-so looks over coffee. And somewhere along the way the petty gripes will wind up on Captain Nelson's desk. He will build on them for his own political ambitions. They will become fodder for his discussions with the City Manager at the Country Club aimed at discrediting The Chief. No, it's best not to grandstand, not to seek credit. Stay out of the limelight. Let the microscope hover over someone else.*——But Reynolds knew O'Brien. He detested that about his partner. He recognized, however, that he could not keep O'Brien from being O'Brien.

The phone rang, and the Chief answered and said, "Thank you, keep up the nice work." He replaced the receiver, "It's preliminary, but Shanahan said that he is 95% certain the prints found on Hal's boot match Givens' prints. This ices it as far as I'm concerned. I want to hold a press conference first thing in the morning and to be the one who breaks this to the press. I know you are not a hundred percent, Morris, but are we ever 100% in this line of work? I have to strike first."

Surely, he is referring to Captain Nelson, but he could have meant O'Brien. Reynolds thought, and nodded his head along with the others as The Chief continued.

"I'll advise them of what we have, and make note that the investigation is ongoing, because, well, it is. You all need some rest, and a change of clothes. I don't want to know how it happened that you two are caked in, what is that smell, blood?" The Chief stood up straight and tall. He shook everyone's hands all around. "Now go home. It's been a long day. Have a beer. I'll see you tomorrow."

"Morris, may I have a word?" The Chief asked.

Reynolds' shoulders noticeably slouched and he turned to face The Chief. Sheila and OB stepped out past the empty secretary's desk and waited for Reynolds in the hallway.

The Chief chuckled, "Take it easy, Morris. I just wanted to confirm that you are coming over for dinner tomorrow night." Before Morris could answer, The Chief added, "Your Aunt is expecting you."

"Sure thing. I'll be there by six, say?"

Chapter Twenty Four

Reynolds opened a beer and walked out to the patio where Uncle Gerry sweated over the grill.

"Why does Aunt Lillian feel the need to blindside me like this? And," Reynolds sipped the beer, "you could have warned me."

Uncle Gerry wiped his brow with the back of the oversized mitt. As if the size were not enough, it was emblazoned with big puffy cartoonish words, BIG MIT. "I didn't say anything, because I knew you wouldn't have come over, and that would have upset your aunt, and I would have had to weather the storm. Alone." And he crooned, "*All by myself.*" Uncle Gerry smiled, "So, it was a no brainer."

Reynolds looked over his shoulder at the prettyish woman helping Aunt Lillian prepare salads in the kitchen. *Kind of frumpy,* he thought. *Not exactly my type.* With lowered voice he said, "Uncle Gerry, I happen to be seeing someone."

"I know. The barmaid."

"Bar owner," Reynolds responded, tiresomely.

"I apologize, Morris. That came out wrong. Please just play along. I know you won't make a scene tonight. She is not someone I'd picture you with. Margaret has been widowed for more than two years now. Actually, I think this is her first so-called date since her husband's death." The Chief raised his eyebrows in pseudo question. "Lillian met her in church and has tried to get her out of the house for months." Uncle Gerry removed the BIG MIT and slapped Reynolds on the back with it. "The steaks will be good, guaranteed."

"Oh. Well, I'm sure the steaks will be great. Not to worry, I'll be on my best behavior," Reynolds concluded the underlying silent quid pro quo. "You and I need to talk later."

"Deal," acknowledged The Chief.

Dinner went well. Reynolds found Margaret, "Call me Peg," to be charming and a bit shy in a vulnerable, and not unattractive, way. He began to re-think his first impression. As the dinner wore on it became clear to Reynolds that Peg was not frumpy at all, but pretty and kind, with a subtle sense of humor, and not the least bit interested in him. For some reason that he could not put his finger on, he felt let down.

After dinner, The Chief and the detective repaired to the study. Peg helped Aunt Lillian with the cleanup and left before Reynolds and Hansen returned.

Uncle Gerry, now The Chief in the study, took a seat behind a desk leaving the detective the couch, which sat much lower than The Chief on high.

"What did you learn today?" The Chief asked Reynolds, anticipating Reynolds' his need for a conference.

"According to inter-jurisdictional notices, we know five other similar cop shootings have occurred in the last couple of years; all unsolved. We contacted each department today, and all the cases are very similar. Each officer was gunned down at night, and four out of five officers were shot twice. All four of the officers who were shot twice were shot once at a distance greater than a couple of feet, and then shot between the eyes, up close. Powder burns on each one. All were killed with large caliber bullets. A pristine bullet was recovered in only one of the cases, a .45 caliber hollow point. The FBI has conclusively connected two of the killings, but speculates that at least four of the five are linked."

The Chief noted the pause, "And?"

"And, in no other cases was a robbery involved."

"Chewing tobacco?"

"None noted in any of the investigations."

"What about Willis Givens?" the Chief asked.

"The departments we contacted had no immediate knowledge of Givens, but they are conducting thorough searches of arrest records, and all are skip tracing the name." Reynolds quickly added, "As are we, but, so far nothing. We have no evidence that Givens was involved in the other shootings. But,

Chief, we found out that Willis was not employed in Corrine laying the new track. So, I have no idea where he came by the money."

"Have you checked Givens' jail records?" the Chief asked.

"We'll get on that first thing in the morning."

"Morris, I know you are skeptical, but I expect you to keep digging. So far nothing you have told me is enough to counter what I told the press this morning. I truly believe that we have our killer. Also, in less than a week, the Freedom Train will come through our state, and we are invested to ensure that the bicentennial celebration goes smoothly. Our city is providing 75% of the security. The city manager and mayor have taken heat over the expenditure of city funds for a private enterprise, although the organizers have promised the city will be reimbursed. It will take at least that much time to wrap up loose ends."

"Sure thing, Chief. We'll keep working."

Chapter Twenty Five

Reynolds parked in his usual place on the second level of the garage and headed down the ramp to The Roof. *Christ, how stupid of me. I always park in the same place. Jesus, we are such creatures of habit. How easy would it be for anyone wanting to know my whereabouts to figure it out? I've got to alter my habits. It only takes a few kidney punches in the night to wake a guy up.*

The rush of welcoming cool conditioned air greeted him as he pushed through the front door of the bar. Sonya glanced his way and without recognition returned to her conversation with a stocky man wearing Levies and a tight black tee shirt exposing a taught heavily muscled frame. With dark hair parted in the middle and hanging below his ears, the man stood with one foot on the brass foot rail and confidently swirled a glass filled with whiskey and ice. He didn't look Reynolds way, but continued with what appeared to be a serious discussion with Sonya, who was not smiling.

Reynolds sat at the opposite end of the bar near the door and ordered a vodka tonic from Milt, Sonya's part-time bartender.

Taking a long sip from the iced drink, Reynolds briefly felt the warm sun streaming into the bar onto his back as someone entered through the door behind him.

Sonya appeared to stop her conversation in mid-sentence and looked Reynolds way as a slap on his back startled him.

"Well, if it's not Defective Reynolds," Big Rick slid onto the stool next to Reynolds. "Where's Defective O'Brien on this fine summer evening?" He bellowed and laughed.

"Well, it seems that for being DE-fective, OB was pretty E-ffective the other night." Reynolds countered. "Wouldn't Big Rick agree?"

"Big Rick would have to agree with you there, Defective."

Reynolds eyed Big Rick up and down and prodded, "For a man of your considerable wealth, there Big. May I call you just by your first name?"

"Sure." Rick smiled broadly.

"Where are your fancy cowboy boots? Look at you. You could have come off a construction gang."

Big Rick softened his tone and looked at Reynolds and shook his head. "Cowboy boots? Hell sakes I wouldn't be caught dead in those things. They are useless. These good old boys have served me well for years." Rick lifted a foot outfitted in a laced-leather work boot as if to show Reynolds. The boot was well worn. The leather scrubbed to suede from use. "By the way, I always dress like a workin' man. Because, well, I am one."

"Okay, good for you, Big."

"Yeah, well look Reynolds," Big Rick, now just Rick looked at his hands clasped in front of him. "I was hopin' that you and mainly your partner were in here tonight."

"Why is that, Big?"

"Enough with the Big stuff, Okay Reynolds? It's just plain Rick. I wanted to apologize to you guys is all. And to Sonya over there, but she looks like she's busy."

Milt walked over and asked, "What are you drinking tonight, Rick?"

"Water's fine. Could I get a glass of water?"

The bartender complied.

Rick held the glass and spoke softly, "Look Morris, do you mind if I call you by your first name?"

"No."

"I heard about what happened the other night to Officer Halverson. It's disgusting. I just want you all to know that old Big Rick here, will never disrespect an officer of the law again."

"Oh? No longer defectives?"

"No man. No more of that crap either. I came in here last night hoping to see you guys, but I guess you been busy with the investigation and all. So that's it. Man, I am so sorry for that man's family. I'm going to start a charity fund for his wife and kids and advertise it in the *Dollar*. Do you think I would be out of line to begin that in the next edition?"

"No. Not out of line at all. I'm sure Hal's family would be grateful."

"I'll do'er then." He stood up hoping Reynolds would too, so they could shake hands.

Reynolds didn't budge. Rick turned and walked out of the bar.

Milt came back over being adept at eavesdropping on bar talk and asked, "What was that all about? A fund? From Big Rick?"

"I don't know Milt, but I suppose it is a nice gesture. By the way?" Reynolds nodded toward Sonya and the man at the far end of the bar. Something caught his eye. Boots. The man wore heavy black motorcycle boots. The memory of the boot on his hand rushed back into his head like a freight train. The boot had a buckle.

"Oh him," Milt lowered his voice. "Sonya's Ex. Came in from California not long ago. Has been hanging around here for the last couple of nights."

Reynolds pulled out his wallet and pushed a five towards Milt and stood up to leave. Milt being adept at maintaining bar integrity and especially that of his boss, he also had a keen ear for rumors, he said, "I don't think there is anything to it, Mo. I think Sonya has nothing to do with him."

"Goodnight, Milt."

PART 6

A Funeral and Flowers

In the nation's bicentennial year, long-standing misogyny ruled over the officers the Heavenly Valley Police Department. Veteran police officers could be heard advising rookies that, "Remember, you can always find a woman, but it is much more difficult to find a job you love." And if a young officer were married, he may be advised to "Insure that your girlfriend is married too, so she has as much to lose as you do." As if one must chose: police work or happily ever after. But an entry in a criminology textbook published in 1975 warned: *Burnout in police work commonly occurs at six years. That which drives young adults into the occupation all too often dissipates into cynicism, alcoholism, and divorce.*

Chapter Twenty Six

Standing in the noonday sun in navy blue dress uniforms that no longer fit and hadn't been worn in years, O'Brien and Reynolds stood shoulder to shoulder with police officers, firefighters, and other law enforcement officers from jurisdictions throughout the state and a few from neighboring states as Officer Halverson's funeral procession slowly made its way down main street. Perspiration mixed with tears dripped from nose and cheek of the men and women standing ramrod straight, hands held in perfect salutes forming the long blue line.

Bag pipers from the area chapter of the Veterans of Foreign Wars followed the horse drawn hearse carrying the fallen officer. The somber piped notes of *Amazing Grace* echoed indiscriminately off the surrounding buildings to add to the perception of ascension, distance, and completion as the slow march turned east towards the cemetery.

It had been a long and dreadful day. Now, back into the cool comfort of civvies, Reynolds waited in the car for O'Brien and Henry, who had gone into the Main Street Deli to pick up dinner. Sheila Henry wanted to look over the menu inscribed on the wall before ordering. The deli was a regular stop for the detectives. No menu necessary. John, the proprietor, joked that they needn't come in. "Just honk. I'll bring the subs to you. No onions on one of them."

Turning away from the menu and the queue of customers in front of them, Sheila faced O'Brien. "I have to admit, Robert, that your partner is a bit odd. He seems so aloof, yet, hmmm. Do you know what he gave me?"

"Let me guess. Something that looks like a finely crafted wooden bowl, that he says is actually an amplifier. Am I right?"

"Well, yes," Sheila Henry replied. "You're correct. I was sitting in my office after the funeral today and before we met, and in pops Reynolds and hands me this thing wrapped in fancy paper. He tells me to unwrap it and, sure enough, it is a beautiful bowl and a small stand. He told me that he 'turned it' himself. I really don't know what that means specifically, but I've a rough idea."

"He is really an accomplished woodworker. Don't ask him about it unless you want a full-on dissertation of band saws, roughers, and lathes."

"I guess," Sheila Henry replied. "I said, 'thank you for the bowl.' And he said 'Bowl? Perhaps to the untrained eye. Feel how thin I have turned the sides. Put your transistor radio in it and, voila! Great sound, big volume from a cheap radio.' He turned and walked out of the office. I'm a little confused by the gesture. I thought that perhaps I should return it. I don't know what to make of it. We need to keep this on a professional level and all that. Tell me what you think. Am I making too big a deal out of this?"

O'Brien thought for a few moments and then responded. "I think, that he meant it as a 'welcome to the team' type of gift." O'Brien looked out at his partner sitting in the car outside the deli and shook his head. "Sheila, don't put too much into it. He has given us at least two of them. He enjoys making the things, and I'll bet he has a stack of them in his workshop. My wife, Suzy, uses the ones he gave us as popcorn bowls. They are perfect for that too. Don't give it back to him. You don't want to hurt his feelings. Know what I mean?"

Sheila Henry nodded and turned back towards the line in front of her.

"Unit 216, Notifier Alarm. Sample Sporting Goods."

Reynolds thought, *that place is just around the corner.* He looked into the deli and saw that O'Brien and Sheila Henry were still waiting in line, at least six people back. He mumbled to himself, "oh hell, it's probably a false alarm. Ninety-five percent of them are…" But knowing that it would curry favor with the patrolmen—a detective not being above answering a routine call—he reported back to dispatch that he would check it out.

He walked around the corner towards the shop and saw two men coming toward him in the shadows, each jogging and carrying an armload of clothing. He quickly ducked out of sight and into the alley. The men turned and entered the same alley. Reynolds hid behind a dumpster.

The men slowed to a walk as they reached the end of the alley, and they stopped and stepped back away from the headlights of a passing car before exiting to the right. They ambled casually along the sidewalk of the tree-lined, quiet, street, hugging the shadows, and Reynolds, following behind, heard their muffled laughs.

Stopping in front of a brownstone apartment building, one of the men turned, and saw Reynolds not twenty feet behind them. Clothes in arms, they bolted up the short flight of stairs and into the apartment building, and attempted to slam the door. Reynolds closed quickly and jammed the door open with his foot. The men entered the first apartment on the right that Reynolds burst into. There, he saw two older Hispanic women and four frightened children huddling together on a large overstuffed couch.

"Where did they go?" Reynolds demanded.

The women said nothing, but one of them started to cry.

"¿Dónde están? los dos hombres?" Reynolds demanded.

A girl of about five years old pointed towards one of the closed doors on the far end of the room. Reynolds tried the knob but the door was locked. He stepped back and kicked it with all of his might. The doorframe splintered, and the heavy door fell from one of its hinges and landed on one of the men, who looked about nineteen and frightened. Reynolds pulled his .38 snub-nosed Detective Special from his shoulder holster, and pointed it at the boy's face. Clothes still on hangers were strewn about the room and he could see that one of the men had crawled under the bed. Reynolds reached down and grabbed the man's foot, clad in a worn work boot, and yelled at the man to "get the fuck out from under the bed!"

The teenager who had been lying beneath the broken door scrambled to his feet and jumped on Reynolds' back, flaying his arms wildly. Reynolds ducked and spun. The boy tumbled over his back, landing on top of the man who had crawled out from under the bed. The man was on his knees, and screamed something in Spanish at the boy. The boy scoffed, and jumped into a defensive position, knees bent. Reynolds saw the knife in his right hand. He felt a warm moist oozing from his thigh and left arm. He glanced down and saw the expanding blood stain on his right pant leg.

"You stabbed me, you asshole!" Reynolds screamed.

131

"Vete a la mierda!" The boy screamed back at him.

Reynolds then screamed at the boy to drop the knife. The older man, still on his knees, yelled at the boy, and although Reynolds could not understand the words, he knew the man was telling the boy to put the knife down. Cautiously, the boy took a small step towards Reynolds. Reynolds raised his left hand, palm facing the boy, and told him to stop or he would shoot.

"Parada o me va a tirar!" Reynolds yelled.

The boy looked frightened. Reynolds thought that he would drop the knife, but instead, the boy let out a yelp like a wounded animal. Before he could complete his lunge towards the detective, Reynolds fired. The bullet entered the boy's left upper chest, exited his back and shattered the mirror hanging on the wall behind him. Stunned, the boy looked at Reynolds and appeared to smile hesitantly. His knees gave way, and he collapsed to the floor. The older man, still on his knees, clung to the boy, cradling his head in his hands, and let out a wail.

Reynolds shoved his gun against the man's right temple and ordered him onto his stomach. The man didn't move. Reynolds heard a small voice from behind him. The five-year-old said something in Spanish, and the man let go of the boy and lay on his stomach. Reynolds handcuffed the man. The small girl said, "He doesn't understand English."

"And I've exhausted my Spanish," he said apologetically.

Reynolds asked, "Do you have a phone?" The little girl said no, but there was one down the hall. Reynolds directed her to "Go call the police", as he showed her his badge. "Well, GO!" Reynolds commanded. The little girl stood, looking at the blood gurgling from the young man's chest. "It's a pay phone," she said. Reynolds dug some coins from his pocket, handed them to the child and said again, "Now GO! Tell them to send an ambulance. Does anyone else here speak English?"

The little girl said, "My brother."

"Send him in, and you go make the call."

The little girl ran from the room and a boy of about seven or eight years old tentatively entered the room, crying softly. Reynolds ripped the wounded boy's shirt off. He noticed the blood bubbling from the wound, and realized that the boy had suffered a sucking chest wound. Reynolds looked up at the boy and said, "Bring me a plastic bag, or anything you have that is plastic." The boy looked at him dumbly. Reynolds asked, "Do you speak English?"

Between sobs, the boy answered, "Yes."

Reynolds lowered his voice. "Son, bring me a loaf of bread."

The boy lifted his eyes from the wounded man. "Bread?" he asked.

Reynolds spoke softly. "Yes, son. Do you have a loaf of bread?"

The boy said, "We have Wonder Bread."

Reynolds replied, "Perfect. Bring it to me."

The boy returned in a few moments with a half loaf of Wonder Bread wrapped tightly in its plastic polka-dot bag. He watched the detective intently as Reynolds dumped the bread out of the bag, and ripped the bag in two. He then pushed one piece of plastic over the wound in the boy's chest, pressing it tightly against his skin while moving it back and forth over the chest, sealing it to the bloody wound. He gently lifted the boy and placed the other piece of plastic in the same fashion on the exit wound. He turned the boy onto his side, and told the small boy to hold the pieces of plastic as tightly as he could to the other boy's chest and back. The child was reluctant to follow the detective's orders. Reynolds sat holding the plastic against the wounds, and asked the small boy who the wounded man was. The young boy said, "He's my brother," and pointed to the older man lying handcuffed on the floor. "He's my father."

Reynolds asked, "Do you want your brother to die?"

The little boy shook his head violently. "Then hold these two pieces of plastic on his wounds while I make a bandage."

The little boy responded. "Now hold tight. Push with all your might," said Reynolds as he tore a strip of material from the wounded boy's shirt, and wrapped it around the boy's chest, tying it as tightly as he could over the plastic patches.

As Reynolds stepped to the bedroom door, two uniformed officers entered, guns drawn. Reynolds said, "Put those away. Come on in here. Did anyone call an ambulance?"

One of the patrolmen responded, "It's on the way. We've got this now." Looking down at the detective's leg, he said, "Is that your blood?"

"Yeah, the fucker stabbed me," he responded. "You'll find the knife under the bed, where I kicked it. But don't touch it. It's evidence."

The patrolman lifted the bedspread and looked under the bed. "You talkin' about that steak knife?"

"Yep."

Reynolds and the wounded boy rode in the same ambulance to the hospital. Reynolds was treated for a wound in his left upper arm and a deeper wound in his right thigh that severed a tendon and was far worse than he thought. Above his wishes to the contrary, he was admitted to the hospital.

The wounded boy would recover, over time, and the ER doctor complimented Reynolds for his fast action and medical knowledge in bandaging the boy's injury.

The doctor asked, "Where did you learn how to treat sucking chest wounds?"

"I once worked for Wonder Bread."

Chapter Twenty Seven

Reynolds opened his eyes. Disoriented, he surveyed the hospital room. His drowsy, hooded eyes found Suzy O'Brien staring back at him from the leather easy chair on the left side of his bed, opposite the door.

Tranquil and looking as fresh as a silvery mountain stream, Suzy leaned closer to the patient. The first thing that one noticed about Suzy, of course, was her eyes, which seemed capable of recording and understanding everything with a quick sweep of all that lay before her. They were at once mesmeric and magnetic. Once locked on you, the trap snapped shut. Luminous in the stark bright light streaming through the partially opened door, those wide, almond shaped, deep-set camera lenses revealed striking brown pupils bordered in gold. She glanced over the adjustable hospital bed, the tray containing a plastic water container, the man lying atop the blankets and sheets, the heavily bandaged right thigh, and then captured Reynolds' eyes. An uncomfortable miasma settled over him, but he could not look away.

She wore her hair pulled severely back into a short auburn ponytail, revealing a square hairline, above dark heavy brows, small straight nose separating high cheek bones, wide mouth, and narrow, pointed chin. Her trim figure nicely filled out a button-down collared white shirt with sleeves partially rolled, and she wore perfectly a medium length dark pleated skirt revealing crossed knees.

Her full lips spread in a wide toothy smile. Reynolds' malaise evaporated at the splendidness before him. He noticed as if for the first time, but it wasn't, that her left eye narrowed more than her right eye when she gave her all to a smile. Then, he admonished himself for what was going through his mind. *Whoa, man. Fucking OB is a lucky guy.*

"Good morning, Morris."

"Um, morning Mrs. O," Reynolds' voice thick, hoarse and barely audible punctured the scene.

"How are you?"

"Not as good as you look, Suze."

"Looks deceive, Morris." The smile was gone. Suzy O'Brien leaned forward locking her hands, elbows on knees. "Okay, Morris. What is going on?"

"Huh?"

"Sheila Henry, Morris."

Oh Christ, what have you done, now, OB? Reynolds thought. He was fully alert now, tried to buy time. "She's the Assistant District Attorney, Suze. She has been working with me and OB," Reynolds said lamely. He had interviewed too many guilty suspects, who gave themselves away by avowing the obvious when silence would have better served them. He mentally kicked himself for not thinking before spouting. *Suzy knows what Sheila Henry does for a fucking living, you idiot. And Suzy's here at the hospital, questioning me. A phone call would have updated her on my condition. Hell, OB could have. Think!* Reynolds fury pressed against the top of his skull. *Fucking OB always puts me in these situations. Why do I have to bail him out? I shouldn't. If he is fucking Sheila… Wait. I don't know that. Yeah right. Calm down. I don't know ANYTHING. Be cool, dick head.*

Suzy leaned back, hands together prayer-like under her chin. Her eyes darkened and narrowed, knowingly. Reynolds squirmed and tried to sit up in the bed. The air grew heavy with anticipation.

Raised in cosseted privilege, cultivated, and supremely confident, Susan Winston had it all, and did it all. Born into one of the most powerful families in Northern Utah, who owned two of the largest newspapers in the state, Susan was the only daughter in a household of men. If her four older brothers watched over her like Swiss Guards, it was her father who carefully orchestrated her life. She not only skied almost before being weaned, Susan raced and won, always. She topped honor rolls for as long as anyone could remember. Daddy Winston insured that her name frequented the society pages of his newspaper, publicizing her hosting soirees, showers, and charitable events, although just in her teens.

She took up space in high school. Few clubs, student organizations from chess to golf and ski did not contain her membership, and her leadership dominated student government. Then, she allowed star quarterback Robert O'Brien onto her super charged life at the beginning of her senior year at Heavenly Valley High.

It wasn't as if she did not know O'Brien before then. Everyone knew him. He was brash and defiant. Suzy had always thought him too full of himself to make a good boyfriend. She even told herself that she principally despised him. He had none of the qualities she thought she wanted in a boyfriend: studious, smart, humble, and romantically poetic... Robert Browning.

Robert O'Brien took to study even less than to humility. Poetry? He knew bawdy limericks, "There once was a man from Kent..."

He didn't laugh. He roared. He grew a full mustache before most boys his age needed to shave. People liked him. Other students wanted to be his friend. Men thought of him as a "remarkable kid." "Irresistible, a heart breaker" were words used by most women of any age to describe him. He allowed everyone in. He seemed not to care about social status or position, athlete or egghead. He simply liked everyone. Though he was quick to anger and "go fist-city" with quite literally anyone, he was quick to forgive and forget after a brief skirmish "on the hill" behind the school which was just off campus, so it served smokers and a place to settle arguments with bare knuckles. Of course, he always won. Strangely, seldom did anyone call the confident young man "conceited." No one, that is, other than the equally confident Susan Winston.

"You are beyond belief, Robert," Suzy noted one crisp October morning long before the start of the school day. It was her senior year, and there wasn't a moment to lose. Secretly, Suzy could not bear the thought of graduation. High school or just "school" to her meant everything. The cyclone of activities that made up her day paled in comparison to the energy with which she had to devote. No activity was too small or too large for her. Prioritizing was easy for her. She attached top priority to everything she took on, and she tackled everything. She, of course, was put in charge of decorating the school for homecoming. He, being the star quarterback, was assigned to help. Which meant posing on a ladder for the photograph that would make the yearbook.

"Why? I'm doing what the coach told me to do. I'm here in the middle of the night, hanging posters and signs. You know, like, any of this crap means anything to anyone. Know what I mean?"

"Doesn't mean anything? Really?" Suzy stood by the ladder, looking up at the football star. "You apparently have no sense of tradition and history. My mother was homecoming queen. Here. That's right," she said with breathless zeal. "At this grand old, really splendid, school. She... She met my father right here in these marble halls in this school, which has always been considered the crown jewel of high schools in the state, throughout the west, no less. We, Mr. Big Shot, we will continue the practice of celebrating the tradition, and not just because the coach ordered it. We will do it proudly. Now reattach that. It is crooked, can't you tell?"

"It's a football game." O'Brien noted with wry smile while re-hanging the far end of the banner announcing the event. "Nothing more, really. A football game that I fully intend to win. Know what I mean?"

"You have to be... No... You are the most conceited boy I have ever met. Just a football game that YOU intend to win. Shouldn't that be WE intend to win, or are there no other boys on the team?"

O'Brien smiled down at her. "I'm sure that you have met a lot of boys there, Winston."

"I, well, I imagine. I... uh," her voice trailed off. She was caught between her self-imposed obligation to honesty while trying to maintain her exasperation with the big jerk.

He was also caught by an empathy drilled deep into his soul to rescue her. That's just the way he was, and would always be. "So, your mom was homecoming queen here? That is very cool. Why aren't you?" He immediately noticed that she recoiled at that. "I mean, why aren't you... in a way that I mean, well you know. You're so... Well..."

It was her turn to rescue him. "I didn't try to be." Her eyes shone as she looked up at him in the glare of the rising sun perched in the large windows at the east end of the marble hall that smelled of polish and gleamed with

138

each stroke of the large buffer that the janitor worked side to side down the far end. She smiled, and said more softly than she intended, "I have never been interested in such things, to be honest. But I'm glad you think I could have been... the queen." The words tumbled out huskily, and she blushed.

He stepped down the ladder and they were very near each other. He could smell the lavender shampoo she liked to use. She noted his dark features, straight nose, the mustache, and something that she took for compassion in his eyes.

"Hey, Bob," queried the school photographer. "Can I get another of you up on the ladder, and Suzy beside the ladder handing you something? Tape maybe?"

Not taking their eyes from one another, O'Brien climbed a couple of rungs and turned and held out his hand. She extended her hand as she handed him a roll of tape. Their fingertips met and a warm shock wave flowed between them. Suzy jerked her hand away as one would upon touching an exposed electrical wire. She then pushed her hand back to meet his.

"Rodney, you'd better get another shot." Suzy ordered, unable to resist a broad smile that was matched by O'Brien's.

They became inseparable after that. It was all so easy. Perplexed by her surprising passion, Suzy found it downright difficult to talk about him. She feared what it all would come to. Talking about him might make it too real, too true. She passed off what her friends were saying. "No, we aren't going steady." But steady they were. "Have you introduced him to your parents? Your DAD?" "Heavens no. Why would I do that? We are just friends." Eyes rolled, but she maintained the fraud. Inwardly, she knew that her life's dream of becoming a doctor would be destroyed if she allowed herself to acknowledge what O'Brien meant to her. She also thought that her father would not approve of him. He would be disappointed in her and that would be devastating. She had always sought to remain in the spotlight of her father's sanction. She thought of her father as more than parent, mentor perhaps. In fact, she fantasized her young life as that of a well-trained figure skater who had been taught each and every move by her coach-father. But, mostly now, she anguished over whether Robert O'Brien, conceited footballer, rough edged, not in the least bit studious—*in fact, did teachers pass him as her friends suggested because of his ability to throw a football?* Who knew nothing of Robert and Elizabeth Barrett Browning—felt as much for her as she for him. Would he give up his dreams for her? She did not know and it was all she could think about.

They made love for the first time in her father's cabin in Park City after skiing there during Christmas break. Thereafter, they made love any place private enough, like the janitor's closet in the basement of the high school or the darkened after-hours gymnasium, but not in the back seat of Robert's Buick—Mother had used "stay out of the back seat of a boy's car" to instill fear and warning in the same vein as looking both ways before crossing the street. Take heed. One could die, or become pregnant, "before her time."—It never occurred to Suzy to ask why her mother equated the back seat of a car with being run over by a bus.

"Oh my God, Suzy," Daddy Winston exclaimed at the end of winter quarter. "A 'B' in calculus? How on earth did you allow that to happen? This may well shatter your chances. Harvard, Suzy. How many times have I told you, opportunity doesn't knock, you have to build a door. I shall have a talk with the Principal…"

"Oh, for God's sake, George, enough with that stupid line," an exasperated Mama Winston burst out. Papa Winston and Suzy both looked at Mrs. Winston, suddenly Norma, as though she were a stranger who had just butted into a private conversation. "Milton Berle, coined that stupid *build a door* phrase. A comic, mind you, not some great thinker and certainly not you, George." Norma Winston heating from within continued, her voice growing stronger. Gone was the lilt. Gone was the precise subtlety of expression that had marked her existence. "For Christ's sake, George, your daughter's pregnant. I should think that you ought question the 'A' in anatomy, more so than the goddamn 'B' in math." Suzy had never heard her mother swear before.

Her life would take on a different reality now. Words, actions, feelings, her life, just like that, transformed with the new life growing within her. Opportunity may be a door, but it comes in many shapes large and small.

If all of that sounds tragic, it was not. Suzy and Robert O'Brien were married in June, two weeks after graduation. Within a year, he joined the Army. Assigned to the Military Police in Fort Benning, Georgia, Robert would chase down deserters and ruffians for the whole of his three-year enlistment. There, he and his wife and twin boys took up residency in a small house in Columbus. In years to come, O'Brien would often refer to their time in Georgia as the happiest of their lives.

Neither Suzy nor Robert ever spoke about unrequited aspirations, which was, frankly, easy for him. He had none to speak of, whereas, she had set aside a boatload. Suzy took on her new role as Army wife and mother with the same zest and energy as she had taken on every other part in her life. And O'Brien, well, he remained true to himself as well.

In the fall of 1967 the O'Brien family returned to Heavenly Valley. He quickly found a position with the police department. Suzy joined her father's newspaper as a beat reporter. Daddy Winston, like almost everyone else, fell through the trap door that was Robert O'Brien's allure. He liked him.

Made to work herself up through the ranks at the newspaper, Suzy again relied on her father's careful tutelage. And that doesn't mean favor. She had to be better than any other reporter. Mediocrity was not part of the bargain; Suzy and her father understood that from the beginning, and besides, she was as averse to commonplace as oil to water.

By the bicentennial, Suzy had her own byline and wide-ranging column known as "Be Choosy with Suzy." She was free to report on anything within the state. And she was a bulldog. With the advent of her column, circulation increased, and that, quite naturally, caused Daddy Winston to bellow the tall tale, "I always wanted Susan to become a part of the newspaper business. She's a natural." Her contacts and sources amounted to a veritable listing as large as the phone books for many of the towns in Utah. Now, she sat in front of her husband's partner in a hospital room without pad or pen, apparently about to interview him. His timorousness became noticeable, and she could use that.

———

"Thank you, Morris," answered the now composed reporter. "For clarifying what Ms. Henry does for a living."

Reynolds said nothing while looking dumbly just above and not into Suzy's eyes.

"Do you mind if I ask you a few questions on the record?"

Reynolds almost relaxed. *So, she isn't here to ask about OB's exploits.* "No. I don't mind. I mean, you know if I say anything, or if you print anything that I disapprove of, or sounds disparaging, I will claim that you barged into my hospital room and harangued me while I was under the influence of strong medication."

"Fear not. I don't use those tactics and everyone knows it. Including your uncle."

"Touché."

"Morris. The only question I have is your uncle and the mayor held a press conference announcing that you had solved the murder of Corporal Halverson and placed the blame one Mr…"

"Givens."

"Thank you. Willis Givens," Suzy continued. "If the case is closed, why is an assistant district attorney still involved, and in fact, working with you and Detective O'Brien?"

"Why," Reynolds eyebrows rose. "Don't you ask your husband?" He figured if she was going to personalize his and The Chief's relationship, then the door had been opened for him to return the insult.

"For all the obvious reasons. The detective is my husband. It would be a conflict of interest for me to ask him about an open investigation. And also, I need to protect him from your uncle." Their eyes were locked. She paused for effect.

So, there it is. Out in the open, finally. I always wondered, about dear old O'Brien using me to stay in good graces with The Chief… Careful Morris. She took a shot, that's all. You have used that tactic many times. Take a cheap shot to get them off balance, then ask the question that you are interested in. Be cool. She is just another reporter now.

Reynolds patiently said nothing.

142

"Givens didn't kill Halverson, did he?"

"What makes you think so?"

"Do you believe that Givens killed the officer?"

"We found Givens dead in his room, door locked from the inside, I might add. Halverson's gun lay beside him. He shot himself with it. He had a wad of money that we have been unable to verify where it came from, although we do know that it was roughly the same amount that Hal was carrying at the time of death when you factor in all that we know about how much he spent at the liquor store and bars along the street, all in the days following Hal's death. Given's fingerprints were found on Hal's boot. We located Hal's wallet in the trash bin behind The James Hotel. Really, who else do you think killed Hal? We are still wrapping up loose ends. That's why Ms. Henry is still on the case, as are we. But really, Suzy, you know all of that. So?"

"So. You do know that half dozen other police officers from... well I don't have my notes with me... throughout the West have been killed in ways that are eerily similar to the way Halverson was gunned down. Do you think, or do you suspect Willis Givens in those other crimes?" Suzy sat back and dropped her gaze.

Reynolds thought and then spoke hesitantly, which drew Suzy's eyes back to his. "We have notified the other jurisdictions, five to be exact, of our findings so far."

"So far? Have you? Hmmm. Or let me ask this, then."

It dawned on Reynolds that Suzy was simply trying to draw an answer from him that she already knew. Of course, her husband had clued her in on all aspects of the investigation. She just needed someone, other than O'Brien, whom she could quote as a source. He thought, *you can't trust anyone really.* And that that included Suzy, pained him, and he felt deceived, and that disturbed him more than he thought that it should have. She will not sail her husband down the river, but... "I'm sorry, Suzy. The interview is officially over."

She did not move, nor did he. "Okay. Understood. Now off the record, Morris, you actually thought that I came here to ask you if my husband is fucking the attorney. Didn't you?" She let that sink in. "But I know you better than that. I should hope you know me better than that."

He didn't move or speak but the thought lingered in his head, *If only I knew you better than that...whoa there you go gain...OB is a lucky son-of-a-bitch...And you, DEFECTIVE Reynolds. Why is it that you never fall for anyone you actually have a chance with? OB's wife for Christ sakes! Your ex-wife! Why do you seem to find a route that takes you past Cheyenne's place? What the hell can come from that? A glance? A chance sighting that will pull her back? Fuck O Mighty, man. Come to!*

With that she stood up and straightened her skirt. She turned to go but spun back. "Oh, by the way, we are barbequing Sunday. Please come over and bring, um, a friend."

"Sonya?"

"Of course, Sonya. Get well soon, Morris." She pushed through the heavy door and was gone.

Reynolds found the button to lower his bed. The door swung open and Suzy re-entered the room.

"One more thing, Morris, and this *is* important, I want you to know that to me, Robert is faithful. Faithful to our boys. Faithful to our home. Faithful to my parents. I know that I can count on him. Always. He would give his life for me." She scowled, angry that her eyes welled with tears. "Just so you know, Morris. For some reason, I find it necessary that you know that is how I feel."

"Okay, Suze. Just so you know, I don't think there is anything going on between OB and Sheila."

Suzy turned on her heel and pulled the door open causing The Chief to stumble into the room.

"Oh, Chief Hansen."

Reynolds roared with laughter at the blushing chief and startled reporter.

"Mrs. O'Brien," The Chief found his voice. "Good to see you." They shook hands.

"Bye-bye, Morris."

"See you, Suze. Oh, Suzy, by the way, I have made you guys something special. I'll bring it Sunday."

"Okay. Bye."

"Chief, nice of you to drop in."

"Yes, just came to see you. How are you, Morris?"

After exchanging pleasantries as The Chief and as uncle, The Chief asked for a full report on how it was that his officer ended up in the hospital, and did not wait for backup before going in after the burglars.

"Hot pursuit, Chief. Simple as that. Had I stopped. Waited. I would have lost any legal advantage of the rules of hot pursuit. Had I waited, do you want a bet on how long it would have taken those guys and their family to somehow get rid of the evidence? I was alone out there. I couldn't cover all windows and doors while searching for a phone to call in for backup. We need those walkie-talkies, Chief."

"And you could have saved your skin, while waiting it out. Get a damned search warrant and then, heaven forbid, go in with full force, and no, by God, injuries." The Chief shook his head.

"I'm sorry Chief. I could have gone that route. It really just didn't make a whole lot of sense to me at the time. I spent less than a second on the decision. Next time, I'll be more careful. Remember the rules. Consider all that should be considered. Make sure I cover all the bases. Keeping in mind, the whole time, that whatever I decide will be deliberated over on Monday morning by…"

"All right, Detective. You're bordering on insubordination, that," The Chief sat in the chair Suzy had vacated and chuckled, "that even your benefactor uncle can't get you out of."

"Sorry, Uncle Gerry."

"One more thing, Morris. The witnesses at the scene, did not recall that you identified yourself as a police officer when you entered their premises."

Reynolds' eyes widened and his anger rose.

The Chief added quickly before the detective could speak, "I'm not making an accusation, here, Morris. In fact, it's best if you say nothing right now. As you're aware there must be an investigation of any police-involved shooting. I," The Chief continued with a hard stare that said far more than the words. "Well, in all honesty, should not have made any reference to the events of last night in this... setting."

Both men said nothing for several long moments.

"Enough said on that topic." The Chief said, lightly. "I spoke to the doctor. They will release you today. And, by the way, your partner has been busy, but that can wait until tomorrow. See you in the morning, Morris. Go home. Get some rest. I'll have someone pick you up. Give dispatch a call when they are through with you here."

"Thanks Chief. See you in the morning."

The Chief stopped by the door and turned, "Oh, yes. The Boss has pulled Ms. Henry off the team. Umm. Morris?"

"Yes Chief."

"Could it be that there is anything to Mrs. O'Brien's fear, you know, about..."

"OB and Sheila? If you're thinking that had something to do with The Boss pulling her from the case, I don't think so."

"You sure?"

No, he was not sure of anything when it came to OB and women, but he tried to assuage The Chief's concerns. "I haven't been with them twenty-four-seven, but last night we were talking in the car—me, OB and Sheila. The conversation got around to women. OB asks us 'you know what I like in a woman?' and," Morris held back the smile. "Sheila says 'personality disorder would be my guess.'"

"Good enough. See you tomorrow, Morris."

Chapter Twenty Eight

A nurse came by with discharge papers to sign and told Morris he could dress and wait in his room for his ride home.

He called the station and was told that a unit would be dispatched to pick him up. He dressed quickly in the bloody garments that he had worn the day before, and lay back on the upturned bed. Browsing the newspaper for any mention of his escapades, he found a short account on page one of the 'B' Section entitled "Officer Responds to Burglary Hospitalized." "Oh, fuck me," he swore when he read that the reporter had misidentified him as "Detective Maurice Reynolds."

A small knock drew his attention to the door and Sonya entered carrying a small bouquet of yellow flowers.

"Hi Mo. How are you?"

"Quite well, actually, I have been discharged and I'm waiting for my carriage to freedom." He smiled.

Sonya looked around, "I guess I don't need a vase for these since you're about to leave. So, I, um, suppose, I'll just…"

She sat the flowers on the tray table and continued to stand. A deafening silence followed. It was not lost on Reynolds that she had not offered to drive him home. He just looked at her. Even though his stare, he knew, brought her discomfort, he did not take his eyes from her.

"Mo, I need to tell you something. This is an odd place to say it."

He said nothing.

"Well, I know that," She slumped into the chair and put her hands to her cheeks. "Rick did not beat you up the other night."

"I know."

Startled, she said, "You do?"

"Yes, I do."

"And…and…do you know who… I mean I came to tell you something…"

"I know who did it and why. So, there is really nothing for you to say. I know who it was, Sonya."

"Uh-huh. Well, I am so sorry it happened." She got up and went into the bathroom returning with tissue and dabbed at the tears below her eyes. "I want you to know that I didn't know that Barry was even in town then. I don't really know of… Well, I'll just say it." She paused and pressed more tears from her eyes. "He wants me back." She studied Morris' face for some sign, recognition. She got nothing. "He is my daughter's father, but what he did to you is inexcusable. Just inexcusable. Unforgivable… But…"

"But," Reynolds said flatly. "You want me to forgive him, correct?"

"No." She cried. "Not forgive. I cannot ask you to forgive him. I just can't ask you to do that."

"But," Reynolds looked out the window into the setting sun. "You wouldn't mind it if I didn't press charges against him."

"I know you can't believe it, but he is a good guy. He really is. I've never known him to be aggressive in that way. And," she repeated. "He is my baby's father."

"I see."

"Do you, Mo?" Anger, or was it desperation taking refuge in her words now? "Do you know about feelings that can't be quieted? Do you know about a daughter's need for her father? Do you know? I think you do. I know you do."

"Okay."

"Okay?"

"I'll not pursue charges against," disgust flowed now. "Barry, is that his name, Barry? Barry Wright?" The alliteration brought an unintended smile to form. "Sorry."

Dry eyed now and in total control, Sonya stood up. "Okay, thank you Morris. I have my daughter to consider. She comes first no matter what. Always. I'm sorry Mo, that it had to end this way, I truly am."

"Yeah. Me too. Goodbye Sonya."

"You know it is interesting," Reynolds reflected.

Sonya opened the door but let it close as she turned back to face him. "Interesting?"

"Yeah. Interesting. Twice in the same day I have heard the same story. In all practical terms that is. As I see it, you will return to a life with good old Boots there, that you ran away from, or so I assumed. Maybe not. I have to ask though. Is it worth it? Really?"

"Me choosing him over you?"

"No. Forget about me in this equation. We are done. I get that. What about when you are fifty? Have you thought about that? You and Boots will still share the bond of parentage. Will that be enough? Will that bond never be broken? Can it be broken by infidelity? Abuse?"

"Wow. So, you are a seer, now? Infidelity? Abuse? Who said anything about that?"

"Someone else," Reynolds replied. "Someone, like you, who is apparently blinded by the afterglow of the creation of children. Infidelity was her word, and her problem. You were driven away once before for enough of a reason to be driven off, now you return. Both of you cite children as the reason for remaining with someone that I can't for the life of me figure out why. But I have never fathered a child. So, I am in the dark on that front. I just don't understand it. Why would two clever, attractive women stick with such assholes?"

Anger rose, but Sonya did not take the bait, if that is what this was. She chose not to respond, in kind. She felt it was the least she could do, under the circumstances. She had no idea about whom he was referencing other than her. She was annoyed by the reference to someone else however.

"Really Morris, can't you at least be angry at just me? I have no idea who the other woman is that you are talking about, but you know, maybe that is your... was our problem. You can't even be intimate in our break-up. Think about it, Mo. I tried to choose an easy way out. Less hurtful than I could have been. Fair enough. I shouldn't have used my daughter in that way. My going back to Barry has more to do with us than our child…though that is a pretty good reason.

"I see."

"Do you Mo? I don't think you do. For once, goddamn it, let yourself go. Frankly, like now, I always felt like there was someone else in the room with us. Can't you just, at least, be pissed at me? Me, Mo. Don't' diffuse your anger, your passion. Don't divide it up. Let go. Find that ONE. Be with someone. I hope for your sake that you can find that one who you can give your all to."

Silence followed. Morris could not remove his attention from the parking lot through the window.

"It is just you and I here now," Sonya sighed. "Is there anything you want to say? Just to me?"

Sonya was right. She and Reynolds' intimate moments were shared. "Reynolds curse," as he had labeled it, or was he as he mostly thought "just too much of a romantic." Whichever, it was always the same. Whomever Reynolds shared a connection, whether acted upon or not, up sprung the fantasy, the myth created in Reynolds' mind. There was Sonya and there was Reynolds' romanticized version of Sonya. The fantasy always overrode reality. No one can compete with that. Sonya, or anyone for that matter, would be forever destined to finish a distant second to Reynolds' wishful thinking. How could he possibly explain to Sonya that she simply could never compete with his version of her and how he thought they should be? It was impossible. It was debilitating. And there was nothing he could do about it. It was a spigot that he could not shut.

"Goodbye, Sonya."

Still looking out the window he heard Sonya walk out clicking down the hallway as a black and white police car parked in front of the hospital. Reynolds picked up a plastic bag containing his belongings and discharge papers and limped to the door leaving the bouquet of yellow flowers on the tray stand.

"Another day," he said aloud as he left his room. Allowing the creeping self-pity to continue its course, he thought of Suzy looking like a shiny new penny defending her promiscuous husband, and there was Sonya who decided to return to a relationship she had once described to him as abusive, while he remained, yet again, on the outside looking in. "Enough of that shit. Feeling sorry for yourself is counterproductive, man. Chalk it all up as just another strange fucking day in the life of *Defective* Morris Reynolds."

PART 7

The LTE and Horace

Time at last sets all things even
If we do but watch the hour
There never yet was human power
That could evade, if unforgiven
The patient search, and vigil long
Of him who treasures up a wrong.

- Byron, *Mazeppa's Ride*

Chapter Twenty Nine

Tuesday, June 29, 1976, Denver

The Freedom Train

Dear MMI,

Goddamn, Conway. What got into him today? I clearly gave every signal, did I not, that I did not want to talk? Not today. Did not want to be disturbed. Did I not turn away whenever I felt a personal conversation coming on? Not even insinuating that it was my time of the month worked to dissuade the talkative bastard. Jesus, I could not shut that fat fuck up.

He kept going on and on about how he raised his two daughters on his own after his wife died. He had to go there again today—of all days. Here's the thing, MMI, I could have shut him up. But, I couldn't hurt the man with words who I intend to kill with a bomb in a few days. Oh, fuck me. The train will be in Utah in a couple days. Now is the time to distance myself from all of them, which I should have done a long time ago. I screwed up.

Can I go through with it? Jesus, now is hardly the time to have second thoughts; I must finish it. I have no choice, do I? There's always a choice. It's as simple as that.

Chapter Thirty

Horace sat at the desk, gently fingering his hat on his lap. "Mom, I heard great news on the radio this morning: The police reported that they solved the murder of the Heavenly Valley cop. Maybe we can stay here for a while. I have been thinking about how this fortuitous turn of events might make it possible for me to finish up my degree at the University of Utah. This could be the break we have been waiting for. I am going to call an old professor and get his thoughts on my returning to school in September."

Horace went to The Elms Café and General Store three miles away. The pay phone hung from a wall by the restrooms. After three attempts, he connected with the professor, who Horace spoke with enthusiastically. They exchanged pleasantries and caught up on each other's lives while avoiding the topic of Horace's parents. The professor expressed delight and offered encouragement upon learning that Horace planned to return to school.

"Horace, we would be delighted to offer any assistance possible to see that your dream of returning to the U is fulfilled."

"Thank you so much, sir. I knew you would be supportive of my desire to return to school. I suppose I just needed to hear it." Horace found it difficult to suppress the glee he felt. "Thank you so much. Best wishes to your family. Good day, sir."

Before hanging up, the professor asked a question that flummoxed the big man.

"Horace, was that you at the memorial for the fallen officer in Heavenly Valley?"

"Officer ... what? The memorial service? Yes, well ... "

"Last night I saw the news coverage of the officer's memorial parade in Heavenly Valley. They panned the audience along the route, and there you were, at least, I thought it was you. The camera caught someone with a hat in hand standing in the crowd as the procession went by. Your obvious expression of grief caught the cameraman's attention, and he zoomed in on you."

"News coverage?" Horace stammered.

"It was you, was it not? My wife and I were so moved by your anguish. Did you know the officer?"

"I felt compelled to attend the service." Horace was recovering slowly from the cacophony of alarms going off in his brain. "I did not know the officer, and I had no idea that I was on camera. I guess I felt particularly close to him ... call it professional courtesy."

The professor didn't comprehend what Horace meant by professional courtesy, but concluded, "I did not mean to embarrass you, Horace. Whatever your reasons, your outpouring of sentiment tore at our hearts. My condolences, Horace."

A long pause followed, and Horace's morning of hope faded into the shadows.

Finally, the professor spoke, "Again, Horace, my apologies. I look forward to seeing you again."

"Thank you," his voice strained. "Good day, sir."

Professional courtesy? Good day, sir? Chrissy thought as she overheard most of the conversation. She was returning from a morning run through the canyon, and as she approached her goal of 8,450 paces, she noticed Hoss' truck in the parking lot of The Elms.

She was done-in by the June heat. She veered from her normal course that offered more shade, but the detour had discombobulated her. Still hundreds of paces from the cabin, that caused her to panic, she passed The Elms and saw Horace's truck parked at the general store. Relieved, she knew that Horace would give her a ride home.

Chrissy looked around and asked the woman behind the counter if a big cowboy had come in. She was told that he was using the phone. Chrissy's mood turned dark as she listened to the phone call. *Who the fuck are you, Hoss? Or is it Horace? Shit.* She hurried out into the summer heat.

Horace hung up the phone and sauntered into the café. "Thanks, ma'am, for lettin' me use yer phone. 'Preciate it," he said with a tip of his hat.

155

"No problem, cowboy. I should tell you that some girl listened to your call. She left in a huff," the woman said.

"What did the girl look like?"

"She came in here lookin' for you. Stringy hair, skinny. One of those runner types. Sweatin' like she was runnin' from a pack o'dogs."

"Chrissy," mumbled Horace.

From the woods across the street, Chrissy watched as Hoss walked out of the café, looking around before jogging to his truck.

Chrissy looked around frantically and picked a handful of wild flowers and hurried out across the street.

"Hoss. Hoss," Chrissy shouted and waved.

Horace looked up from inside the truck and saw Chrissy running towards the truck.

She approached the driver's side and laid a hand on Horace's elbow that rested outside the truck window.

"Can a girl get a ride back to the cabin for a small offering?" Chrissy held up the flowers.

"Sure thing, hop in." Horace picked up his hat from the passenger side of the bench seat and put it on the back of his head. He knew she had seen him inside the café and had waited for him.

"I thought it was you the woman said came in lookin' for me."

"Yep," Chrissy replied, smiling inwardly.

Horace eased the truck onto the road and proceeded toward the cabins. Horace thought about saying how the woman thought Chrissy looked pissed after listening to his phone call, but didn't. Instead, he brought up something else that troubled him.

"I thought I saw a female cop drive up to yer cabin this mornin'," Horace said tentatively.

"A cop?" Chrissy was taken aback momentarily. *Beatrice*, and then added, "She's no cop."

"I thought she was wearin' a uniform of some kind."

"Yes, she is employed by the Freedom Train. I'm assume you've heard of it," Chrissy said flatly. Her suspicions about Hoss were growing.

"Oh, I thought she was a cop by the color of her uniform. She's awful pretty. I didn't think the train was here yet."

Chrissy took a deep breath and let it out slowly, "Yes, she is awfully pretty. Her name is Trish, and she's Bingo's babe. Be careful, cowboy, Bingo can be pretty jealous."

"I think Bingo can be many things." Horace caught himself, and grimaced inwardly for speaking without thinking.

Chrissy turned towards Hoss and eyed him carefully. "Yes, I think we are all capable of being many things." She quickly added, "The train is in Colorado. Trish has a couple days off before the train leaves Denver, so she drove over to visit Bingo. She'll rejoin the train when it gets here." She wanted to confront him but knew this was not the place or the time. They both sat quietly as Horace pulled over the bridge and parked next to his bungalow.

"You're a life saver, Hoss." Chrissy handed him the bouquet and opened the door and climbed out. "You better put those in water. Thanks again." She walked swiftly around to her cabin.

Holding the flowers carefully, Horace unlocked the door and entered the cabin. He filled a tumbler with water and gently placed the flowers in the glass. He got the key to his mother's room and placed the glass of flowers on the ornate top of the desk.

"Compliments of Chrissy, the unusual woman next door. The woman with a troublin' secret. I'm thinkin' it may concern us, Mom." Horace sat in the chair and rocked back and forth for a while, thinking. The more he replayed the events of this morning in his mind, the more distressed he felt.

157

He was at odds trying to figure out his next move. The joy he experienced earlier rocked away in that chair. Finally, it came to him: Grand Junction, Colorado.

"Okay, yer right," Horace, said aloud. "I have to finish this full circle."

Chapter Thirty One

Drinking coffee and speaking in low voiced huggermugger, three-fourths of La *Ligue des Terroristes Environnementeaux* poured over the assorted documents strewn about the kitchen table. Pages torn from spiral notebooks contained rudimentary hand drawings of parking areas, rail tracks, switches, a train containing two dozen cars and rectangles replicating platforms containing the number of visitors. Strewn among the handwritten pages were several photographs of the massive steam locomotive and images of its component cars. One of the cars was identified with a large red "X." Hordes of people, young and old, were pictured waiting in long queues to board the exhibit cars.

"What are you saying, Trish?" Bingo asked.

Jonathon answered, "Everything's ready to go. That's what all that means, Bingo. Right, Beatrice?"

"Yes, that sums it up. I do think … " Beatrice stopped in mid-sentence.

The door flung open, and Chrissy stepped in and leaned back against it, pushing it shut.

"What's wrong?" Beatrice gasped.

"Something. Nothing. I don't know. Everything. Fuck. Not sure," Chrissy stammered.

The three at the table exchanged glances.

Jonathon spoke evenly, "Chrissy, breathe. What is wrong?"

Chrissy scrutinized her coconspirators. She sought to overcome what she knew to be her mates' perception of her. She realized long ago that the other three members of the LTE knew she could be erratic, but they also knew to trust her judgment; when she worried, they should be concerned. Above all else, she sensed concern in their eyes. Searching her psyche for ·calm, she breathed deeply to gain purchase of her emotions.

"Our neighbor may not be who we think he is," Chrissy said, voice quivering. She then related to the group what she witnessed and overheard at the café.

All three sat silent and motionless for a few moments.

"So, he's not the country bumpkin that he portrays," Beatrice began. "How does this concern us?" Looking around she added, "What am I missing here?"

"Why would someone want to portray himself as a fucking bumpkin?" Bingo asked. "I'm with Trish. I don't think we need to worry about him."

"Why indeed, Bingo," Jonathon broke in, measuring his words. "Why indeed? He moved into our little enclave after we did. He seems to have come from nowhere. Anyone know where he hails from?" Jonathon answered the question before the others dared to respond. "No, we have no idea. Why would we care where some apparent bumpkin came from?" His voice rose, the others looked away, "Is that what you called him, Bingo?"

Jonathon stood up and regained control. In a hoarse whisper, he continued, "What do we know? He seems to come and go whenever he pleases. Is he really a shit thrower at the stables? He says he is, but he goes to work at odd hours. He has no friends that we are aware of. No one comes to visit him, right, Chrissy?

Flushing, she nodded.

"He comes off as this big country boy, and, according to what Chrissy heard today, he is anything but what he seems."

"That's correct, Jonathon," Chrissy cut in, and she blushed, trying to regain control. "He comes across as someone who is easy to ignore. Maybe, I am overreacting." She was hoping for agreement, playing to the others' perception of her.

"The perfect cover, not like others we have encountered in the past," Beatrice concluded. She looked at the others.

"Well, I know one fucking way to solve this," Bingo said.

Chrissy scowled at Bingo.

"Really, Bingo? You're so fucking insightful, aren't you? Need I remind you of the debacle in Denver?" Chrissy was referring to Bingo's attempt to bring a young man into the LTE while they were planning an assault on the Federal Building there. Beatrice and Jonathon had followed the recruit for days before seeing him meet with detectives of the Denver PD.

They fled. Months of planning ruined, and even though Bingo vigorously claimed he had not told the man of the plan or of the history of the deadly group, they went into hiding in Bozeman, Montana. Beatrice, whom the recruit had never met, stayed behind. She took an entry-level job as a records clerk with the Denver Police Department. She found nothing that implicated any members of the LTE. Satisfied, she quit after six months and joined her comrades in Montana. She hatched the plan to blow up the Freedom Train.

Bingo looked away. The others sat contemplating events of the past; they had been lucky. The bombing of the government building in Omaha had cost them Beatrice for four years, but it had gained them Chrissy. Chrissy "The Chemist," so named by Jonathon after he met her while visiting Beatrice at the prison in York, Nebraska. Six months later Beatrice was released. Seven weeks after that Chrissy was paroled. La Ligue des Terroristes Environnementeaux became a formidable bomber group.

Over the next three years, the LTE scourged society of two rail bridges, two small government buildings, a tobacco processing plant and weapons and C-4 plastic explosives.

It was Chrissy's bomb making that made the difference. Chrissy was incredibly important to the group, but she was also the only member of the group actively wanted by authorities. Luckily for her, parole violators were not generally highly pursued.

Jonathon broke the hush, "We have to know more. The train will be here in three days. Bingo, keep an eye on our good ole boy next door. I don't need to tell you to be the stealthy son-of-a-bitch I know you can be."

Bingo beamed. He knew an endless discussion would ensue, so he was happy to be shed of all that. Action is what he longed for, even if it was surveillance. He would be *doing* something, and besides Chrissy was *freaking* him out, even more so than normally. He had grown increasingly annoyed with her incessant speed induced cackling.

A soft knock on the door, against which Chrissy she leaned, caused her to gasp, exhale, and stop breathing momentarily.

Beatrice peaked around the blind over the small window. "It's an old woman," she whispered.

Chrissy opened the door slightly. It was Mrs. Burke, one of the elderly couple from next door. Chrissy stepped out and closed the door behind her.

"Mrs. Burke, how nice to see you," Chrissy breathed impatiently.

"Yes, nice to see you, too," the woman replied while trying to peer around Chrissy.

Irritation found its way into Chrissy's voice as she asked, "How can I help you?"

"Well, I don't mean to be a snoop, but Owen and I noticed a young Negro woman over here," Mrs. Burke began.

"Oh, yes. Well that would be a friend of ours, Trish," Chrissy's eyes narrowed. "Not to worry, it's okay Mrs. Burke."

"Oh my, we are not worried," Mrs. Burke responded. "We are not like that, dear. She's very lovely, tall too. Owen and I were just talking. We hate to admit it, but we do not know one single Negro. Only spoke once or twice to any one of color actually. We were wondering if you and your friends would like to join us this afternoon for a little wine on our porch."

Chrissy smiled, "And you would like to meet a real live Negro, I suppose?"

"Oh my, I've upset you. Owen said that might happen. I do apologize." Mrs. Burke looked down and said, "I'll be going now. I meant no offense, dear. Please believe me."

"I do believe you, ma'am," Chrissy's tone softened. "You're very sweet and charming, but we have other plans today. Sorry, maybe some other time."

Chrissy entered the cabin and eased door shut behind her.

"What was that all about?" Bingo asked.

"Oh," Chrissy giggled. "Our little elderly neighbors from Salt Lake wanted to meet Beatrice."

"Me?" Beatrice looked surprised.

"Never mind," Chrissy replied, as she slumped onto one of the chairs at the table, "It has been a very strange day. Bingo, make sure you take a roundabout way up to your observation post. The cabins around here have eyes."

Bingo, cum Nathanial Bumppo, found his way up the hillside, stepping carefully. After the fact, he thought that he should have removed his boots before walking up the hill. However, he was certain no one had seen him or heard him.

Two hours later, Bingo grew restless sitting cross-legged watching the scene below. He wondered what the others were doing, when he saw Hoss exit his cabin carrying a large wooden box and place it in the back of his pickup truck. Bingo straightened his leg, and then Hoss suddenly looked up squinting at the hillside near where Bingo was perched.

Bingo froze. He watched Hoss scan the hillside and go back inside the cabin. Momentarily, he returned to the truck with a canvas bag and placed it in the cab of the truck.

Cramping, Bingo straightened his other leg. His foot slipped in the loose pine needles covering the ground beneath him as he braced himself. Startled by the sound of movement above, Horace stopped and again scanned the area where Bingo sat. Bingo breathed shallowly and tried to make himself small. He felt that Hoss looked directly at him, into his eyes. He did not blink. His heart raced in anticipation. Yet, Bingo thought it odd that Hoss locked the doors of the truck before hurrying back inside the cabin.

"What you got in that bag?" Bingo whispered. "What is so important that you would lock your truck? Gettin' paranoid?"

Horace was back outside. He locked the cabin door, and looked over the hillside where he had heard the sound. He entered the truck and drove slowly off.

Bingo stood and watched as Hoss eased the truck over the bridge and turned westbound towards the mouth of the canyon and the city.

Bingo hurried off the hillside to his cabin. The others looked up from a spiral notebook on the table, over which they had been examining like three surgeons gathered around an operating table. Beatrice placed a protective hand on the notebook as Bingo entered.

"He left. Drove away," Bingo informed them with a wave of his hand.

After listening to Bingo's detailed report, Jonathon quickly decided to search Hoss' cabin after dark.

"And, if he should happen to come home?" Bingo asked, excitedly.

Jonathon glowered, "Bring the gun."

Jonathon turned to the others, "Great notes and sketches, Beatrice. As always, your preparation is meticulous. What do you think, Chrissy?"

"Lovely," Chrissy announced. "Exactly what I needed, Trish."

Chrissy was now within her element. Precise thinking eased her anxiety. Her eyes danced across the sketches in the notebook. "Tomorrow, I'll test the fuses. Time it all out. To the fucking second." Her eyes gleamed with excitement. "Yes, we will test it all. Measurements must be exact. To the fucking inch. It will be like nothing you have ever been a part of. Ever seen. Elegant. Stylish. Masterful. It will be…" she looked up.

Although this was a familiar scene, the others were captivated by Chrissy's calculating excitement. Beatrice coughed, breaking the spell.

Jonathon turned to Bingo. "Get the tools. It's time to see what Hoss has been hiding over there."

Chapter Thirty Two

Bingo had a small pouch of tools and the gun tucked into the waistband of his jeans.

"Okay, we all know the drill. Bingo and I will go over there and gain access," Jonathon ordered. "Give us ten minutes, then join us. Everyone get a headlamp. Let's go, Bingo."

Ten minutes later all four were inside Hoss' cabin. Beatrice and Chrissy searched Hoss' bedroom while Jonathon worked on the padlock that secured Hoss' secret room.

Jonathon removed the padlock and swung the hasp open. "We're in, boys and girls."

The desk loomed at the far end of the room. Jonathon approached it and eyed the lock.

"Put a light on the lock right here, will you, Bingo?"

Bingo did as he was asked, and Jonathon opened the lock quickly. "Oh my, what have we here?"

The other three moved behind Jonathon, and all four focused on a picture of a woman clad in western wear standing next to a horse. A paper taped on the interior of the desk read, "Our time came, and we left mourning in their tribe -Kit Carson."

Beatrice verbalized what the others were thinking, "Who is that?"

"Look at the little cubbies, there are bullets in some of them," Bingo remarked.

Jonathon carefully pulled open the top drawer to ensure not to disturb the little standing sentries. The drawer contained three yellowing newspapers all dated from 1974. The top one contained a large photo of the woman in the picture on the desk. Below the picture was a smaller photo of a football player.

Jonathon read the story and passed the paper over his shoulder to Chrissy. Beatrice read it as well. Bingo waved it off, "Just tell me what it's all about."

"Meet Hoss' mother, Mary Paulson, Bingo," Jonathon said pointing to the picture in the desk. "She was killed by cops in Colorado a few years ago."

Chrissy and Beatrice pulled open the other desk drawers and found more newspapers. These were more recent and from different locations: Oklahoma City, Lubbock, Shreveport, Garden Grove, Carson City and Heavenly Valley. Each contained similarly headlines about the murder of a police officer.

Beatrice paged through a notebook and located a columnar list in neat handwriting on a folded sheet of graph paper. She called the others attention to the list, "Jesus, look at this you guys. This guy has planned all of this out. Notice that the locations noted in this list coincide with the newspapers reporting cop killings in each place. He has methodically plotted all of this and carried it out."

The other three looked over her shoulder as their headlamps played over the page.

"We have the locations and names of cops killed in each place listed here, and newspapers verifying his actions," Beatrice said.

Jonathon said, "He planned all this out and followed through. You have to hand it to him; he identified his objectives and toiled to meet them. Hoss certainly has left the pig tribe in mourning."

Chrissy and Beatrice were now seated cross-legged on the floor reading and passing the newspapers back and forth, not a word was spoken.

Jonathon rocked back and forth, staring at the desk. "Well, well, well. Six dead cops, six little brass sentries, as you so aptly put it Bingo, surrounding dear old mom. What do you know about that?" He inquired of no one. Then he murmured, "Hoss certainly has left the pig tribe mourning."

Jonathon stood quickly and ordered, "Put everything back where we found them, and let's get out of here. We have to think this through."

PART 8

Scare Canyon

Amid the pizza boxes and beer bottles strewn about the small cabin, the members of the LTE recounted memories of their past activities. Laughing now and then, but a melancholy atmosphere engulfed them, as each talked about his or her revolutionary beginnings, all except for Bingo that is. Then it was Beatrice's turn. She filled in the gaps that she had not previously shared with the others concerning her past.

Chapter Thirty Three

Chrissy and Jonathon found the cabin by accident while searching for places to set up a makeshift lab for Chrissy and to hide the plastic explosives far from the Wasatch canyon bungalow. They happened to glimpse the small building barely exposed amidst quaking aspen trees. Their hearts leapt.

It was perfect. Jonathon researched the cabin thoroughly. It had belonged to a man, who died the winter before and his only remaining relative was his sister. Jonathon contacted the woman who gratefully agreed to rent the stone hut. It had small tight windows, a knotty pine floor over a rock foundation and a solid wood door.

There was also a large lean-to about twenty yards from the cabin where wood was stored. Chrissy and Jonathon wrapped five boxes containing six kilograms of C-4 each in bags and buried them in four different spots under the wood.

No detail was too small for Jonathon. He intentionally left backpacks, fishing rods and tools outside the cabin.

Weeks later, Jonathon thought they had destroyed more than just a small pine tree while testing Chrissy's bomb. The test was conducted downwind from the cabin. The ranger showed up on horseback about an hour after they had detonated a smaller, but identical device they planned to use on the Freedom Train. While speaking to the ranger, Jonathon tried to remain nonchalant, but his gut twisted with each gusty breeze. If the wind direction changed, he knew the ranger would get a whiff of residue from the detonation. The ranger didn't appear to notice, but Jonathon remained disquieted by the encounter.

———————

They had decided to spend their last night together in the Scare Canyon cabin.

"For me it was Mexico City, 1968," Beatrice began.

Chrissy whispered, "Tlatelolco."

Jonathon concurred.

Bingo sat cross-legged, head down, studying the knotty pine floor in front of him.

"The palace doors opened. We all thought that someone from the government, perhaps the president himself, was coming out to address us. People were singing and waving flags and signs." Beatrice continued in a soft voice befitting the surroundings, "We had had a marvelous summer. Thousands of students gathered from all over. Petitions, painted signs, black armbands, sit-ins, and inspirational speeches. Everyone was so involved and confident. Hell, we thought we had won. Finally, our demonstrations would bring real change to the country, and autonomy restored to the universities."

"You didn't see good old El Presidente come through those big old gates, did you Trish." Jonathon sneered.

"No. El Presidente de Mexico, Gustavo Diaz Ordaz," Beatrice spat, "chose not to address the crowd. Instead, hundreds of soldiers double-timed through the gates and formed a line in front of us. At first, they just stood there, eyes black under helmets worn low, bayonets glistening in the afternoon sun, causing the plaza to grow quiet. A man in a suit and wide brimmed hat stood by the big gates smoking a cigarette. Suddenly, a screamed command reverberated around the plaza. The soldiers responded with resounding, "Yo. Ha!" lowering their bayonets. The line marched in lockstep towards us."

"We moved closer together in the center of the plaza. There were thousands of students in the square. Someone searched his pockets and found the only weapon that perhaps we all had in our possession: twenty-cent pieces, which are rather large coins. After the first one was thrown, the air filled with coins as the students tried to fend off armed troops by zipping money at them."

"Jesus, Trish." Chrissy asked, "Is that when the soldiers fired on the crowd?"

"No," Beatrice chuckled, soft and low. "What happened next was actually kind of funny and sad. The soldiers stopped their advance, broke formation and began walking around picking up the coins. We realized they were much like us: young and poor. Unlike us, they were uneducated peasants who were ill paid. The twenty cent pieces meant more to them than following orders from screaming officers or pushing around a bunch of students."

Jonathon, leaning back against the stone wall sipping at bottled beer and staring at the candles on the mantle of the darkened fireplace across the room, said, "The massacre would come later, right, Trish?"

"That's right," Beatrice confirmed. "The word passed that another rally would be held on October 2 at the Plaza de las Tres Culturas, just ten days before the start of the '68 Olympics. After three months of rallies and protests, many of the students left, so there were fewer of us who made our way back to the plaza. The soldiers were already there, lining the plaza and waiting with tanks. You could sense something bad was going to happen. We were tense. The soldiers were grim, but nervous. Coins would not interrupt their job on this day. It had been a great summer, and we thought we were making progress and that real reform would come to Mexico. We just didn't realize that greed and power conquer idealism every fucking time."

"Protests don't work," Jonathon summed up flatly.

"No, they do not work," Beatrice, agreed. "The cards were stacked against us. We were playing in the government's house, and the government had had enough of the street scene. They wanted to end it that day, and they did. A shot rang out. I am certain that it came from the snipers positioned on the rooftops surrounding the plaza. They were government snipers, I might add. The general, commanding the troops on the ground, went down."

"Are you saying soldiers fired on their own commander, Trish?" asked a bewildered Bingo.

"That's exactly what I am saying, Bingo," Beatrice snapped. "The government didn't want any disruptions during the Olympics, don't you see? They were through pussyfooting around with a bunch of 'commie agitators,' as they called us. They fired the first shot. An expendable general, but a leader nonetheless, went down. The soldiers on the ground, thinking the students fired on them, started spraying bullets into us. Jesus, it was awful." Beatrice pressed her fingers into her temples and closed her eyes. "Dying

170

cries for help and booming rifles. The soldiers went crazy. Blood everywhere. Bodies everywhere. People running around. Exits blocked. We dove for the ground, and the shooting continued. We crawled, then jumped up and ran, and then dove back to the ground. You had to keep moving. Fucking bullets ricocheted from every angle. For more than two hours the troops just went nuts and kept shooting. My friend Leonardo, whom I met at the university and with whom I went there, stood up as a young soldier advanced near the stone column where we were hiding. Leonardo pounced on him and wrestled the rifle from the trooper. Leo wanted to fight back. Before he could raise the rifle to his shoulder, they shot him until he was unrecognizable."

"How many," Chrissy choked, "did they kill?"

"Oh, God," Beatrice sighed, tears rolling off her cheeks. "So many, no one will ever know. The official report by the government claimed four protesters killed. But that's a lie. A big fucking lie. We saw trucks carrying bodies. No one will ever know. The next day women came carrying mop buckets and cleaned up the plaza. No blood to be seen. No reform. Fear replaced fervent protests. Corruption bloomed once again. The people returned to the squalor that is still their lives. The Olympics went on as scheduled, and two black men with raised fists got more press than the hundreds killed in Tlatelolco."

"How the hell you get out of there?" Bingo asked.

"I laid on the ground until the shooting ended. I did not move for what seemed like hours. Then, I looked up and soldiers milled around the square with a bunch of suits. Surviving protesters were kneeling near the fallen, crying and feeling for heartbeats. I just stood up and walked out like a zombie. All I remember is the fat man in a tan suit standing near the gate. He had a big floppy hat, no eyes, no face, just Cheshire teeth. He flipped the cigarette he had been smoking at me as I walked by him."

"And you came back to Nebraska where you met me," Bingo completed her thought.

"Yes," Beatrice sighed, "I met you, then Jonathon and then——"

"Me," noted Chrissy quietly.

171

Beatrice looked at her for several moments and smiled, "Then I met you."

Jonathon coughed and interjected, "Chrissy, walk us through the operation once more."

Chapter Thirty Four

After organizing her thoughts, Chrissy began, "As you know, the material I used came out of the Compton raid and is high quality." She picked up a soda carton empty of the twenty-four cans of Coke. "I filled eighteen of the cans with the explosive material, and I placed them in a container similar to this one, Beatrice. I left three cans of Coke not filled with explosive on each end of the case, just in case one of your workmates might actually want a real Coke and reaches in."

"'Cause 'Coke Adds Life,'" laughed Bingo, referencing the ad campaign introduced by Coca-Cola in May as part of the nation's bicentennial celebration.

"Well, it will certainly add life to our campaign against the pigs," scorned Jonathon, which drew an eye roll from Beatrice.

"Quite," Chrissy added. "Beatrice, all you need to do is carry the case, which will be somewhat heavier than a regular case of Coca-Cola, to the location in the third car from the engine, as you pointed out."

"Yes," Beatrice said. "That's where the beverages are stored. I will have no problem with that step. I have been bringing a case of Coke to work almost every night. No one will suspect me carrying yet another case. Where is the actual bomb? I want to pick it up to determine how best to carry it and compare it to the weight of a regular case of Coke."

"The bomb is about two hundred yards from here, hidden in an outcropping of rocks. Only I know where." Chrissy glanced at Jonathon. She picked up the empty box. "The trigger mechanism is actually a cheap timer that I bought at an appliance store. It is located on the right side of the box, and this is important, Beatrice. If you look at the box from its top, it looks like this." Chrissy displayed the box to the group. Beatrice stood behind Chrissy to gain the correct perspective.

"Now," Chrissy continued, "I have preset the timer for 2 P.M. That should be the time of day when the most people are present." Chrissy let that sink in.

"All you have to do, Beatrice, is push in the cut-out handle located on the right side until you hear the click, do you understand?"

Beatrice's eyes were glued to the box. She said nothing.

"Do you understand?" Chrissy repeated hoarsely.

Jonathon exchanged a look with Bingo.

"Yes, of course," Beatrice mumbled.

"What's the matter, Bea?" Bingo chimed in, knowing Beatrice hated the name Bea. "You getting cold feet?"

"No." Beatrice leveled her eyes at Bingo, and smiled sardonically. She calmly added, "My feet are not cold, Bingo."

Beatrice turned her attention to Chrissy. "How do you know that the so-called cheap timer will set this thing off at 2 P.M."

"That's the most important piece to this exercise," Chrissy said smugly. "It is set for six hours. Your shift begins at midnight and ends at 8 A.M. When you leave for the day, press the timing mechanism. Six hours later it will go off. The timer is attached to primitive, but effective detonators that I bought at a fireworks stand in Evanston, Wyoming, last month."

"Primitive detonators? Cheap fucking kitchen timer?" Bingo was instantly livid. "All that fucking C-4 that we risked our asses getting? And you are telling us that this homemade fucking thing will work? How the fuck do you know that?"

Jonathon moved between Bingo and Chrissy. "Because," he jeered, "first, Chrissy fucking said it would work; that should be good enough for you. It is for me, because she has never constructed a device that did not work. And second, Chrissy and I tested the fucking thing last week. Yes, that's right, Bingo. We used one of those primitive detonators and the same type of timer and blew up a fucking can of C-4 Coca-Cola. Do you follow?"

Bingo wilted under Jonathon's glare. His eyes, however, burned in a sidelong stare at Chrissy.

"Okay, we have what we need," Jonathon said. "We have a plan. We know what we have to do. We are willing. Now, we must act."

Chapter Thirty Five

"Okay, freedom fighters, today is the day," a buoyant Jonathon exclaimed as the team began stirring about in the cabin. Jonathon had been up for hours, drinking coffee and planning the final moves for the operation.

Bingo shared Jonathon's ebullience. He had slept little overcome by the knowledge that they would be on the move once again. He had grown restless in the passing weeks while holed up in the cabin in Wasatch Canyon. He was sick of it all. "Let's just get on with it," was his mantra; therefore, his opinion mattered not a smidgeon to the others. But, Jonathon knew when to listen.

He listened this morning when Bingo joined him on the hillside while the others slept.

"That's what she said last night, Jay."

"Bingo, when exactly did she share that with you?" Jonathon asked. "I don't think I slept a wink. I heard nothing."

Bingo said, "We both heard you get up. She just laid there in her bag, and I heard her crying. You know she doesn't cry. So, I asked her, what was wrong? She didn't know I was awake."

"You're good at that, Bingo," Jonathon encouraged. "Please, what exactly did she say?"

"She said, 'Bingo, this plan is becoming a fucking nightmare.' I said, 'What do ya mean, baby?' She said, 'I'm supposed to plant the bomb tonight when I start my shift at midnight.' She was sobbing by this time. She says, 'So, I'm going to change the plan just a bit. The bomb will go off at 6 A.M., three hours before the public is allowed in. That way, the bullshit artifacts will go up in flames, and the train will be blasted out of our national fucking narrative. Our objective completed, but with no dead kids, which is not what the LTE is all about.' Got to admit, she made sense."

"Think, Bingo," Jonathon added sharply. "What exactly did she say?"

Bingo, noticeably recounting the conversation in his head, continued cautiously, "She said, 'I'm not doing it, Bingo.' I said, 'You can't mean that,

Trish, not after all we went through to get the explosives and all.' And she said, 'I'll plant the fucking bomb, but I'm not going to start the six hour timer at 8 A.M.' I said, 'But, you got to. That gives us six whole hours to get the hell outta here. Boom! The thing goes off, and we're almost to Las Vegas.' You know I'm not one to rat out a friend."

Jonathon eyed his minion. "It's okay, Bingo. A man's got to do what is best for all, even if that means betrayal of a friend. But, we all agreed, right from the start, that we would sacrifice ourselves for the operation. Remember, the operation comes first."

"I know; I remember the oath," Bingo sighed in relief. "She says, 'I saw the itinerary for tomorrow. There's going to be a shitload of school kids, elementary-aged kids coming to Promontory at 1 P.M.' And now she stops crying and becomes the Beatrice we all know; the one who can figure anything out."

Jonathon nodded.

"She says, 'Bingo, you got to promise me one thing. I need to know that you will do me this one favor, for all the time we've been together.' I say, 'Sure, Trish, anything for you.' She says, 'I'm going to set the timer at midnight when I report for work. I say, 'that will mean the thing will go off at around 6 A.M.' And then she said, 'Tell the others of my change of plan tonight, just after midnight. That will still give you guys the six hours head start. At about 5 A.M., I'll step away from the security car with all those fucking closed-circuit TVs. I'll say I have to pee. There's always a lot of commotion at 4:30 A.M., that's when the rest of the security crew shows up. No one will miss me. I'll dump the car off at the Salt Lake Airport and take the morning flight to Las Vegas. It leaves at 6:40 A.M. I know that is cutting it close, but they will not figure things out since most of the security detail will be dead or injured in the explosion. It'll take them a while to sort things out. I need your help in this, Bingo.' I say, 'That seems like a better plan than Jonathon's.' I pretended to go along, but that ain't all. I found this under her pillow."

Bingo handed the small leather bound diary to Jonathon. "The lock was easy. I used a hairpin to unlock it. Look at the more recent entries."

MOURNING IN THEIR TRIBE

Paging through the diary, Jonathon read the entries quickly. "You read this, Bingo?"

"Yeah, I knew as soon as I read it that it meant trouble. Add that to what she said last night, and I think we have big trouble."

"Good thinking, Bingo. That is a high-risk plan that she came up with. Not a bad one, mind you, but not what we all agreed to."

The conversation with Jonathon had not gone as he had planned. He had hoped that Jonathon would agree to Beatrice's plan and change of heart. Bingo had not thought about the casualties or who they may be. Killing kids did not sit well with him. Troubled thus in his revelation, he trusted Jonathon completely. He would do whatever his leader catechized.

PART 9

Grand Junction

Horace knew what he had to do; his course predetermined by the momentum of the past. It was time to begin the final leg of his journey. Carefully, he took the big Colt from its place in the desk and cleaned it. Satisfied, Horace loaded the weapon and slipped it back into the leather holster. He placed the pistol on top of two black western shirts, two pair of black socks and two pair of undershorts inside a small blue canvas bag along with a shaving kit and zipped it shut.

Chapter Thirty Six

Horace carried a large wooden box from his mother's room and skidded it into the bed of the black pickup truck parked just outside the kitchen door. A sudden chill crept up his spine, telling him he was being watched. Lastly, he retrieved the small canvas bag and placed it carefully inside the cab of the truck on the passenger side, but he needed to go back into the cabin to secure everything.

Movement from above stopped him. He zeroed in where he sensed it had emanated. Warily, he made his way around the truck, locked each door and quickly stepped back inside the cabin.

He locked everything, looked around, turned off the lights and went to the window of the darkened cabin and again examined the hillside. He scanned the mountain, looking for anything that did not belong. Nothing. Nerves bared, he felt certain that someone was watching.

Senses on full alert, Horace locked the cabin door and slowly walked around to the driver's side of the truck, eyes scanning the hillside from under the brim of his Stetson.

Horace started the truck and backed it slowly over the munching gravel drive and then forward down the short clay driveway over the bridge and onto the paved canyon road. Tranquility eased into his shoulders, arms, and slackened his grip on the snakeskin-wrapped steering wheel as each curve of the canyon passed behind him. The rearview mirror confirmed that no one followed.

A sense of freedom enveloped him as he drove the winding road. He settled back, tuned to his favorite country station and headed for Colorado. The soothing sound of wind rushing through the open windows of the truck's cab mesmerized Horace on his final journey of redemption and revenge. His head clear, the decisions made.

The summer sun still hung high at this late afternoon hour as Police Captain Myron Gibson stepped out into the glare and heat. He walked to his car, which was parked in front of the police station.

Parked across the street, Horace sat perspiring copiously in the black truck and watched as the captain eased into the police cruiser.

"Well, well, well, Cap'n Gibson. It's about time." Horace started the truck and waited as the captain pulled away from the curb. "Are we goin' home, Cap?"

It had all been too easy to locate his mother's killer. The phone book provided the man's address. A call to the police department told him that Lieutenant (now Captain) Gibson was on duty on day shift, which ends at 4:30 P.M. Horace waited and watched.

Now, he followed. He knew Gibson lived west of town in a new subdivision. Earlier, Horace had driven by Gibson's new home. "One way in, one way out," Horace said aloud as he swung around the area and drove into Grand Junction.

Horace followed Gibson to the shopping area about six blocks from the police station. He parked several rows away from Gibson's car and watched the officer stroll into King Soopers. "Aha, groceries. Okay, that means you're a headin' home. Well, no use me sittin' here, and then riskin' bein' seen follerin' ya home. I know where you're goin' there, sheriff. Ole Hoss will be a waitin' for you."

Horace pulled out of the parking lot and drove to Gibson's house.

"Hey, Cap. How's it hangin'?"

"Gomez," replied Gibson.

Gomez, wearing the same uniform as the captain, but his trimmed with silver appointments, stood behind the captain in the checkout line.

"We had a good day at the range, eh Cap?"

180

Gibson hated talking shop, especially at the grocery store and with a guy he knew to be *a* brownnoser. He wondered: *Hell, I'll bet he followed me in here just to chat.*

"Yes, Gomez, a pretty good day." The captain lowered his voice, "Hell, I even ended up shooting most of my own ammunition as well." He tapped the ammunition pouches on his Sam Browne belt.

Both carried small baskets of groceries. Gibson noticed contemptuously that Gomez' basket contained three oranges and a pack of gum. *Couldn't have handled that without a basket? Yeah right, he saw me come in here and followed me.* He looked into his own basket and noted the gallon of milk, two packages of Oreos and a loaf of Wonder Bread.

"Oreos, eh Cap?" noted Gomez. "They are my favorite as well. Only I stick to fruit because I need to watch the old waistline. Unlike you, that is. You work out a lot, Cap?"

Gibson stood a little taller, pulling his shoulders back ever so slightly and sucking in his gut. "Every chance I get."

"It's sure paying off for you."

Gomez, to Gibson's relief, allowed a young woman with a baby, squirming uncomfortably in the child carrier of her cart, to go in front of him.

Captain Gibson sat his cap next to the check-writing podium on the check stand and reached for his wallet when it was his turn. He glanced back at Gomez who quickly looked away.

Gibson paid for the groceries and, without looking back, hustled out of the store to his car, happy to get out of the store well ahead of Gomez.

Gomez watched the hatless Captain hurry from the store carrying the heavy bag with both hands.

"Captain. Captain!" Gomez yelled causing the baby to erupt again. The woman scowled at him. "Your hat, sir." Gomez said quietly.

The clerk gave Gomez a sympathetic look as he pushed his oranges up for checkout. He read the woman's nametag and said, "Lena, I work with Captain Gibson. I'll take his hat to him, if you don't mind."

Lena handed him the hat that she had stashed under the counter.

"Thank you," Gomez replied. He smiled and decided to return Captain Gibson's hat to him at his home.

Horace pulled the truck over next to a massive sandstone marker imbedded with the name of the subdivision. The road to get to Gibson's house was secluded. He got out of the truck and walked up and down the road two hundred yards in each direction. No homes were in view. Gibson's house was to the left and just out of sight. He had conjured his plan earlier in the day.

Horace turned and climbed the small rise so that he could see the entrance road to the subdivision. He nestled down in the shade of a spruce tree and watched for the police cruiser.

Horace watched the cruiser pull off the highway and watched Gibson pick up and sort through his mail. He waited until the captain reentered the cruiser before dashing to his truck. He hurriedly climbed in and grabbed his gun from the glove box. He positioned the truck to block the road and turned off the motor. He intentionally left the driver's door open after he jumped out and knelt behind the sandstone marker.

Captain Gibson swore as he approached the truck, blocking the entrance to his cul-de-sac. Gibson could clearly see that no one was inside the truck.

"Oh, for Christ's sake. Where the hell are you?" He honked several times before laying on his horn for ten seconds.

Horace grew fidgety. He peered around the bottom of the sign, and he sighed in relief when he saw Gibson emerge from his car and approach the driver's side of the truck. Horace stepped quietly around the sign, so he would come out behind Gibson.

Gibson looked around as he approached the truck. He leaned in and noted the keys still in the ignition. "Well, that's convenient. I don't know who the fuckhead is that owns this thing?" He blurted. In a louder voice intended for anyone close by, he bellowed, "Okay, wherever you are, whoever you are. I'm gonna move this piece of shit out of the road."

"I wouldn't do that if I was you, sheriff." Horace stepped between Gibson and the police cruiser. His right hand rested on the butt of the holstered Colt.

"Oh, I shouldn't, should I?" The captain, face reddening, spun out of the truck to face the man. He stopped quickly. A chill ran down Gibson's spine as he took in the scene: A big man dressed in black, wearing a cowboy hat pulled down shading his eyes and his stance wide, and armed.

Horace was about to say something, but Gibson did not give him the chance. Gibson fell to the ground and rolled under the truck while simultaneously pulling his service revolver from its holster as he went down. He scooted to get in a shooting position.

Horace was quick. He fired off two rounds at Gibson under the truck. One round slammed into Gibson's right thigh as he kicked, rolled and turned towards the cowboy. The second round kicked off the pavement right in front of Gibson's nose. Returning fire without taking proper aim, Gibson yanked the trigger three times.

Horace retreated around the rear of Gibson's police cruiser, ducked down and made his way to the front of the vehicle keeping the car between him and Gibson. Gibson used the opportunity to scoot painfully to his left and positioned himself behind the wheel of the truck. He knew where the cowboy would emerge on the other side of the squad car. He carefully aimed at that spot.

Horace sat on his heels behind the car and leaned into the fender. "You shoot pretty good, sheriff." He noted the small round hole in the top of his hat that just missed his head. He called out, "You ruined a perfectly good hat."

Gibson steadied his aim and retorted, "Who are you? What the hell do you want with me?"

Chuckling loud enough, Horace responded, "Don't you remember me there, Gibson?"

"No."

Officer Gomez pulled off the highway and down the lane. He heard little above the sound of the air conditioner running full blast and the radio tuned ever louder. He drove slowly thinking of just how he would approach Gibson at his home. As he made his way around the bend, he saw the rear of the captain's police unit and the black pickup truck parked in front of it. He could make out from that distance a man in dark clothing kneeling on the left side of the police car. "Captain Gibson?" he asked aloud. He thought *he needs help*.

"You ought to remember me, sheriff. You killed my mother," Horace yelled over his shoulder.

"Paulson?"

"That's a fact, Jack," Horace yelled back. He thought, *OK, it's now or never*. He prepared to turn and fire, and determined that his best chance would be to rush the captain by firing on the run, cut to the right and dive low, thus achieving full view of the captain under the truck. He heard the second police vehicle coming towards him. The unit screeched to a halt and a hatless, young, thin officer emerged from the car and ran towards him.

"Captain, what's going on?" Gomez gasped as he approached Gibson's car, stopping dead in his tracks when he realized it was not Gibson crouched behind the left fender.

Without hesitation, Horace squeezed off a round, striking the young officer in the stomach. The officer fell to one knee and went to the ground, falling behind the cruiser.

Horace cautiously approached the shot officer. Gomez pulled his revolver and, from his position behind the car, he could make out the lower half of the approaching man. He fired striking Horace just below the left knee. Horace folded to the ground. Now, the young officer had clear view of the cowboy. But, he hurried his next shot, striking the under carriage of the car.

Horace did not hurry his next shot, and it punched a hole in Gomez's forehead, killing him instantly.

Struggling to his feet, Horace approached the dead officer. He kicked him and got no response. He returned his attention to Gibson. Cautiously he made his way around the fallen officer and along the right side of the captain's car. He fell to his stomach to attain a view truck ahead. Gibson was gone.

He searched the area. Nothing. Horace stood and staying low, limped towards the truck and peeked into the cab. Nothing. Movement up the road caught his attention. The captain limped quickly across the road and disappeared toward his house.

Horace did not follow. He clambered into his truck and sped away.

Chapter Thirty Seven

Flinging the door open with a crash, Gibson called out, "Doris! Doris!" He slammed the door shut and turned the dead bolt lock. He stumbled to the large living room window, knelt and positioned his eyes just over the window stool, watching for the cowboy.

"Myron, what is wrong? Oh my God, you're bleeding." Doris steadied herself against the entrance to the living room, dropping the hand towel with which she had been wiping her hands.

"Call 9-1-1. There is a maniac out there. I've been shot."

"You're shot? Oh my God!"

"Get me the goddamn phone now, Doris." He turned to see his wife leaning heavily against the wall. Gibson softened his tone, "Come on, baby, get me the phone. I'm not hurt bad. I need to keep watch."

She picked up the phone from a small table in the hall to her right and pulled it cautiously towards her husband.

"Stay down, baby. Crawl it over here."

Doris complied.

Gibson dialed the number and was patched through to his police station. "This is Captain Gibson. Send all units to my house. An ambulance. Yes, all units. We have a shooter out here, about two hundred yards from my house on Red Rock Circle. Officer Gomez is down, and I've been shot. Yes, through the leg, bleeding like a son-of-a-bitch. I don't know the condition of Gomez. I'll stay on the line."

The dispatcher did as instructed, and was back. "Now get this," the captain said between pangs of throbbing pain. "The shooter's named Paulson, Horace. I do not have a visual. Got that? No visual from here. I'm in my home. Gomez is out on the road not far from here. I don't know if Paulson is still out there or not. He is driving a black Ford pickup truck with Colorado plates. Early seventies model. I didn't get the plate number. Early seventies model with a short wide bed and chrome wheels. Got that?"

"Check. Hold." The dispatcher came back on line. "All units are responding, sir. Do you have a description of the suspect?"

"White male. Big. Six foot-four or five. Well over two hundred twenty, thirty pounds. Around twenty-five years old. Wearing a black cowboy hat and black western shirt, long sleeved. Blue jeans. Armed with an old west style six shooter ... Advise all units, he is one dangerous motherfucker."

Doris returned with a first aid kit and flinched at her husband's language, which brought a nervous laugh from Gibson. He had promised Doris, as a condition to her accepting his proposal of marriage, that he would never use profanity in their home. He had kept that promise, until now. Not taking his eyes off the entrance to the cul-de-sac, the captain sat down, straightening his wounded leg while Doris cut off his pant leg with scissors.

Gibson relaxed a little as he heard the approaching sirens. He remained on the line with the dispatcher. When dispatch advised him that the black truck had vanished, Gibson slumped back against the wall, and his head thumped against the heavy glass window.

Horace sped out of the subdivision and slowed to the speed limit once he pulled onto the highway. He knew it wouldn't be long before every cop and highway patrolman in Colorado would be out looking for him. They had the description of his truck and of him. It wouldn't take them long to find his license plate number, if Gibson did not already have that.

Horace knew that his best chance of escaping the dragnet was to stay on busy thoroughfares, but Horace had a larger problem. If escape was even remotely possible, he needed to tend to the bullet wound below his left knee.

"Let's pray," Horace whispered, "that Wade's home." Secondly, he thought, *hopefully McCandle had not heard the news of the shooting in town.* He rebuffed himself and said aloud, "Do you think that, if there is a God on high, He would answer the prayers of a killer?"

Horace drove through the traditional ranch gate constructed of large pine logs. Nonetheless, Wade McCandle had always been a friend. As the story went, he had courted Horace's mother and was devastated when she chose to marry Ben instead of him. But, that was ancient history. McCandle had become a veterinarian. McCandle leaned against the entrance of the large barn watching the approaching dust cloud caused by the dark colored pickup truck coming up the drive. He sensed danger when he recognized Horace Paulson emerge for the truck. McCandle stepped over to the small radio and turned it off, and he calmly walked out to meet the big cowboy.

"Well, as I live and breathe, if it isn't Horace Paulson. I haven't seen you since—"

"The funeral," Horace concluded.

Horace stood awkwardly, favoring his left leg. His pants severely darkened by the blood streaming from the gunshot wound in his left calf, Horace tried in vain to conceal the wound with a crossed leg and beneath a dirty red oily rag that he had found in the bed of the truck.

The veterinarian's eyes were immediately drawn to the wound, but he said, "How've you been, Horace?"

Horace noted the slight nervousness in the man's words. He knew.

Horace smiled and with a small laugh replied, "Well, Mr. McCandle, as you can see, I screwed up." He looked down at the darkening pant leg and removed the rag from the wound. "I was out shooting bottles and shot myself, if you can imagine someone being that stupid."

Horace looked the man in the eye in an imposing way. He continued, "I was close by, so I came here hoping you could help me until I could get myself over to the hospital."

The radio had said nothing of the suspect in the police shooting in town being wounded, but it had broadcast the suspect's name and the description of the truck, and here they were in his driveway. The incongruous thought that passed through McCandle's mind initially was of Dr. Samuel Alexander Mudd and how administering treatment to an injured John Wilkes Booth had ruined his life. He also realized he had little choice than to treat the man. "Come on in, son and let me have a look at what you've done to yourself."

188

The two men walked to a clinic in the barn.

"This is where I treat my four-legged patients, Horace. Hope you don't mind."

"I would be much obliged if you could just fix me up best you can until I can get to a hospital before I bleed to death."

Horace declined having his jeans cut off. He gingerly took them off and laid them aside. McCandle pulled a clean sheet from a cabinet and spread it over a bench and told Horace to lie down, and then he washed his hands thoroughly in the nearby sink and put on a pair of surgical gloves.

"Wade, Wade! Are you in there?" came a woman's frantic voice from the front of the barn. Before he could answer, the voice blurted, "Did you hear about Horace Paul..." Mrs. McCandle stopped, mouth agape, as she entered her husband's makeshift operating room where lay Horace Paulson.

Calmly McCandle said, "Yes, I did honey. Now, if you wouldn't mind, open that box of gauze sponges there on the shelf and set it next to Horace's leg."

Sadie complied, and said, "I'll go inside and boil water to sterilize the instruments you'll need."

"No, ma'am, you stay in here," Horace said firmly, not malevolently. "There is a kerosene stove over there."

"Oh, of course, how silly of me." She lit the burner and placed a pot of water on the flame.

Silence filled the space as the small group waited for the water to come to a boil. Finally, Horace broke the spell.

"Look, folks, I mean you no harm. I'll not hurt you in any way." He could see that they did not believe him.

"You already have, just by being here," an indignant Mrs. McCandle exclaimed.

"I know, ma'am. I didn't know where else to go. I can't go to the hospital. I will be gone as soon as Dr. McCandle bandages my leg."

189

Mrs. McCandle wasn't finished. "Horace, for goodness sake, why did you do it? One of the officers is dead. Why would you do that?"

With growing fear, Wade interrupted, "Now, Sadie, you don't know that Horace here committed the crime."

"Gibson got away," Horace said. "It was the other one, a young guy, who died."

The husband and wife exchanged horrified looks.

"That's right, I did it."

Horace lay back and fixed his gaze on the ceiling, and he spoke unguardedly gently, "Mr. and Mrs. McCandle, I'll bring you no harm. I have been on a vengeful path for ages now. I want it to be over. Oh, how I want it all to be over."

Mrs. McCandle pulled a chair next to Horace and took his hand. "We believe you, Horace. We truly do." She looked at her husband who gave her an affirming nod. "We can help with that. All we have to do is call the police, and it will all be over."

Horace looked at her and then at Dr. McCandle who stood preparing a needle. "No, that's not the way to end it. I will not turn myself in. I can't be put in a cement cage."

"But, what will you do? Where will you go? You may end up harming other innocent people. Just like those two poor officers today," Sadie cried.

"Innocent?" he scoffed. "No, they're not innocent. No one who puts on that uniform and straps on a gun is innocent. Know this," Horace looked Dr. McCandle in the eye, "each one of my battles with the men in blue has been a fair fight. I meant to shoot Gibson. He killed Mom. Did you know that?"

"Is he the one who fired the fatal shot that night?" Dr. McCandle asked. He then advised Horace, "I'm going to give you a series of shots that will deaden the area around the wound. I will have to extract the bullet."

"Yes, he's the one who gunned down my mom. And, she was the one who called for the cops in the first place. The young guy stumbled into the battle with Gibson. He had no idea what he got himself into."

190

Horace looked at the needle that McCandle was about to insert into his leg and asked, "You wouldn't put me out would you, Doc?" Horace's voice had hardened, "Let me see the bottle where that medicine came from."

McCandle dropped the needle in the wastebasket and said resignedly, "You caught me. I really am trying to save your life, Horace. If you walk out of here, they'll catch up to you and kill you."

Horace's anger subsided. "OK, Doc, I understand. Now, let me see the bottle before you mix up another brew."

"Novocain. That's more like it, Doc. Now, do your job and make it quick."

After the procedure, Horace forced the McCandles into his truck and ordered them to bring a large canteen of water.

"Sorry, folks, you're coming with me," Horace told them. Mrs. McCandle began to weep.

"You said you weren't going to hurt us, Horace. Where are you taking us?" Dr. McCandle demanded.

Horace drove into the area known as badland; the outlook seemed very bleak to the McCandles. Mrs. McCandle now sobbed. Dr. McCandle thought of jumping from the truck as his only hope, but he could not leave Sadie behind.

In a remote, desolate place sparse of trees but teeming with doom, Horace pulled over. "This is it folks. End of the line."

"Horace, I beg of you. Don't do this. There's no need. Please," said Dr. McCandle.

"Take the canteen," Horace said. "I figure it'll take you at least an hour to walk back to the nearest farm. By that time, I'll be long gone."

Chapter Thirty Eight

After leaving the couple to walk home, Horace did not attempt his escape from Colorado right away. Instead, he drove to an old hideaway where he knew he could easily conceal the truck in the thicket along the river bottom. He considered correctly that law enforcement would be flooding the highways watching all escape routes, especially once the McCandles made their way to a phone.

The next morning he left his hideaway and made his way toward US 50. As he approached the town that stood between him and the Utah border, he was confronted by a parking lot full of Utah and Colorado Highway Patrol vehicles at a dealership.

Turning into a nearby residential neighborhood from which he could view the dealership, he planned his next move. He decided to walk to the farm store, acting like a local. Troopers, who stood in small groups in the parking lot out front of the business drinking coffee and talking in serious tones, did not seem to notice the big man wearing torn and stained jeans as he passed within a few feet of many of them. Walking without a limp required all of his concentration.

Horace entered the business and approached the clerk at the information desk. He and his discolored, soiled and torn jeans looked right at home in here. Few of the customers milling about wore jeans or overalls that were not soiled.

"What can I do for you?" asked the clerk.

"Well, I'm looking for a back hoe for a little project I'm working on. Do you rent them?" Horace asked while looking around at the police activity in front of the building.

"No, sir, we don't. I would suggest you try Triple A Rent-All over in The Junction." The man added, "I know they rent almost anything we sell."

"Okay, I'm looking to rent. Thanks a bunch, mister." Horace turned to leave. "What's all that about?" he asked, nodding towards the activity in the parking lot.

"Manhunt headquarters, I'd say. Man, have you not heard that a couple of cops were gunned down yesterday?"

"Yeah, I did hear something on the radio about that. Just terrible."

"I'll say." The clerk leaned in and lowered his voice, "I heard some of those fellers out there talkin'. Seems the man who did it made old Doc McCandle fix him up yesterday not too far from here. So, the cops out there have road blocks set up on all the roads leaving Colorado."

"Oh, yeah?"

"Yep, and this here," the clerk said proudly waving his hand in the air, "is their stagin' area, as they call it."

"What's this here suspect look like?" Horace knew he was pushing it, but he was enjoying the exchange and that puzzled him.

"Big dude, like you," the clerk smiled, "except he's a cowboy-lookin' feller, wearin' a black cowboy outfit. Horace Paulson."

Horace wearing a dingy white tee shirt, standing with his hands in the pockets of his stained and torn jeans, topped off with a Denver Bears minor league baseball cap, said, "Okay. Well, I hope they get the dude."

Taking an indirect route back to his truck, Horace climbed in and sat fiddling with papers. Suddenly, the patrol cars in the parking lot peeled out in all directions except one.

Horace drove slowly along the road until he got near the Utah border. From a small rise, he watched a roadblock form about a mile ahead.

Paulson left the highway taking a jeep road, crossing into Utah undetected. He relaxed some as he got farther from Colorado.

Horace stopped at the stables and lingered in Junior's stall. Sitting against the rough wall, he slipped into a fitful sleep. Awaking early, before dawn, he stood up and stroked the old horse and brushed him down a final time. Completing what he came to do, he drove his truck out of the stables only moments ahead of the stable manager who had parked in his usual place and didn't notice the black truck leaving by the back gate with lights out.

For the first time in two years, paranoia swept over him. Horace stopped driving during the day. When he did drive, he obeyed every traffic ordinance real or imagined: He signaled his turns long before he needed to and maintained the speed limit by closely watching the speedometer needle.

Letting out a huge sigh, Horace finally got to his cabin. Once inside, he pulled off his jeans and elevated his leg onto the kitchen table. He examined the stitches and noted the swelling and erythema around the wound. Overtaken by exhaustion he remained in that position and dozed fitfully. After what seemed like an eternity, he opened his eyes fully and was startled to see Chrissy standing over him, probing the wound.

"Gunshot wound, eh, Hoss?" Chrissy said as she unwrapped a roll of gauze.

"Yes, it is."

"Cops?"

Thinking lying was pointless, Horace replied, "Yes."

"Figured," Chrissy replied. "We know everything, Hoss. We broke into your private room while you were gone."

Horace tried to stand, but Chrissy pushed him back into the chair. "Not to worry, Horace. Your secret is safe with us. Trust me, Horace, you'd be shocked to learn who we are."

She washed her hands and bandaged his leg.

"Nicely done, Chrissy."

"In my line of work, Hoss, you pick up a few things," she said dryly.

He asked, "What line of work might that be?" Their eyes locked for a long moment.

"Never mind that now. We have to get you out of here."

"Right now?"

"Right now. Let's go. Grab some pants. That's it. Now, Horace, let's go."

"Horace, not Hoss?"

"I know all about Hoss," Chrissy pointed at the padlocked room with her eyebrows. "And a little about Horace. I prefer Horace. Now, let's move."

"Wait. Chrissy, please wait a minute." Intense pain radiated through Horace's leg, almost causing him to pass out.

"Horace, there is no time. We've got to go," Chrissy implored.

"Oh, Chrissy," he sobbed. "They know my name. They know my truck. The description will certainly have been broadcast all over the country by now. It is only a matter of time. I'll go alone."

"No. I know a safe place, but we have to go there now."

Horace hobbled to the truck with Chrissy's support. Above, Bingo watched as Chrissy and Horace drove away.

Chapter Thirty Nine

Quietly, Horace stared out the passenger side of the truck as they drove by the entrance sign to Scare Canyon. When they got to the cabin, Horace thought it was marvelous.

"Come on in. We need to get you off that leg."

Once inside, Chrissy lit several candles, unrolled two of the sleeping bags and gently tried to help Horace onto them. He flopped down with a groan.

"Sorry, Horace."

"No need to be sorry. I'm fine."

"Fine doesn't grunt the way you did. But, I'll take your word for it. I'll fire up the stove over there. Pancakes okay for you?"

"Pancakes sound great."

"Good, cause that's all we got."

Horace watched Chrissy putter about. She expertly fired up the small wood stove and told Horace how she and Jonathon had found the cabin, leaving out key details.

He smelled coffee and listened to the batter sizzling on the griddle. Inexplicably, Horace sensed a fleeting belonging that he had not felt in years. Nothing mattered outside of the two hundred square feet of knotty pine and stone surrounding him and this strange woman at this moment. Content, he dozed.

Shaken awake, Horace found a paper plate piled high with pancakes sitting on his chest.

Chrissy laughed, "Don't move; you'll spill. I'll get those for you. Can you prop yourself up against the wall?"

Pancakes dripping with maple syrup followed with huge gulps of steaming coffee brought life back into Horace one mouthful at a time. Chrissy picked at the single barren pancake on her plate with her fingers. She sat the plate aside and sat cross-legged next to Horace holding a mug of coffee in both hands.

Horace finished off the flapjacks and let out a satisfied sigh.

"Okay. You're welcome," Chrissy responded playfully.

Silence closed in on the room. Neither spoke. The only noise came from the occasional slurp of coffee.

Finally, looking straight ahead at nothing, Horace asked, "How is it that we are here? You making me pancakes. You knowing who I am: Hoss, the cop killer. Why are you not frightened by me?"

"I guess I'm not scared, because I'm not a cop," Chrissy said and immediately realized she shouldn't have been that flippant; although she felt what she said was true.

"Horace, why aren't you scared of me?"

"Well, maybe I am. I figure anyone who is not afraid of a self-avowed killer must have a reason and that would be reason enough to frighten most folks."

"You remind me of someone I knew many years ago," Chrissy reflected. "They killed him for no reason at all. I have been waging war on them ever since."

"Well, I guess I have nothing to worry about, since I am not one of *them*."

Chrissy turned and faced him. "You are right. You are not one of *them*."

PART 10

The Bomb

The most interesting thing about the terrorist movement…is that while women have been approaching equality with men in other fields of crime, this is the only one in which they have come to be dominant. – *San Antonio Express. Thursday, February 10, 1977.* **Excerpted from "Women: The New Criminals"; Copyright 1977 by Richard Deming; Published by Nelson**

Chapter Forty

"Fuck! Gone where?" Jonathon fumed.

Bingo said, "Chrissy was out by the cars when the cowboy drove in. She finished packing and hurried right over there. She helped him to his truck because of a bad leg. Then they drove off, eastbound; Chrissy was driving."

Jonathon frowned, "Scare Canyon."

"What does it matter?" Beatrice questioned. "Her part in this is over, right? I mean, for now, anyway. Let's hope she is taking that guy away for a good reason. We have to trust her."

Beatrice wanted nothing to interfere with her plan at this stage. She knew she must allay Jonathon's fears and knew that he did not deal with adversity well, especially when their scheme was close at hand. "We know Chrissy. She did what she had to do. Let's stay focused. My car is loaded. Time to move. The plan continues. Am I wrong?"

Smoothing his beard, Jonathon agreed. "You're right, Trish. Chrissy is a damned good soldier. She did what she needed to do. We can all agree to that. It's almost 10:30 P.M. Trish, this is it. You should get going. On to Promontory!" Jonathon intoned.

Bingo summarized quietly, "And leave mourning in their tribe."

Jonathon and Bingo watched in silence as Beatrice drove toward Promontory Point.

They did not move for several minutes. Jonathon, satisfied that she was not coming back, said, "Well, she's gone. Let's get on with it."

Returning to the cabin for one last look, they were convinced that the cabin was clean, and that they had forgotten nothing. Jonathon had attended to wiping down all surfaces that could possibly contain fingerprints. The cabin reeked of vinegar and ammonia, but looked spotless. Jonathon thought with a certain irony that the owners would be pleased.

Activated by Beatrice's attack of conscience, Jonathon and Bingo put their revised plan into action. They hurried off to the jeep that held their bags, ammunition and weapons. Jonathon drove quickly, following the route that Beatrice had taken. They pulled off into the parking lot of a supermarket, and parked next to a 1963 Chevrolet. He and Bingo had stolen a car earlier that day from a college parking lot. It had been too easy, even for Bingo's skills. The keys had been left in it.

Bingo drove off in the stolen car towards Promontory, followed at a safe distance by Jonathon in the Jeep. In a last-minute change of plan, prompted by Chrissy's sudden departure with Horace, Jonathon blinked his lights twice to signal Bingo that he was turning off and heading back towards his ultimate destination, Scare Canyon.

The parking lot of the visitors' center at the Golden Spike National Historic Site had been temporarily expanded to accommodate the throngs of people that would pour in the next morning to view the Freedom Train. As he turned into the parking area, the sight of the Freedom Train struck Bingo. The sight of the silvery train sent a wave of goose bumps over his body for two reasons: one, the otherworldly apparition before him aglow under the bright lights and two, knowledge that he would destroy it.

Distracted by the sight, he drove by Beatrice as she walked through the same parking area. He had wrongly assumed that she would park closer to the train.

Beatrice did not bother a second look as Bingo drove by her. Bingo breathed easy as he parked two rows behind Beatrice's Vega. Something was wrong. Beatrice should be carrying the bomb encased in the Coke box. Panic seized his stomach. He felt for the gun in his waistband and jumped from the car. He sprinted after Beatrice.

Beatrice stopped at the entrance road that separated the temporary parking lot and the main lot. She looked around and turned to go back to her car and abruptly came face-to-face with Bingo.

Fear gripped Beatrice. Bingo simply looked at her with no expression at all.

Beatrice quickly regained her composure, and coolly asked, "What are you doing here?"

"Well, Jonathon sent me out here to back you up. Just in case you needed it," Bingo lied, and Beatrice knew it. "But, aren't you supposed to be taking the … " he looked around to see if anyone was within hearing distance, " … bomb in with you? Wasn't that your plan?"

"Yes, it was and is. I am just making sure no one will see me carrying it. It weighs more than you think, and I didn't want to draw attention. Okay? Now, I'm going back to the car to get it."

Bingo stepped in front of her. "Actually, it's best if you don't take it in right now. Why don't you go on into work, and I'll see you at 8 A.M. I'll keep an eye on your car and the bomb. We'll trigger the timer at eight, according to the original plan." Bingo stood menacingly, feet wide apart.

Two more cars drove into the parking lot. Each driver wore similar uniforms as Beatrice. One waved through an open window while looking suspiciously at Bingo.

Beatrice gave him a wave and smiled to signify that she was all right.

Beatrice hissed, "Goddamn it, Bingo. We agreed. You told Jonathon and Chrissy, didn't you?"

"No. Not Chrissy, anyways."

"Of course, I was stupid. What was I thinking? You would follow your leader into the depths of hell, wouldn't you?"

"Well, I know you wanted to change the plan, Trish. We can't allow that," Bingo tried to give his best Jonathon impersonation.

"Oh, really. We?"

"That's right, we," Bingo countered. "We'll just leave the bomb in your car until your shift ends."

Beatrice eyed Bingo then smiled. "Okay, the original plan it is. But, there is one thing you should know."

"What might that be?"

"I didn't notice before," Beatrice said, warily looking about, "but I don't have a key to the trunk of that piece of shit rental car."

Confused, Bingo responded, "So?"

201

"So, I can't lock it. You don't know, but there is a roving guard who walks around here at night. The case of Coke is in plain sight under the hatchback. The rover checks to insure the employees' cars are locked. It's part of the procedures. What if he is thirsty? Just our luck, eh, Bingo? Months of planning, burglaries and conspiracies all exposed because some cracker wants a Coke."

"Yeah, I see your point." Bingo asked himself, *What would Jonathon do?* "I have the answer. Let's put the damn thing in my car."

"That isn't a bad idea. Was that you in the white sedan that parked back of me a few rows?"

Feeling good with himself, Bingo smiled, "Okay, I can get it. Why don't you go on inside before you're late."

"Oh, no. I'll carry the thing to your car. I know you're damned strong, but the box is bulky. We can't have you dropping it out here, can we?" Beatrice asked, noticeably lowering her eyes to Bingo's prosthetic arm.

"Let's go."

Beatrice opened the hatchback and leaned in to pick up the box. Bingo stuck his head in and said, "Careful now. I paid attention to the lecture. Don't stick your paw into the right handle and touch that mechanism. That-a-girl, pick it up by the bottom."

Beatrice walked in front of Bingo as they made their way to his car. Bingo opened the rear door on the driver's side and motioned for Beatrice to place the box on the back seat. The box slipped. Beatrice caught it by compressing the handle on the left side and made a show of it. "Not to worry, Bingo, left handle. The switch is on the right, right?"

"Right. Yes, right side," Bingo said with trepidation. "Well, I'll just slide into the front seat and keep an eye on things."

"Okay," Beatrice said. Her voice quivered, suddenly overcome with sorrow. "I'll see you, Bingo."

Bingo noticed, and said, "Oh, don't worry, Trish. It'll all be all right. We're still friends, ain't we?" He smiled broadly.

"Yes, Bingo. We're still friends." Beatrice turned quickly and hurried off.

Bingo stepped into the car and scooted down as another employee parked a few spaces to his left. He didn't see Beatrice quickstep back to her car.

Tears streaming, Beatrice turned and quickly glanced back at the white Chevrolet before jumping into her car. She gunned the engine and headed for the exit.

Bingo heard a car start-up and bobbed his head back up above the steering wheel in time to see taillights of the Vega heading towards the exit of the parking lot.

"What the hell?" Bingo searched his pockets for the car keys. These were the last words that Bingo would speak.

The explosion was said to have broken windows as far away as twenty miles to the east, but that was never verified. The remains of the man in the stolen Chevrolet were never identified. Stuart Smith, a full-time police officer with the Heavenly Valley PD, said to be a distant relative of the Mormon Profit, Joseph Smith, and who was moonlighting as temporary employee by the Freedom Train, and who had parked near the stolen Chevrolet, would die two weeks later from multiple "shrapnel wounds." Seventeen parked cars were damaged, seven beyond repair. The next day's event was called off.

Beatrice heard the massive boom and never looked back.

"Actually, there was another change of plan, Bingo." Beatrice sobbed as she pulled over to keep from running off the road.

Yes, but it was a failsafe plan that Chrissy had put in place, and that she had shared only with Beatrice. Chrissy, being true to herself, had never constructed a device without building in redundancies. She had placed another arming mechanism under the left compression handle of the Coca-Cola box, but with a short timer that once compressed, "will give you a up to two minutes and three seconds before it triggers the device," Chrissy had confided with Beatrice late last night. "So, Beatrice, use it if you have to; you never know what will happen out there, then run like hell."

Chapter Forty One

Jonathon stopped at Denny's. He needed to stop and think about his next moves. Beatrice's reluctance to carry out the original plan cast a shroud of doubt and foreboding over him. It marked the first time in the history of the LTE of a break within their ranks. His confidence in Bingo being able to handle that situation ebbed as he thought more about Beatrice as an adversary. *No*, he thought, *Bingo versus Beatrice, Bingo loses!*

Sitting in a booth, Jonathon placed the shoulder brief next to him. The waitress set a white mug in front of him and poured coffee into it. Sirens shrilling and red lights flashing drew her attention to the highway. "Well, something big is going on out there tonight," she said to anyone within listening distance as she walked back to the waitress station.

Jonathon stared out the window at the passing traffic, letting the coffee cool. Rooting within the bag, he pulled out a mechanical pencil and a sketchpad. He slowly turned pages of what would appear to be nonsensical drawings to anyone else, but were well thought out plans to him. Losing all sense of time, circling this, crossing out that and mumbling to himself, his thoughts took him back to the late 1960s: the night that he and Bingo met Beatrice, and her persuasion not to join the Weatherman. It was Beatrice's sacrifices, judgment, and ability that had pushed the LTE to this point.

In a painful moment of reflection, Jonathon, with head in hand, admitted to himself that Beatrice was the de facto leader of the LTE. *She became the glue for the LTE. For us. No, Bingo will be no match for her.* Jonathon thought as he doodled in his sketchbook.

Two highway patrol troopers walked by Jonathon and sat at the counter. He returned to his notes. More details. More plans. Suddenly, he froze. *Promontory?*

"Yeah, one big assed explosion out at Promontory," one of the troopers was saying to the waitress at the bar.

"Is that what all the sirens were about, oh, maybe an hour ago?"

"Yep," the other trooper responded. They lowered their voices conspiratorially. Jonathon leaned toward the conversation at the bar. He could not hear all of what was said, but he heard enough.

Slowly rising, he dropped a few dollars and all the change in his pocket on the table and left the restaurant.

Jonathon sped south towards Heavenly Valley and then east through Wasatch Canyon. Finally, he pulled off the road at a campground not far from Scare Canyon. Perspiring, he tried to gather his thoughts. The plan had called for all of them to meet in Las Vegas tomorrow night, taking separate routes and modes of transportation: Chrissy by bus, Beatrice by plane and Jonathon and Bingo by car.

Chapter Forty Two

Chrissy eased away from Horace on the floor covered with sleeping bags. She heard his deep breathing morph into snoring. Not taking her eyes from the man, she slowly slipped on her faded jeans and red and black checked flannel shirt. Barefoot, she picked up her sandals and padded to the cabin door and stepped outside. She leaned against the cool stones of the cabin wall and looked up at the universe narrowed by dark brooding pines and aspen trees. Finding the small tin of speed in her pocket and without lowering her eyes, she removed two little white pills and placed them under her tongue.

The night sounds of the forest ceased with the crunching of tires and headlights. Stumbling over rocks and loose gravel, Chrissy scampered to the road and stopped at the sight of the jeep parked in a pull out above the driveway to the cabin.

"Chrissy."

She turned quickly. Jonathon stepped from the darkness. "Jonathon, what are you doing here? You weren't supposed to come up here until tomorrow morning."

"Morning will come soon enough. It's all gone to hell, Chrissy. First the cowboy, then Beatrice having an attack of conscience, then the detonation."

"What are you talking about? Slow down. You're making no sense."

Jonathon walked back to the jeep and sat on the bumper. Head in hands, he recounted the events of the past twenty-four hours. Chrissy paced. The forest watched, and from behind the curtain of trees, Horace listened.

"We don't know that they didn't blow the train, right?" Chrissy spoke frantically, "You know, with the two-minute fuse I built in maybe Beatrice used it to get the fuck out of there. What about the train, did she blow the train?"

Jonathon leaned back against the grill of the jeep. Suddenly exhausted, he murmured, "What two-minute fuse? Chrissy, what the fuck have you done?"

As Chrissy explained, Jonathon dropped his head back into his hands. "I should have known you had a backup plan. So did I in sending Bingo to make sure Trish did what she was supposed to do. Sounds like your plan held, and mine fell through." He sat up, pushed his head back and closed his eyes.

"No, Chrissy, she did not blow the train. I picked up the police bands on the scanner in the jeep. The fucking train is not scratched. They blew up a parking lot."

Chrissy sat next to Jonathon on the bumper and leaned forward with elbows on knees, and said almost to herself, "All our work. Everything we hoped to gain, gone. What of Bingo and Trish? Where are they? They should be here by now. We agreed to meet up here, if things went wrong. I'm worried, Jonathon."

"Yeah."

They sat staring at their feet for a long time. Finally, Chrissy stood up and turned to face Jonathon, "They're dead or, worse, captured. Let's hope dead."

Jonathon looked at The Chemist, pale and smooth complexioned in the forgiving light of the waning gibbous moon that blended and evened the edges and creases; Chrissy appeared more her age, soft and pretty. Her cold sense of reality pricked him, but brought him reassurance. "You're right. We go on. Let's see, we need a new plan. What about the cowboy down there?"

Chrissy quickly briefed him, and then she said firmly, "Listen, Jonathon. I had to get the man and that truck away from the heart of the group as quickly as possible. The last thing we needed the day before D-Day was to have the cops crawling over the Wasatch Canyon bungalows looking for a cop killer. Give me a gun. I'll handle the cowboy. You get out of here. Go to Vegas. I'll meet you there as planned. If Bingo and Beatrice are POWs, they will not talk. We both know that. Best that we split up. You still have remaining C-4 in the Jeep and the rest of it. Take it and go. That's important shit we have in that jeep. It is more important than Bingo or Beatrice, or you and me for that matter. The war goes on, Jonathon.

Remember that is what we are all about. Casualties happen in war. Battles are lost. The war goes on."

Strengthened by Chrissy's words, Jonathon agreed with a simple nod of the head and handed her a gun. They did not hug, shake hands or say goodbye. Jonathon climbed into the vehicle, turned the jeep around and disappeared over the hill.

Chrissy turned and walked cautiously to avoid stumbling back to the cabin. She stopped and hid the pistol under a flat rock by the door. Easing the door open, she attempted to lessen the scrape of the metal on metal hinges. Horace appeared to be sleeping soundly. She slipped out of her clothes and lay down next to him, but did not sleep.

Chapter Forty Three

Sleep found them. Bright sunlight streamed through the small window settling on Chrissy's face. She struggled for consciousness, and tried to wipe away the glare with her hand. Horace rolled over slowly and faced her. She opened her eyes and shaded them with her hand.

"I slept," Chrissy whispered with disbelief.

"You don't sleep much, do you?" Horace responded with a smile. He, too, was astonished by sleep, but for other reasons. He tried to sit up but felt feverish and dopey. Instinctively, he reached for the wound.

Chrissy sat up and blanched at the sight of the cowboy's leg. It was deep red and had ballooned overnight. The bandage that she had applied the night before did little to hold back the swelling. She gently touched his leg, and then put a palm to his forehead.

"You're burning up, Horace. Let's have a look at the wound."

He rolled onto his back as she cut the bandage off. She sat back on her haunches and looked troubled. "You need a doctor."

"Right."

"Okay, let me think. I will brew you up a poultice." She smiled at him, but she could not hide the concern in her voice.

"Well," Horace smiled back at her, "you could always shoot me." The smile fell from her face. "That's what they do with horses, right?" Neither smiled while their eyes locked for a long moment. Horace smiled broadly lightening the mood. He laughed at her expression.

"Chrissy, don't worry about it. I'll be fine. You know what I would like more than a poultice right now?"

Her eyes narrowed, and she assumed the answer, but she replied, "Really? In your condition?"

"Pancakes. I could use some pancakes."

Chrissy laughed heartily. "That, I can do." She helped him to sit up against the wall and elevated his leg on rolled sleeping bags.

"What do they say about a fever? Feed? Starve?"

"I don't know. I'd say by the way you destroyed that stack of pancakes, it must be feed. Can I get you more coffee?"

"No, Chrissy. You've done plenty for me. Believe me."

"Okay, then." She filled a kettle with water and set it on the hot stove.

"I'm going to find the plants for your poultice. Your fever seems to have subsided a bit."

"How is it that you know so much about poultices?"

"Chemistry," Chrissy said. Strangely, the word evoked memories of her family. "I'm a chemist, Horace. A good one at that … " Her voice trailed off as she pictured her mother saying those words so long ago. She wiped a tear from her cheek and headed for the door.

Chrissy shut the door behind her and leaned over and removed the rock exposing the pistol. She picked up the gun and slid it under the waistband of her jeans against her back hidden by the tail of the too-large flannel shirt. She marched around the cabin and into the forest.

It took all of his strength and willpower, but Horace got dressed. He heard Chrissy crunching around outside the cabin and caught a glimpse of her through the small window as she headed into the trees.

Hesitating for a few minutes, he eased out of the cabin and looked about as he opened the passenger door of his truck and reached into the glove box. His hands shook as he strapped on the gun belt. Deliberately and painfully he followed Chrissy's path through the woods.

The pain that gathered in his stomach then invaded his chest overcame the pain of the wounded leg. He watched as Chrissy stopped by a stream. Finding a tree, Horace leaned against it and pinched the bridge of his nose. *It doesn't have to end this way. All I have to do is get back to the truck and drive off.*

PART 11

Three Hammer Falls

The events of Scare Canyon unfolded with the tragic syncopation of Mahler's Symphony No. 6. Three gigantic hammer blows would resound through the canyon to be heard only by whoever may survive in the dying sun. The composer, himself, refused to add the third hammer blow to his symphonies, because he worried terrible consequences would result as the Scare Canyon participants in July 1976 would discover.

Chapter Forty Four

It was 6 A.M. The Freedom Train event the community had been so heavily involved with for months had been cancelled. The organizers had issued a press release at 4:37 A.M. that in the interest of public safety, the train was moving onto its next location at Reno, Nevada.

———————

Reynolds and O'Brien stopped for coffee following meetings with the detective staff, officials from the Department of Defense bomb squad and the special agent in charge of the local FBI office.

"Two?"

"No doubt in my mind," O'Brien quipped.

The well-endowed hostess showed them to a table, and glared at O'Brien, but said sardonically, "Cute."

He sat down with a self-satisfied look. Naturally, O'Brien interpreted the exchange as flirting.

Reynolds looked on disinterestedly. He had heard it all before. "What do you think?"

"The bomb was no car bomb, contrary to what the Feds have said," OB replied, still gawking at the young receptionist.

"I agree, but whether it was or wasn't, what was he doing out there at 11:30 P.M.? Another thing, if a guy intended to blow up the train, why would he park so far away from it? I agree with the DOD in one aspect, the bomb went off accidentally. It was a mistake."

"The bomber was an employee," O'Brien concluded.

Reynolds thought that over and mused aloud, "Shift change was taking place, so that would make some sense. The FBI noted that only one employee did not show up for work for last night's shift. A woman by the name of ... " Reynolds pulled the notebook from his pocket and paged through it.

"Beatrice Donaldson," O'Brien said taking a sip of coffee. "Could be she's the body parts found at the scene."

"Maybe. FBI said they are not sure if what they have is male or female yet. She's a full-time employee. Had been with the train for months, since it left back east. I don't know."

"Could be that was the idea."

"So, if that is so, that would mean the plan had been in place for months," Reynolds said. "That would certainly mean that others are involved. I still don't know though. With all that planning, you'd think they would know better than to set the bomb off accidentally, don't you think?"

O'Brien was still distracted by the receptionist who purposely refused to look in his direction.

"You with me, OB?"

"Yeah," OB replied. "Mo, I think we have our own fish to fry. Know what I mean?"

"Yeah, yeah. Hal's murder. I do know what you mean, this Paulson fellow out of Grand Junction. What have you got?"

"While you were lazing around in the hospital and after we got word of the shooting over there, I phoned Detective Mortonson with Grand Junction PD. He said that they have confirmed that the truck and the big cowboy, who shot up their department, may have been involved in the Garden Grove shooting." O'Brien stopped and looked at his partner for recognition.

Reynolds nodded.

"Large caliber weapon was used in Grand Junction, probably a Colt .45. Garden Grove PD has a pristine bullet.45 caliber, and, get this, a parking ticket issued to a Ford pickup truck with Colorado plates and registered to Paulson. So, if that's the case, maybe this same fucker gunned down Hal. Know what I mean?"

"Impressive, but I thought all along that Willis Givens did not shoot Hal with his own gun," Reynolds added his own smirk. "I wish we could get our hands on the FBI lab report, but it'll take a while. If Paulson came through here on some kind of anti-cop rampage and killed Hal, he must have stayed near here for at least a few days. Maybe worked here."

"Out in Davis County, as a matter of fact."

"What?"

O'Brien sat back in his chair and, with his best upside-down smug smile, was thoroughly pleased with the way in which he had set up the conversation.

Reynolds knew this was pure O'Brien: Self-aggrandizing always and with investigative instincts that Reynolds admired.

Reynolds said nothing. He waited for the other shoe to drop.

Satisfied that he had constructed the discussion to his best advantage, O'Brien dramatically marched to the finish line. "Seems that one Horace B. Paulson owned a horse named Junior." He let that sink in.

"It seems that someone shot Junior a couple of nights ago. Right between the eyes."

"No shit?"

"No shit. A stable owner out in Davis County said that he found the horse yesterday and that its owner, Paulson, worked for him a few days a week and boarded the horse there. He told a Deputy Harris that Junior had been sick, and probably on his last leg, but he didn't think it right that Paulson should just shoot him."

"Wait, how do we know that Paulson shot the horse?" Reynolds asked.

"Left a note and two fifty dollar bills on a nail in Junior's stall. The note said he had done it. Paulson used his real name on his application for employment at the stable. Shot the old horse to put it out of its misery and left money to cover the cost of disposing of the remains. Signed it, Hoss. The stable owner called the sheriff's office to report it. Later that day, the sheriff's office got the Teletype on Paulson. Gave the lead to Grand Junction."

"And you found all this out through Detective Mortonson," Reynolds concluded.

"In case you're wondering, the Davis County Sheriff said that they could find no crime in the shooting of the horse."

"Really, not even like illegally discharging a firearm?"

"Nope," O'Brien replied. "That's a city ordinance here. The county has no such law."

"Did Paulson happen to list a home address?"

"He did. They checked it out. Phony. It would have placed his residence in the middle of the Great Salt Lake. But what it does mean is that Paulson made it safely out of Colorado and was in Utah after the gunfight in Grand Junction. He is wounded as well. Of course, all law enforcement agencies in Utah are on the lookout for him."

"Detectives O'Brien and Reynolds?"

They both looked up at the buxomly receptionist.

"That's us," O'Brien smiled dreamily at the woman.

"You have a phone call. You can take it at the front desk."

O'Brien didn't move. Reynolds stood and made his way to the phone.

"Like I was telling Mo on the phone this morning," Park Ranger Art Hadley began, "It's probably nothing. You know, but with the train thing last night and all of that, I just thought I'd run it by someone. Me and Mo go way back."

Reynolds nodded. He had known Hadley since high school. They met up again four years ago at the Police Academy. Though operated by the state with an assist from the FBI, Reynolds had taught a class on bloodstain analysis for the first academy class that also included park rangers. To Hadley's way of thinking, it was about time that the state trained its park rangers in police work. He had long advocated for rangers to carry guns and be given full police powers. Rangers often confronted all types of criminal activity in the campgrounds, and for the past four years, the Park Service Rangers were de facto police officers.

Reynolds and Hadley arranged to meet for burgers at The Elms Café and General Store in Wasatch Canyon at about 5 P.M. Although out of the city's jurisdiction, it was one of Mo and OB's favorite eateries, and it was located equidistant from the city and Art's assigned state parked that abutted Scare Canyon.

"That's okay, Art," O'Brien said wiping his mouth with a paper towel that served as a napkin. "We never pass up an opportunity to eat at The Elms."

Reynolds cut to the chase. He pulled the small spiral notebook from his shirt pocket and read from his notes. O'Brien rolled his eyes. "So, this morning, Art, you said that a couple of weeks ago you heard an explosion."

"Nope, about a week or so ago."

Reynolds edited his entry, "All right, a week or so ago."

O'Brien and Hadley exchanged a look. O'Brien shrugged.

"All right, a week or so ago, you heard an explosion near a small cabin in Scare Canyon. And you noted that it was not a cherry bomb or some sort of fireworks." Reynolds turned the page of the notebook. "Okay, you thought, or think it could not have been a rifle shot. Too big, yes?"

"Yes."

"What did you do then?"

"Well, Mo, as I told you this morning," Hadley responded flatly, "I wasn't sure where the explosion had come from. I was like in the next canyon. I rode my horse over to where it may have come from. It took me some time to get over there. Once I got to that area up in Scare Canyon, I talked to a couple of hippies that had rented a small cabin over there. They had heard the loud noise as well, but thought it was fireworks. They swore it wasn't them, and said I was free to have a look inside the cabin if I wanted to. I thought that was an odd thing to say 'look *inside* the cabin,' but I sort of passed it off. I did want a closer look at things *outside* the cabin, but it was a day or two before I got back over that way. No one was at home in the cabin when I went back, and so, I nosed around. About a hundred yards

216

away, I found a midsized pinion blown to shards. Now I don't know of any fireworks sold that could have done that to a tree. Do you guys?"

O'Brien and Reynolds said nothing in return, but both formed essentially the same conclusion.

O'Brien spoke first, "Why don't we go have a look?"

Reynolds concurred, but with reservations. "I don't suppose it would hurt to drive up there and have a look, although it's out of our jurisdiction and not exactly our case."

O'Brien frowned and cocked his head.

Reynolds caved, "But … okay … let's do it."

"Why don't you guys follow me. I have four-wheel drive, and I don't want you to get stuck or high-centered. The terrain up there is rugged, to say the least. I'll show you where to park. Then we'll go the rest of the way in my truck." Hadley stood and was about to leave when he remembered something. "Oh, by the way, I drove by the place after we talked today, Mo. I think the hippie couple moved on. They drove a jeep. Now it looks like someone else may be renting the place. A black pickup truck was parked in there this morning."

217

Chapter Forty Five

Hadley motioned for the detectives to pull over. He walked back to their car, pointing to the steep incline of the Scare Canyon road. "Park it here. We'll go the rest of the way in the four-wheeler."

The three men in the Park Service truck rumbled to the top of the hill and slowly proceeded down the other side.

"Stop," O'Brien yelled. Hadley braked hard, and the truck lurched to a stop and settled back. "Look there."

"That's the black truck I was telling you about."

"When you were up here before, did you get a plate number on that truck?" Reynolds asked.

"No."

O'Brien was out of the truck in an instant and spoke to the others through the open window, "Wait here. I'm going in a little closer to see if I can get a plate number."

Before the others could answer, O'Brien jogged down the driveway stooping over and staying close to the trees on the right. He stopped about thirty feet from the truck. He turned and in the same manner, jogged back up the hill.

Out of breath, O'Brien wheezed and smiled, "Colorado plate," and spewed out the number. Reynolds paged through his notebook.

"Fuck, OB, that's Paulson's truck."

"Paulson?" Hadley asked. "The guy involved in the Colorado shooting. Holy shit. We got that APB. I should've been more attentive to details this morning. Shit. I'm still a lot more park ranger than cop."

They discussed their options and realized they had few. Backup was needed, but the radio in the car would be out of range up here. The Park Service radio was in range but had to be at the top of the hill to get a signal. From there Hadley could not see the cabin, but could make out the driveway to the cabin and the meadow in front of it. They quickly decided that the

218

detectives would take up positions where they could cover the truck and cabin. They all agreed to maintain in visual contact with one another. Hadley told them the cabin below was made of stone and had one way in and out. Hadley would back the truck up to the top of the hill and call for help. They would wait for the cavalry to arrive.

Chapter Forty Six

A spring gurgled up from an outcropping of large boulders under the shade of ash and aspen trees. Catching the cool water in cupped hands, Chrissy dashed the water onto her face repeatedly. Perspiration mixed with the water stung her eyes. She bent low and submerged her face in the small placid spring pool until she could hold her breath no longer. Sitting up quickly, the cool water drizzled down beneath her shirt and over her chest and stomach causing a slight tremor. She lowered her face to the pool and drank deeply.

Refreshed as she had ever felt, Chrissy instinctively rolled onto her left buttocks and reached for the little tin of speed in her right rear pocket. Twisting the can open, her eyes searched the surrounding area for vegetation that she could use for a poultice. She caught herself and momentarily stared at the little white pills in the tin container. Delicately holding two of the pills she gently rolled them between her thumb and forefinger.

"What's the point?" she said aloud. Fingering the pills, she eased back against the rock, and the chill of the granite boulder seeped through her shirt, as she looked skyward into the infinite blue. To her right her eyes found the branches and twigs robust with finely crafted and perfectly formed leaves separating her from the limitless sky. Her gaze pinpointing the one small branch containing a few curling, withering leaves among the sea of health and perfection left her uneasy. As the small curling stem held her focus and the endless number of flawless leaves became a blur, her disquieting sensation progressed to desolation and anguish. "Is that withered branch, us?" she whispered.

"Danny, tell me, please. What is the point?" The sound of her voice broke the trance.

She shuddered. "Oh, my God," she said more loudly. A small alarm sounded in her mind and clanged louder and louder until she could no longer hear the bubbling spring, the rustling leaves, or the troubling thoughts that sprouted from the appearance of the dying twig above her. Once again, her standby defense mechanism kicked in to rescue her from the perceived harmful stimuli. She had forgotten to count the number of strides that she had taken from the cabin. Sitting straight up, she pressed her hands to her temples and frantically tried to calculate the distance to the cabin.

"Let's see. Come on, Chrissy, you can do this," she said. "Thirty-inch steps … Thirty-inch steps … How far am I? Fuck. How could I be so stupid? Three hundred, four hundred yards from the cabin? Fuck, that is a big difference. How many steps? What if I am short on my estimate? Fuck. What if it's four hundred twenty-five yards?"

She bent over until her head was between her knees and her nose inches above the wild water crest. In her panic the two little white pills had slipped from her fingers, and now they lay staring back at her. She plucked them off the damp soil with trembling fingers and pressed them under her tongue.

"Okay. Okay." She sat slowly up. "Four hundred yards from here back to the cabin. That's four hundred eighty strides, give or take. Count the steps from here along the spring and gather what we need. Come straight back to this spot and then four eighty back to the cabin. Okay. Okay. That's my plan."

Satisfied that she had what she needed, Chrissy trudged back up through the trees towards the cabin.

"Four forty-eight, nine, fifty. Shorten the strides. Cabin's just ahead," she breathed.

"Chrissy," came a harsh whisper from behind. She froze. "Chrissy."

Not turning, she responded weakly, "Horace? Is that you? You following me?"

"Shhhh. Yes. Back here."

She turned. Horace crouched partially hidden behind an aspen tree not more than ten feet from her. She could see that he was fully dressed, including the gun belt. He motioned to her to come to him, but she did not move. The small branches, sticky with sap, bulbs and other plant life that she carried by rolling them in the front tails of her shirt tumbled to the ground. Her eyes met his, and she slowly reached for the automatic pistol tucked in the back of her pants.

"Chrissy. Don't. Somebody's up there." Horace pointed up the hill. "Really, a truck came down the road a bit, then backed up the hill. I heard voices."

She didn't want to believe him, but she whispered, "What are you doing out here, Horace?" She knew the answer to her own question.

Muffled voices came from behind her, and she ran around the other side of the tree next to Horace.

"We know you're in there, Paulson," came a loud voice near the cabin. "Come out; we've got you surrounded."

Chrissy pulled the .45 automatic from the back of her pants and crouched lower. Neither she nor Horace said a word. Their eyes met. He lowered his eyes to the gun in her hand then back to her eyes. She glanced down at his gun belt then retuned an icy stare. Almost simultaneously, they shrugged slightly, before returning their attention to the cabin not more than twenty yards in front of them.

"What the fuck are you doing, OB? Stay back here." Reynolds breathed an undertoned shout.

O'Brien stepped out from behind the cover of the tree line and walked towards the cabin and began yelling for the occupants to come out. Reynolds limped after him. As he neared, O'Brien turned his head slightly towards Reynolds and said quickly, "It'll be dark soon, Mo. We got this."

"Fuck you, OB. You're going to get us killed."

"You should listen to your partner, there, sheriff." Paulson stepped away from the cover of the tree into the clearing and faced the detectives. As instructed, Chrissy stayed back in the trees. "I see you got nothin' in your hands. Hah. A fair fight. Draw, sheriff."

O'Brien stepped towards the cowboy. "A fair fight, you say. I'm not armed." OB lifted his jacket and spun around to prove his point.

"Oh, Christ," Reynolds profaned and quickly strode to join his partner, but stumbled and sprawled behind him. He rolled over and pulled his snub-nosed .38 caliber Detective Special revolver and sighted it towards the cowboy. But OB took another step towards the cowboy and partially blocked Reynolds' view of the big man. Off to the right, he saw a woman emerge from the tree line holding a pistol.

"You know, maybe some people have to take that shit from you, but I'm not of them, Horace." OB took another side step towards the cowboy, although a large boulder six feet to his right was his goal.

If O'Brien calling him by name took Horace aback, he did not show it. The big man's nose flared and his brow furrowed. He bellowed nasally, "Your pard' over yonder is armed. Same difference. Makes it a fair fight. Bye, Sheriff." Hoss snapped his wrist and smoothly pulled the six-shooter from the black holster.

A shot rang out and echoed through and around Scare Canyon.

O'Brien crumpled to the ground.

Mystified, the big man looked at the gun in his hand. "Chrissy," he screamed. He thought she had shot the detective. Chrissy came running. "No, stay back."

Reynolds fired again. He knew his chances of hitting anything at that distance with the short-barreled gun were slim.

Horace quickly turned back toward the detectives. He raised the pistol and carefully cocked it and aimed it at Reynolds.

The big cowboy did not flinch as the third and fourth shots from Reynolds' gun spat up dirt yards from him. He evened his breathing and sighted down his outstretched arm, down the seven and one half inch barrel at a spot just under Reynolds' chin twenty yards away. He let out his breath evenly and started to squeeze the trigger, just the way his daddy had taught him those many years before.

Stop pulling the trigger, idiot. You're jerking rounds all over the place. You have one chance left. Cock, aim and squeeze. Reynolds cocked the little pistol and carefully aimed at the man in black. *You've got one chance.*

Chapter Forty Seven

Ba-boom!

Horace's right arm dropped like it had become unhinged. The pistol he held fired into the rocky soil in front of him. Knees gave way as if the puppet strings had been severed as he collapsed onto the ground.

Ba-boom!

A second gunshot rolled through the canyon. Reynolds watched and didn't realize as he tried to wave it off. His scream drowned out by the blast of the rifle.

Chrissy collapsed and died next to Horace.

Reynolds wrenched around and squinted up at Park Ranger Hadley who was surveying the scene below through the scope of the rifle. Hadley perched the killing machine on his hip and stepped back to brace himself against the Park Service symbol emblazoned on the driver's door of the faded green pickup truck. Reynolds watched as the ranger raised his free hand to the bridge of his nose, removed the John Lennon glasses, and slumped to the ground, sobbing noticeably, and pointing the rifle at the silent grey-pink sky.

O'Brien, supported by his left elbow, took in the scene around him. He said nothing as Reynolds removed his shirt and used it to tightly bind the wound on O'Brien's right calf.

"Fuck, Mo, I can't believe you shot me," O'Brien sniggered through the pain. "I didn't know you had it in you to pull something that …"

"Stupid?"

"No," O'Brien whispered through clenched teeth, "bold."

Neither detective paid much mind to Ranger Hadley as he walked slowly down the hillside, passed them, and bent over the girl, and then moved cautiously around to the big man.

"Hey," cried Ranger Hadley, "the big guy is still alive."

Ba-boom!

224

A nearing thunder rolled up through the valley absorbed by flora, fauna, and topography. The men of Scare Canyon scarcely noticed the final tragic hammer blow.

EPILOGUE

MOURNING IN THEIR TRIBE

December 1985

Susan O'Brien received a phone call that she hesitated to take. It was late. It was Friday night. She had a head cold. It was snowing.

Her secretary stood in front of her desk and implored her to take the call. "Susan, there was something about the woman's voice. Really, you need to talk to her. I know it's Friday and late and all of that, but when did that ever stand in your way? Just give her a few minutes."

"Oh, all right. But, if I'm not off the phone in 15 minutes, you come back in here with an emergency. You got that?"

"Fifteen minutes. You bet, boss."

Susan picked up the receiver and punched the blinking button. "This is Susan O'Brien. How may I help you?"

Silence. "Hello, is anyone there?"

"Mrs. O'Brien, thank you for taking my call. I'm Beatrice McCovey."

Susan stiffened. A jumble of thoughts ran through her head.

Beatrice broke the silence. "Perhaps, I need to tell you who I am."

Susan recovered. "I know who you are. Everyone knows who you are. The Feds have been trying to locate you for ten years. I know who you are, but I don't proclaim to know you."

"Yes, well, that is why I'm calling. I want my story told. And I want you to tell it."

Silence.

"Mrs. O'Brien, are you still there?"

Susan let out a slow long breath. "I am. With the national coverage you could gain by going to any of the news giants in the country, why would you choose me?"

Beatrice laughed gently. "I've done my homework, Mrs. O'Brien. I know who you are as well. I sought you out based on your past articles and because of your connections to our little group."

227

"Please, call me Suzy. I did have an indirect connection I suppose. My former husband was involved with the ... apprehension of one of your comrades."

"Apprehension? Okay, well I wouldn't refer to Chrissy's murder that way."

"I'm sorry. I meant no offense."

"None taken. Believe me, with what I have been through the past ten or so years, words mean little to me now."

"How do we begin? May I call you Beatrice or Ms. McCovey?"

"Trish is fine, Suzy."

"Trish, I do have a question that I just have to get out of the way before we go any further."

Her secretary opened the door, but Susan impatiently waved him off.

"You want to know if I'm turning myself in, correct?"

"Correct."

"Let's take it a step at a time."

"Okay, where do we start?"

"I have thought this out for many months, years really. Of course, I need to trust you completely, but having thought that through as well, one can never be sure about that."

"You can. But, I do understand your trepidation."

"Here's my plan, Suzy. I will mail you several of the diaries I have maintained for several years. From those, I'm sure you will get to know me better than, my guess, anyone has ever known me."

Suzy was breathless. *Diaries!* She tempered her excitement. "Trish, I have to tell you that I will not divulge my sources or addresses, but I will write and report without your permission."

Suzy thought she had overstepped, and perhaps was frightening Beatrice away.

Trish said after a long pause, "I would have it no other way. I will not give you my address, and I have edited out any location identification or other ways of identifying me, or my current... circumstance. So, where would you have me send my diaries?"

"Before we get to that," again Suzy held her breath in anticipation of Beatrice's response. "What can you tell me about the ever mysterious and elusive Jonathon Wainwright?"

Acknowledgements

Years of sitting alone converting thoughts into words. Listening to other media. Picking up a phrase here and there. Continuous editing. Never ending restructuring. Re-writing. More drafts. All of that is only a part of the process of producing this work. It could not have happened without the support, and criticism—some welcome… some not so much—but all of it contributing to this book. I thank all who took away from busy lives to assist in this work.

Without the love, understanding, time and considerate listening of my wife, Marilyn Foss, this book doesn't happen.

A Special thanks to my editor Kiana Kekauoha, DLA Editors for lending her considerable talents and energy to this project.

Marsha Foss, Patricia and Greg Foss, Tom and Mara Eckhardt, Janet Sherwood-Holst thank you so much for the guidance and support. Jeff Carter, Deb and Rocky Hayner thank you for lending an ear.

Made in the USA
Columbia, SC
01 December 2018